LOVE ON A WINTER'S WIND

THE WITCHES OF LOVING BOOK II

TIMBER PHILIPS

COPYRIGHT

Edited and book design by Maggie Kern at Ms.K Edits

Cover art by Dar Albert at Wicket Art Designs

Models - Tyler Smith King and Tionna Petramalo

Photographer - JW Photography and Covers

PROLOGUE

*B*lyn...

Ceaseless ringing in my ear. On, and on, finally the ringing cut, suspending mid-tone and before the person on the other end could speak, my circle sister's name escaped my lips...

"Miri?"

"Blyn? What's wrong?" She sounded bewildered, sleep addled, and I hated that I was doing this to her after everything that'd happened. I broke down in fresh sobs and told her:

"I-I-I c-c-can't any more... I just can't *see* anymore! It's horrible!"

"Oh, love, calm down. Talk to me." Her voice was sympathetic, empathy traveling down the magic line that bound us together in a wash of comfort and grace I didn't deserve.

I talked to her. I told her everything, and she was silent for a time on the other end of the line, absorbing it all.

"Okay, this is what we're going to do... Come *home*. I'll cleanse your family's cabin before you get here. You need a break. Let's make that happen."

I closed my eyes, fresh tears tracking down my cheeks, and I nodded, realizing belatedly that she couldn't see it, so I murmured, "Okay."

*B*lyn...

My family was rich. Filthy rich, actually; and it didn't have a thing to do with my mother, who had been the witch and a descendant of one of the Originals of Loving. The Originals, as they had been coined, weren't really – they had just earned the nickname after abolishing Jenny's curse over the town. The families of Eilish, Courtney, Tremblay and Roth.

The Roth's died out last century, unfortunately; so just the three houses remained. It'd been difficult. There hadn't been a circle or coven until my generation's circle, and we'd lost *it* when Oaklyn had died from cancer.

It'd been just me, Miri, and Ash that were left. Ash and I had allowed ourselves to be blinded by grief and the wickedness of an interloper. What had remained of our little circle went crumbling under mistrust, tumbling from the cliffs of the little seaside town we'd all grown up in to be swept away.

It'd been both a blessing and a curse. A blessing, because without the backing of a full circle, my power had been somehow less, and I was unrealistically powerful to begin with. All of us were.

When we had been a full circle, during the worst of it with my sister's help, we'd performed a sort of binding which had been great at keeping my powers in check; but when Oaklyn passed beyond the veil that binding had been proven to be little more than a Band-Aid and that Band-Aid had been unceremoniously ripped off with her death.

However, her passing had been much the same when it came to all of our powers, so there had been that. Without a full circle, my powers had been limited or diminished again, so even though the binding had fallen away, by virtue of our circle having been broken, not much had changed for me. I'd been fine.

I mean, I was still extraordinarily powerful with the gift of air and sight; a clairvoyant matched by no other. I could see things as they were and as they are now with the simple touch of an object, but I could *handle it*. I controlled the power; the power did not control me.

Then, last Spring, Miri, in a time of deep desperation, had reached out to Ashlyn and I for our help. Of course, we'd heeded her call. How could we not? We were her sisters. Except she'd bound us back into a circle, throwing roots deep, binding us to the earth. She'd somehow found a fire-worker, his magic strong, and she'd bound us into a *full circle* again. One of the elements – earth, air, fire, and water.

What's worse, or best, depending upon how you looked at it, she'd done it during Spring, close enough to the equinox and the festival magic that it'd given things just that little bit extra. That added oomph, if you will, and my power had *loved it*. It had roared out of its slumber and when I had gone back to work, I couldn't pretend that things were the same. My powers had suddenly become limitless, reaching far beyond my control, far beyond anything I'd ever experienced before.

I wasn't just *seeing* the things that I needed to see to catch a killer. I was *feeling them*… and I just couldn't deal.

So, I had called my sister-witch, the healer of the lot of us, and I was eternally grateful that she had answered my call.

She'd been right. I'd needed a break. A safe place to be, and she had done me an even bigger favor by cleansing and readying my family's cabin up in the mountains for me. Or, well, at least what *passed* for mountains in the area. I was well aware that by most people's standards, the mountain areas and cliffs around Loving were more like foothills at best anywhere else.

The point was, the cabin, while boasting every modern comfort and a lot of windows, did sit in the middle of the woods, off the beaten track by enough to feel isolated. It was peaceful here, a lake nearby, hiking trails a plenty. It was a rich person's getaway and my family, as I'd mentioned, happened to be filthy stinking rich – and right now, that worked for me. Rarely had it ever.

I stood at the windows that wrapped around the entire bottom three quarters of the first floor and stared out over the trees that stretched as far as the eye could see. The cabin had the high ground, though mostly for the aesthetics. I couldn't deny the view was spectacular, though. Just as I couldn't deny the freshly falling snow outside the glass, coating everything in a blanket of cold falling white, had the desirable soothing effect that I needed right now.

Despite being cozy in my thermal black leggings and my thick, cowl-necked gray sweater, I was *still* restless.

With an exasperated sigh, I turned from the window and the gentle trickle of snowflakes falling from the leaden sky to go find a pair of boots and my coat. I needed to breathe, and a walk sounded like just the thing. Sometimes, just connecting with nature did me a world of good and to be honest, I was out of any other ideas at this point.

Stepping out onto the deck, I paused, the cold wind soothing to what felt like an over-heated soul. Which is exactly what it felt like, actually. Like my powers had been superheated with the reconnection of the Circle, like the power that had rushed through me, through my other-worldly channels had scorched them, scorched *me* from the inside where it wasn't visible, but *damn*, I sure *felt* it.

I mean, no, I wasn't *literally* burned from the inside out, I just didn't have any other way of explaining it to a mundane or non-magic user. This was just the best alliteration I could come up with.

I sighed out and stuffed my hands into my puffy white down jacket after drawing up the faux-fur-lined hood.

I could never do real fur, not without some heavy magical

cleansing done by another witch. I would touch it, and all of the animal's pain, all of its suffering… I would have to *live* that. Kind of hard to appreciate a mink jacket when the dozen or so mink's that went into it are all screaming out in animalistic pain and panic in your head the second you put it on. It was something I *never* wanted to experience again.

I mean, I wasn't a vegetarian, but it was definitely annoying casting spells over your food every time you sat down to eat. Thankfully, it wasn't too awkward. Most of the Christians at the table would usually bow their head and pray with or against you depending on their moral bent toward other faiths. Sure, the latter had its awkward moments, but usually the former provided the opportunity to cast what needed to be cast in order for me to be able to eat in peace.

I stood and listened to the silent snowfall, the flakes drifting by ones and twos, lazily tumbling from the sky. The clouds were threatening more, but I wouldn't be out too long. Just a quick walk to hopefully cleanse my soul and speak to the Goddess.

Well, beg her mercy was more like it.

I loved the sounds my steps made as I went, crunching softly through the snow crust. The faint whispering grate of it beneath my UGG snow boots was so satisfying. I loved the wintertime. Granted, the cold could be deadly, but I just loved the gentle hush of the world. How silent and beautiful everything became, blanketed in all that soothing, calming, white.

I struck out along the trail leading into the trees, listening to the sounds my breath made; thinking about what I wanted and what I needed. I mean, I would be lying to myself if I said my latest meltdown had *everything* to do with my powers going berserk. It both did and didn't… where it didn't? Well, that had everything to do with my partner.

Richard Dax wasn't magical by nature. Quite the opposite, actually; he was about as psychic as a rock – but he didn't, for one second, doubt my ability. We worked well together. Exceedingly well, to the point it grew into a dangerous infatuation. An attraction which eventually led to some poor life decisions on both of our parts.

You see, Dax was married and there was absolutely nothing worse than feeling both your own guilt and emotions over that, than knowing *exactly* how he was feeling, what he was thinking, every time we made love. I used to be able to shut it out... but not anymore. I couldn't shut *anything* out anymore.

Perhaps that was my Karma, my penance for loving a man who was already taken. His wife was actually lovely. I bore her no ill will, but I was certain she knew and it hurt her deeply and believe it or not, that hurt me too.

God and Goddess, I was such a trash human being. I deserved every ounce of pain my powers brought me, but I couldn't help myself. I was breaking. I was hurting beyond any measure I'd had before, and I didn't know how to hang on anymore. I just knew I needed to. There were people out there who depended on my ability to tell their stories, to bring them home to their loved ones. Granted, more often than not, I was just bringing their body home, their husk... but my job was as much for the living as it was for the dead. For the loved ones who still breathed and needed that closure.

I was just grateful the dead didn't talk to me. Not like they had Oaklyn, which is how I'd fallen into this line of work in the first place.

"Goddess, I miss you Oak," I murmured.

The whispering snowfall was my only reply. Oaklyn had found her way across and was firmly behind the veil. So far behind the veil, that I didn't even see or hear her around All Hallows. Her sister, her twin, hadn't either; and I worried about Ash. She bore an impossible weight of grief and my heart went out to her. Her *and* Miri, who had thought we had abandoned her... and after a fashion, we had. We should have known better than to have let Gwen so deceive us.

Guilt swirled inside me like the little eddies of snow up against the tree trunks. I didn't honestly know what to do with myself. It seemed, despite any good intention I might have had, I just went from one thing to another thoroughly fucking it up. My pride would never allow me to say it out loud, but yeah... seemed like every decision I made was a bad decision lately.

Like this walk, for instance, I had meant to pray for guidance and all I was managing to do was drown in my self-pity going over and over my mistakes. I could say it was so I didn't repeat them, and it was probably true that I wouldn't – repeat any. That didn't stop me from making whole new ones, though.

The wind picked up and buffeted me, blowing sharp crystalline flakes from the drifts of snow already in existence into my face. I threw up my arms and staggered at the power of nature's touch and made for the tree line to the side of the game trail and stepped right into a legit trap.

There was a pop under my foot, a metal twang, and both sides of the trap came up and clamped firmly around my ankle with a sharp thwack and a searing pain, like when you bark your funny bone – only there was nothing funny about this. I yelped and landed hard on my ass in the powdery snow.

I whimpered and tried to suck in a breath where all had been driven out of me with the pain. My ankle throbbed, and I tore away the white plastic trash bag around the offending metal jaws that held me fast. It didn't look like the teeth penetrated my boot, and I didn't *feel* like anything was broken, but I wasn't about to try and stand on it to put it to the test.

"Oh, shit..." I stared at the little circle with a line through it where my signal bars should be on my phone.

Panic bubbled up in the center of my chest and I tried to force it down. I swallowed hard and took off my gloves. I didn't want to touch it, but I had to figure out how to free myself, and the bulky snow gloves I'd put on to keep warm weren't going to help.

"Okay, Blyn. You can do this."

The wind whipped yet more snow right into my face and I spit and sputtered, crying out, "Come on!"

I didn't know what all I had done to deserve this, but whatever it was, I was heartily sorry. I gritted my teeth and reached for the icy metal of the rusting trap, trying to remember when I had my last tetanus booster just in case it *had* chewed all the way through my boot and into my skin.

"Okay, Blyn. Gird your loins," I murmured to myself, psyching myself up to deal with whatever animal pain and suffering may be residual to the trap. I squeezed my eyes shut and touched it; the frozen metal so cold beneath my fingertips it almost burned.

I waited for the onslaught of visuals, the sounds, the torment… but nothing happened.

I opened first one eye and then the other, staring stupidly at my fingers in contact with the trap.

Nothing. There was nothing there.

"What?" I emitted, surprised.

Never mind. I had to pry it apart somehow. I tried. Oh, Lord and Lady, I tried, but to no avail. I didn't know how this damn thing worked!

"I'm all for every lesson you wish to teach me," I murmured and let out a scared huff of a breath. "Just please, don't let me die out here."

I mean, I thought I was ready… but there was still so much for me to do. *I just needed a* temporary *break from it all,* I thought. *Not a permanent one.*

2

*J*ayse...

The rumble of the snowmobile's motor underneath me broke up the silence of the winter wonderland around me. I checked the sled was coming along from behind, hauling my catches and my gear; getting a little worried about the load my motor was under with how deep the snow was piling up. We were getting dumped on, *hard*. A hell of a nor'easter blowing in, and before long it'd be a full-on blizzard with whiteout conditions. I aimed to have me and Shep inside the cabin before it really hit.

"C'mon, Shep!" I hollered at my Husky up ahead, but he was steadfast, pawing at the snow on the trail up by where I had my wolf trap set.

"We got something, buddy?" I called out, pulling up alongside him and the lump in the snow.

"Ha, ha – oh, my God, no! Holy shit!" The laughter died on my lips when I realized it wasn't a wolf in my trap but a *girl*.

"Jesus! Shep, move! Get out of the way!" I barked at my dog, inspecting the woman's ankle, ripping off my right glove with my teeth and putting my cold fingers to her icy flesh, against the side of her neck, looking for a pulse.

My breath whooshed out of me in a plume when I found one that was thready but there. I got the trap off her foot, hitting the mechanism and prying the jaws apart. It took some elbow grease. These traps were meant to catch and *hold*, which it sure did its job. Definitely *not* the way it was intended – well, yeah, maybe *exactly* the way it was intended, just certainly not on its intended prey, *holy shit.*

Her snow boot was mangled, and I winced, not sure what kind of shape her ankle underneath was going to be in but… triage. Treat the most life-threatening injury *first,* and that injury would be hypothermia. She was freezing, her lips a pale shade of blue, her sun-kissed complexion washed out.

She was beautiful, no doubt about it, and it was an alien kind of beauty. Not as in extra-terrestrial, more like not from America, or more like only half white. Gah! My internal monologue was making me sound like a bigoted asshole.

Anyway, I didn't know what she was mixed with, but it was exotic to me and striking all the same.

I worked fast, getting an arm beneath her knees, working the other behind her back, rocking her body back and forth in the snow to get her at the right angle for the leverage I would need to get her up. She groaned and I was encouraged. I got her up into my embrace and turned for the sled.

"Shep, get over here." I whistled as I settled her in among the baskets of traps and catches and pulled my old sleeping bag over her.

"How the hell did you even get all the way out here?" I muttered and snapped my fingers. Shep bounded into the sled and I told him, "Lie down." He did as I commanded and laid himself across her lap.

"Good boy."

I retrieved my trap quickly and threw it in the basket with the rest of them with a clatter and a clang before getting back onto the snowmobile and making for the cabin, the snow coming down in fat downy flakes harder and faster, the wind kicking up at our backs.

It was a harrowing three miles back to my trapper's cabin. I pulled the snowmobile directly under the slanted lean-to 'carport' built against the side of it out of some old tin roofing. It kept worst of the weather off my equipment and was steeply pitched enough that the snow slid off and couldn't pile up on it too bad – unless it was a blizzard, like the one kicking up right now.

I didn't have time to worry about it, or any other prep. Instead, I was all about the girl; demanding my dog get up off her. I opened up the cabin, went back out, and lifted her in my arms. Bringing her straight inside to my bed, which was really just a double-wide pallet lifted off the ground, the frame secured to the wall, the box spring a piece of plywood with some foam padding over it to make it marginally more comfortable. I laid her down on it. I was used to sleeping rough and God willing, the girl would survive to get used to it for however long we were snowed in for.

I built up the fire and got to work, unbundling her from her fancy city-slicker clothes. She was decked out for cold weather, I could give her that, but for survival? Not so much. There was no telling how long she'd been out there, but that didn't matter now. All that mattered was getting her *warm* and necessity negated modesty in this situation. I still couldn't help but feel skeevy the more I removed of her clothing and mine, though.

I got her down to just her panties and me down to my boxers. Tucking her beneath the quilts and sleeping bags on my bed. I built up the fire as heavily as I could so that it would blast heat out of my little wood stove, then I climbed into the bed behind her, between her and the wall, the wood stove in front of us. Nestled down into the blankets, her chilled skin against mine, I started to shiver with how cold she was, but I was okay. She needed the transference of heat. I needed to hold her tight and pray I'd get her through this. I did *not* want her death on my conscience, her blood on my hands.

"Hang in there, pretty lady," I murmured against her silky soft hair. "I got'cha."

With nothing left to do except hope and pray for the best outcome, after a time, I fell asleep encouraged by her shivering and light trembling against the bigger spoon of my body.

∾

I WOKE BEFORE SHE DID. That didn't really surprise me, though. What did, and what relieved me to my very core was the fact that she was still with me. Her breath rising and falling in evenly spaced cadence, her body snug and warm up against mine. I smoothed a rough hand over her shoulder and down her arm and sighed in relief. Shep raised his head off of his paws where he lay on the floor and panted, tongue lolling out the side of his mouth.

It was stuffy as fuck in the cabin; dry, the heat oppressive, but I could deal. I slid out from behind her and got on top of the quilts and covers, pulling them up to her chin to cover her nude body as much as possible. I wasn't as concerned with preserving her modesty as I was with keeping her warm.

Smoothing her long, glossy dark hair where it'd fallen over her face was solely for my benefit, though. I wanted to look at her.

Her lashes were so full and thick, I'd almost believe they were falsies, but I was close enough to know the difference. Her lips were so full and lush, kissable if I were being a total perv, which wasn't my aim here at all. She was just that beautiful. Perfect. Ethereal, really. Like she wasn't from this plane or something. Maybe one of the fairies my mom was forever telling stories about to my little sister when we were growing up. Except this was America, and fairies didn't live here.

I got up with a grunt, my body stiff and a little sore from the back-breaking work of trapping and having spent too long, too still in one position. I had to hand it to her. I slept like a rock curled around her. I don't think I'd slept that good since I'd got out here several weeks back.

Unexpected guest aside, no matter how beautiful, there was no rest for the wicked out here or we'd still both be food for whatever critters managed to get into the cabin to eat us.

I moved slowly, as quietly as possible so as not to wake her, and got myself to work, first pulling on clothes, then checking myself out in the cracked mirror over the old enamel water basin I had up on the even older water-damaged cabinet that rested up under that mirror.

I didn't want to scare the shit out of her when she finally did wake up, so I needed to do something to tame my wild appearance at least a little bit. I took the old metal coffee can, rusting in a couple spots, out from under the basin of the cabinet and outside. I scooped it full of snow, came back inside, and set it on top of the wood stove with a hiss to melt and heat.

While that was happening, I had an impressive list of shit to do from coming in last night that didn't get gotten to with my unexpected guest. I let my eyes wander back to her sleeping form.

It was going to be a long day.

3

*B*lyn...

My ankle hurt and I was parched. It was hot, hot as hell, and I vaguely wondered if that was where I was at. The Christian notion of Hell. I groaned and a sharp pain that lanced into my foot from my ankle made me yelp and try to drag it away. A firm, but attempted gentle grasp kept me from jerking it and my eyes flew open on a strangled gasp.

"Welcome back." The voice was a soft baritone and I jumped and pushed myself back from it, eyes struggling to focus in the dim light.

"Easy. You're okay." He chuckled, and I couldn't quite see his face backlit as he was by the lantern hanging from a hook in the center of the small, one-room cabin.

"Where am I?" I demanded, voice strangled with apprehension.

"Trapper's cabin," he answered succinctly. "East coastal woods."

"Don't touch me!" I cried, registering that his hands were on my bare skin, the fear of what I would see choking me.

"Easy, relax. Please hold still. I'm trying to see how bad this is."

I kept myself propped up on my arms and focused on him, my mouth dropping open in surprise. Nothing. There was nothing. Just his calloused fingertips light on my skin as he inspected the deep bruising around my ankle.

He sucked a breath in between clenched teeth in sympathy as he got a good look at what my leg looked like. It gave an angry throb as my own eyes settled on it and I winced, but to me there were more pressing matters at hand...

"What time is it? How long have I been out? Who are you, and *where are my clothes?*" I asked one question after another in rapid fire succession.

He chuckled and said, "Name's Jayse."

"Chase?" I echoed, or at least I thought I did.

"No, *Jayse,* Chase only with a 'J'. What's your name?" he asked.

"Blyn." My name spilled from my lips, sounding almost foreign to my own ears as I homed in on his face.

He was a little bedraggled, his hair a little long where it showed from beneath his black knit cap, his beard haphazardly trimmed – ragged, as if he'd hastily trimmed it with little better than a pair of scissors. But I have to say, if he had, I appreciated it. He looked more... human. No, that wasn't right. *Civilized* was the word for it. The hack job, while hasty, did something to keep him from looking like an arctic version or the wild man of Borneo.

"Yeah, doesn't look like my trap broke the skin, but it doesn't look awesome either. I'm going to wrap it with some Ace bandage and get some compression on it. We'll elevate it and good thing we got access to plenty of ice. It's the best I can do for you until this storm blows itself out and I can get you back to civilization – which, by the way, *where did you come from,* anyway?"

"Um, vacation cabins outside Loving," I murmured. "Family owns one."

"That's over fifteen miles from here. How did you get all that way?" He blinked at me, and I couldn't make out his eye color backlit as he was, just that he had a dashing scar through his left eyebrow.

"I... I went for a walk." *Fifteen miles?*

"I picked you up in one of my wolf traps about two or three miles from here. You mean to tell me you walked thirteen miles out here in *that?*" He jerked his head in the direction of one of the corners made by the wall that held the front door and the wall that held the iron woodstove. Wire had been strung, crisscrossing back and forth, wound around rusting penny nails driven into the raw wood of the logs comprising the cabin. My clothes were flopped over the galvanized wire, hung as a makeshift clothesline to dry in the oppressive heat pouring from the woodstove.

"Can I have my clothes back, please?" I asked, arching a brow.

He laid the tan stretchy bandage against my skin and shook his head. "I got you out of them, and into bed. I just hung 'em a little while ago. Wasn't exactly a priority at the time, so they're still damp. I'll get you one of my shirts in a sec. Just stay under the quilt while I do this."

I worried my bottom lip between my teeth and stayed quiet, thinking furiously, my mind screaming at me that nothing about this was right or okay. How come I couldn't 'see' or 'hear' anything? It was as if a switch had been flipped and my magic had winked out, snuffed out as though it had never existed at all, and I was torn.

While I was upset it was missing, it was so blessedly *quiet,* and the silence was such a *relief* that I was finding myself becoming deeply emotional over it. Tears sprang to my eyes, cresting on my lower lashes and trickling in twin scalding tracks down my cheeks which felt gritty and dry.

"Hey." His hands stilled, and I looked at him. "You're okay. You're alive and you're safe here. I'm not going to hurt you."

"Why am I naked then?" I asked, voice trembling.

"Not my first choice, but necessary," he explained. "You were wet and freezing to death. Hypothermia set in and I needed to get you warm."

"What, you're saying you got in here and cuddled with me naked?" I asked.

He wouldn't look at me, but his ears turned very red. I couldn't help it, I choked on a laugh. His jaw tightened, and he suddenly became overly interested in wrapping my ankle.

"Thank you," I murmured when he clipped the bandage in place and stood in one sinuous, solid movement. "For taking care of me."

He cleared his throat.

"You're welcome. Hang on, I'll find you a clean shirt and step out. Give you some privacy."

"Thanks."

He went over to a workbench built into the back wall of the cabin and pulled a plastic bin out from underneath it, popping the top. He rooted around in it for a minute and came up with a button-up flannel shirt in a plaid pattern, predominantly a blue and gray. He held it out to me, leaning to hand it over. Making sure the quilt was secure to my nude breast, I leaned out to meet him halfway, snatching the offered covering from his outstretched hand and clutching it to me.

He smiled, and it held an edge of sadness to it when he stepped in his heavy boots across the roughhewn plank floor to the front door.

"C'mon, Shep!" he ordered, and I blinked in surprise as a Husky stood up from the floor below the edge of the bed and stretched, yawning.

"I didn't even know he was there," I blurted.

Jayse smiled and said, "He's a good boy," before he reached down and thumped the dog's flank affectionately. "Take as long as you need, I'm going to bring in some more wood. Might take me a minute."

I nodded, suddenly tongue-tied now that I could get a good look at my unlikely mountain man savior.

He was gorgeous. That all-American-white-boy kind of good looks. I swallowed hard, taken aback by just how attractive I found him to be, and managed to nod once. He nodded once in return, tore his eyes off of my blushing face, and opened the door. The wind blasted in, icy, a flurry of snow swirling in with it and pattering to the floor in droplets as his Husky bolted out into the dark.

He pulled a headlamp off a nail by the door, stepped out, and shut the door behind him tightly, barring the elements outside any further entry.

I stared after him for just a moment, before shrugging into the shirt he'd offered me. The fabric soft against my skin, smelling faintly of whatever dryer sheets he used and what I assumed to be just him. *Like laundry and clean male,* I thought to myself. Still perturbed by the fact that I could touch him and everything else around me without curse or consequence.

A Null.

I'd only ever heard of them as stories. A witch's fairytale, or boogeyman, rather. Something to frighten young witches, even with as rare as we were. I didn't think they actually existed, that they were real... I mean, I knew they existed, there were stories, but I didn't think they existed *anymore*. I thought they'd all been wiped out.

The way the histories told it, the church recruited the Nulls, indoctrinated them to use against those of us with the Gift. Our powers rendered useless; it was then that they could... dispose of us. By the time the Salem Witch Trials came around, witches were very nearly extinct. Only the most powerful of us survived, and we had to be so very careful.

We were clever, and in fighting back, had almost wiped out every Null in existence in return. The good old-fashioned way. With our bare hands.

Now, here I was, a witch and a powerful one at that, and here he was a Null and he'd just saved my life.

I was confused, for sure, but it did explain a few things such as why I couldn't feel my magic, hadn't been able to see anything when I'd touched his wolf trap that I'd stepped in. I was still thinking furiously about it all when he returned, kicking the door in a sort of knock that signaled that his hands were most certainly full.

I worried my lip between my teeth but limped to the door and lifted the latch, stepping as quickly as I could out of his way as he shouldered past me and dropped the armload of wood by the woodstove.

"Should have just called out you were good," he grated, but it wasn't gruff, he was just cold.

"Sounded like you had your hands full."

"Get back up there, you need to stay off it," he said, gesturing at my wrapped foot and ankle. I went back to the makeshift bed and sat down as he went to the workbench and slid a gallon Ziploc bag from a box of them on the workbench.

"Be right back and we'll get you fixed up," he said, and I cocked my head.

"Why are you doing all of this for me?" I asked.

He paused at the door and said, "Because it's the good and right thing to do," before he slipped out into the blizzard to a happy bark from his dog.

I sat in turmoil; conflicted. Perhaps he didn't know what I was. Maybe he didn't know what *he* was. I swallowed hard and thought it best to keep my knowledge to myself. At least for now. I worked with the police. I saw firsthand, sometimes through the victim's eyes, sometimes through the perpetrator's, the absolute *worst* that humanity had to offer and I wasn't keen on experiencing any of what I saw ever in the actual flesh.

Additionally, I couldn't believe that if Jayse knew what I was, that things wouldn't go badly for me. No matter the good I used my gift, my powers, for to a fair bit of folks, I was just *evil.*

God and Goddess, what a mess I'm in, I thought to myself just as Jayse and his Husky returned.

"Ah! She doesn't want none of your kisses, dog!" he cried when Shep immediately came to me and tried licking my face with enthusiasm, stepping all over my lap and scratching my bare thigh in his quest for affection from his newfound friend.

I laughed at first, but when the scratch occurred, cried, "Ouch!" out of reflex.

"Get down!" Jayse cried and came to the rescue, grabbing his enthusiastic pupper by the collar to wrangle him off the bed. I took note that he was kind to his dog throughout, but it still wasn't enough to get me to trust him. It was a start, though.

"He's alright," I murmured.

"Nah, he knows better," Jayse said, absently running a light fingertip over the angry red line atop my leg. I tried not to shudder. He was handsome, and the light touch felt nice. Good, even.

He cleared his throat and said, "Here, lean back."

"Actually, um, I could really stand to use the bathroom," I said, biting my lips together.

"Shit," he swore softly. "Uh, I'm *really* sorry, but this place isn't exactly designed with a lady in mind. I have a couple old five-gallon buckets and a few rolls of TP—"

"It's fine, I'm not exactly a shrinking violet. I'll make do. Just, um…"

"No, that's great. I'll get you set up, step out, and let you take care of things. It's no problem. I have a sister, and if um, she was in your situation, I would hope that she'd be treated right. So if you could just hold that thought, I'll be right back, again."

"Okay, thank you, Jayse."

"Sure, it's no problem, Blyn. I'm just awfully sorry you got stuck in my trap."

It seemed to me I should be glad for it. If I were as far from the cabins as he had said I was, then if I *hadn't* been stuck in his trap, I would likely still be out there, trapped in the storm. Lost. Maybe even never to return. It was a grim reality, but then again, everything happens for a reason… right?

He got me situated. I used the restroom, and he didn't comment or complain, just took the bucket outside and returned with it clean to set it in a depressed corner of the floor, a pad of dipped concrete with a pipe stuffed with a rag leading out through the wall. I was curious and as soon as he had my foot propped, a bag of snow chilling my ankle through the Ace bandage, I asked.

"Why is the floor like that over there?"

"Uh, that's sort of the shower. I heat water on the stove, unstop the drain pipe and kind of bird bath it. I can get you set up to get cleaned up later if you want."

"Maybe later," I murmured. Right now, he was fixing up a pot of stew and some coffee atop the wood stove.

"Sure thing."

"You never said how long I was out."

"Almost a full day, I reckon. I don't know exactly how long you were out there."

"Me either," I said honestly.

"Good thing I found you when I did, then."

"Good thing," I agreed.

The silence was surprisingly comfortable, despite how it felt like a pregnant pause. I think both of us were curious of the other at this point, and I'm afraid I broke first…

"So, um, is this what you do?"

"Me?" he asked, a little surprised.

I laughed as he colored with his awkward and bit my bottom lip. "I was asking Shep, actually." At his name, his beautiful brown-eyed dog lifted his head off his paws and cocked his head curiously. Jayse and I shared the laugh that came from it.

"I'm afraid he's not much of a conversationalist, and uh, yeah. I'm giving trapping a shot. This is my first winter trying to do it for an actual profit. The guy who owns this cabin taught me everything. I've been his apprentice for a while. He's finally decided he's too old to keep it up and retired this season."

"He your father or grandfather?" I asked.

"No." He pursed his lips and shook his head, and I didn't need my gift to tell me I'd brushed fingertips over a sore spot.

"Sorry," I murmured. "I didn't mean to pry."

"No, you're fine. Um, my dad took off when I was seven and my sister was two. It was just us and my mom. It wasn't easy on her, you know?"

"My mom was a single parent for the most part too," I confessed, if only to make it a little easier on him, to chase the shadow of a little boy's anger and pain out of the very grown man's eyes.

"Yeah?"

"Yeah."

"Where are you from?" he asked, working his way around a second tin of stew with his can opener, not really looking at me, keeping his eye on the task at hand, but his head cocked just so indicating he was all ears.

"Loving, actually. I'm from Loving."

"Oh, yeah? And your parents?"

I smiled and said, "My mother was from Loving, too. Her family goes back a long way in the town's history. My father is from Persia, but he and his family have never had anything to do with me. In fact, they paid my mother handsomely to keep it that way." I couldn't help the bitterness that crept into my tone. The derision.

"That's messed up," he said, pausing in his task.

"It's… something," I finished lamely. Acutely aware that he was careful not to swear around me. I was unsure if that was because I was a lady or if he had a real aversion to coarse language so I tried to play it safe. I was sort of at his mercy here and I didn't want to upset him. Especially after all of his kindness and tender treatment thus far.

"I'll get this heated up," he said after a fresh silence, a touch more awkward than the last.

"Tell me about yourself while you do," I suggested.

He gave a nod and carried the pot of stew to the woodstove, setting it on top.

"Where to begin?" he asked with a nervous laugh.

"How about at the beginning?" I suggested.

He nodded and I settled in to listen.

4

*J*ayse...

Her dark eyes, while calm, held this quality that spoke volumes about her. A quality that said to cut the bullshit. That'd she'd somehow see right through it anyway. I didn't want to hide anything from her. Just the opposite, in fact. She was one of the first women I'd ever met that I felt like not only could I tell her anything, that she would actually listen without treating me like I was some kind of creeper.

I didn't know what it was about me. I mean, I didn't *do* anything creepy that I knew of. I always remained respectful to a fault. My mamma had raised me right in that regard – still, I just creeped people out, rubbed them the wrong way, got bullied a lot for it growing up and it was to the point with the awkward stares and mistrustful attitudes when I hadn't done anything to deserve it, that I just kind of had it with being around people. Which is why I was out here. As far away from other people as I could get.

"Well," I said, feeling a bit painted into a corner. "I'd like to learn about you, too."

"Quid pro quo," she said with a smile that eased my nerves.

"Fair enough," I said with a nod.

"Raised by my mom with one younger sister," I said, and she smiled wider.

"You've said that."

I raised my eyebrows and said, "Figured it'd bear repeating, get us caught up to date."

"And buy yourself time to think of other things to say about yourself?"

I laughed. "Guilty."

"Raised as an only child, but there were three other girls my age and we were the best of friends. So, it was like we were sisters," she said and something flitted across her face. A sort of sorrow.

I cocked my head. "I was raised around here, too. Not in Loving. Down the coast more, land locked edge of Garamond Corner."

She smiled and it was sweet. "A boy from the wrong side of the tracks, then."

"If by wrong, you mean poor? Then, yeah," I said defensively.

Her features fell and she looked as sorry as the words that fell gently from her lips next sounded. "I didn't mean anything by it," she said.

My defenses were still up and I didn't mean for it come out the way it sounded but my retort of, "Folks from a life of privilege rarely 'mean anything by it' but the reminder that my family is considered poor white trash is still there all the same."

She visibly flinched and her expression became slightly wounded. I cursed myself inwardly.

"Sorry," I grunted. "That came out harsher than I meant it to be."

"No, its fine," she said gently. "I'm sorry. That was an asshole thing to say and I have my moments."

I nodded and accepted her apology silently.

"What do you do?" I asked her, changing the subject.

"I work with the Boston police, actually. A consultant with their major crimes unit."

"Oh yeah? Some *Criminal Minds* type stuff?" I asked, interested.

"Yeah!" she agreed, relieved. "Profiling, um, psych evaluations after a fashion. That sort of thing."

"Sounds important, what're you doing all the way out here?"

She scraped her bottom lip between her teeth. "I made a mistake," she said, her face so beautiful in its naked honesty. "I'm not a good person, and I let myself become…" she sighed, frustrated.

"It's okay," I said quickly. "No judgment here. You don't have to tell me, either."

"Is it weird that I almost want to?" she asked, and she looked troubled. The stew could do without my babysitting it for the time being, so I went over and dropped onto the edge of my bed where she sat and looked her over.

"Sometimes it helps talking to a stranger," I said. "Can't hold all the things in all the time."

"I've made a lot of mistakes," she said, letting out a shuddering breath.

I wanted to help, my heart going out to her with the cloud of uncertainty, the turmoil in her eyes. I reached out on impulse and tucked some of her silky hair behind her ear, out of her face so I could see her, my ears immediately turning vermillion at the overly familiar and generally creepy gesture. I cursed myself silently while she regarded me with wide eyes.

"Sorry," I murmured and she shook her head, barely, almost imperceptibly.

"It's fine."

"I guess I have a hard time believing anyone as pretty as you could do anything intentionally awful. Have an even harder time believing that anyone as smart as you seem to be could make any kind of huge error in judgment."

"Says the guy who pulled me half frozen to death out of one of his wolf traps," she said, her voice trembling faintly.

I laughed slightly and nodded, then asked, "You trying to hurt yourself being out there like that?" I needed to know. If the answer was 'yes', I wanted to get her some help when we got back to civilization.

"No," she said and I stared her in the eyes and I believed her.

"So, what were you doing all the way out there?"

She swallowed hard.

"I really was just going for a walk, to clear my head and to think about things… I guess I just got so wrapped up in my own thoughts, in my own head…"

"I get that," I said.

"Yeah?"

"Oh, yeah."

"I slept with my partner," she blurted. "My *married* partner – with the police."

I struggled not to give a low whistle. That was pretty bad, alright, but surprisingly, I wasn't judging. I didn't know the whole story and things like that happened all the time, I mean long hours together and so it goes… Still, I could see how much it was tearing her up on the inside and so I tried to keep my face neutral, nodding gently.

"Not sure what I should say, I mean, that's pretty big but I'm sure there's a lot more to it than that."

"Yes and no," she said averting her gaze.

"One of my childhood friends died from cancer and it really created a rift between the rest of us. I'd never really had no one to talk to before and Dax… Well, Charlie listened." She swallowed hard and tears threatened.

"It's a big mess and I needed a break from it all. From the job, from my personal life, just from all of it. I have a lot of making up to do with my sisters and we're going to be okay but the thing with Charlie – they don't know. I can't tell them, and the job just got to be too much and I just needed a blasted break."

I nodded slowly, surprised she was telling me all this, but the power of strangers, you know? Sometimes, you just needed to pour your heart and soul out.

"Say something please?" she asked.

"I'm not sure what you want me to say," I told her and it was probably the second worse thing I probably could have said. She brought her knees to her chest, wincing at her ankle and hugged her legs. She wouldn't look at me and I sighed.

Shit. Could you be any more awkward, dude?

"Again, not judging you—"

"Aren't you?" she asked softly, and the stew glopped in the pot, hissing and bubbling.

I got up and stirred it and said evenly, "I'm not. I don't really people very well. That's to say, I think there might be something wrong with me but hell if I know what it is."

She looked up at me then, her interest piqued. I gritted my teeth and took in a slow and deep breath. "Sorry, that's probably the last thing you want to hear being trapped in a cabin with me. Isn't it?"

"Quid pro quo," she reminded me, and I nodded.

"That's fair."

"Why would you say something like that?" she asked. "I don't think there's anything wrong with you."

I shook my head. "It's nothing, but everything at the same time." I sighed. "I don't know what it is. I've just never been able to make friends that easily. Everybody accuses me of giving them the creeps but I don't *do* anything. You know what I mean?"

She nodded slowly and something about it – I believed her. I believed she understood and wasn't just shining me on because she was afraid of me. Which, believe me, I didn't want *anyone* to be afraid of me. I was just your average guy. Hard to be outgoing anymore, but still trying.

"Here." I handed her a steaming mug of stew with a spoon stuck in it. I dished myself up some in a bowl and took my fork with me to sit in the rickety old wooden kitchen chair I had in here and to give her some space.

We blew on the hot stew and took tentative bites in silence. Finally, she said, "What else should I know about you?"

I chuckled. "Honestly, I don't know. For the most part, it's just me and Shep and the woods outside."

"What about your sister?"

"Married, living in Boston with her husband. He's in construction but, like, management somewhere. He doesn't swing a hammer. Doesn't like me much because I give him the creeps."

"Sounds like she may have made a mistake in marrying him."

"No, not at all. He's really a good guy and good to her. It's all I can ask, really."

"You really are a good man if that's the point of view you have about it," she murmured.

"Thanks."

"You're welcome."

Peace was reestablished, and I didn't want to mess it up.

"I'll make a pallet on the floor for tonight for myself," I said.

She frowned. "That won't be necessary."

"Look, I feel like I've already pushed my luck with—"

"I said it's okay." Her tone was gentle but brooked no argument.

"Okay." I capitulated way too easy, but I didn't want to wreck whatever fragile peace we put into place over something so trivial. Besides, there were worse things I could think of than sharing the small bed with her for another night.

"I'll check the weather after we eat," I said, sure she wanted to get back to her life. I mean, she had to have people worried about her.

"Okay, how are you going to do that?" she asked. "Look outside? The Farmer's Almanac?"

I laughed at that and shook my head. "Wind up radio, I get some stations out here."

"Ah." She nodded, her slow teasing smile so lovely and setting my heart to beating faster.

We finished eating and I dug out the emergency FM/AM radio and handed it to her, flipping out the crank and letting her have at it while I cleaned up and did the dishes.

"Okay, what channel?" she asked.

I told her and she twisted the dial, skipping through stations and static until the regular weather announcement came through. It wasn't good. A storm of the century type of deal. Record snowfalls, the weather out there calm only because we'd reached the eye of the storm. The second wall should be sweeping over us starting late tonight, early tomorrow morning and last all the way through the next day.

"Sounds like at least another night after this one," she said and trapped her bottom lip between her teeth.

"Got people missing you, I reckon," I said and she nodded.

"Probably my sister, Miri, and her man, Kavion." She thought of someone else but didn't look too happy about it, so as much as I wanted to know, I didn't bring it up fearing it would be that guy she'd had the affair with. Mixed bag of bricks on feelings, I'd imagine.

"I bet they're all worried, and I wish I had a way for you to let them know you were okay but I kind of intentionally don't bring anything out here to communicate with."

"What about your sister?" she asked softly.

I wiped off my hands with a dish cloth and took the still steaming metal pail of dish water up to take it outside.

"She knows if I don't make the rendezvous to send search and rescue out to look," I said and I knew it sounded harsh, cold, even… but it was the way I preferred things. Doing them as old-school as possible.

Blyn arched her brows and didn't say anything, mulling that information over while I set the pail aside and shrugged into my outerwear.

"Be careful," she said, and I smiled. The wind wasn't half as bad as it'd been out there, moaning through the cabin eaves, but it was still rustling pretty significantly.

"I'll be back before you know it. I promise. Stay here with the lady, Shep."

I went out and tossed the dishwater beneath the trees, preferring to keep the food bits clear of my indoor drain. I scrubbed the bucket out with snow, and on impulse, brought a pail full of snow back in with me to melt.

Blyn sighed when I came back in, tension easing out of her shoulders and I realized that she was really nervous, really depending on me to come back each time I went out. She was a lot more scared than she was letting on, and I decided that I needed to be more cognizant of that fact.

She was a city girl, through and through. Made me feel sorry for her.

"Is that it, then? For tonight?" she asked, and she meant for it to sound light, which she succeeded on that front but her hard swallow belied her worry.

"Worried about me?" I teased lightly, unable to resist poking at it. She met my gaze, her eyes lovely, dark, twin deep pools.

"Yes, but I can't say it's entirely selfish, though I'm pretty sure that was where you were going with that question," she said.

I believed her. I believed her so hard it almost rocked me back on my heels.

"I don't freak you out?" I asked. "Make you uncomfortable?" My curiosity driving the words off my tongue like a runaway carriage off a cliff in some of the old cowboy movies I'd enjoyed growing up.

"At first, maybe," she said reluctantly, *truthfully*, "but no, not anymore. You've been anything but kind to me. I owe you more than I can repay at this point."

"You don't owe me anything," I said, setting the pail over on the concrete pad near the cabin's drain.

"We'll have to agree to disagree on that," she said and I nodded.

"Okay," I agreed. To disagree, apparently.

She was both beautiful and strange to me. I could feel this invisible push and pull with her and I have to say, all it really did was intrigue me. Made me want to know more. Guess I had like another day and a half or so to figure her out, at least according to the weather service.

What I wouldn't give for longer.

5

*B*lyn...

I couldn't get enough of the fact that Jayse could touch me, even the simplest touch, and there was just nothing... I was convinced, by this point, that he had no idea what he was. It had a strangely calming effect.

The fact that we could brush fingertips and I *couldn't* see a thing had made me a little reckless, and I had spilled one of my deepest darkest secrets. The one about Dax. Mostly because I just hadn't felt like I could keep it in anymore. I needed it out, into the light, so I could bring that short chapter of my life a touch of closure, but also because secretly, there was a part of me that wanted to know if it would be a deal breaker for a man like Jayse.

I had mixed feelings on that. One, why should I care? Other than I found him insanely attractive, and not at all because he was a Null and I was seriously craving the casual contact. To touch in even the slightest way, without a barrage of his life story in living color, searing into my mind. All the loneliness, the pain of a misunderstood... I didn't know if being a Null could be considered a gift.

It certainly had been used as a weapon. Of course, where mankind was concerned, *everything* could be used as a weapon. Witches had been able to use their powers as weapons for centuries, but there were consequences. The rule of three... if you abused your power, it could and would come back in horrible ways, which was an unsettling thought and one I had had before where I was concerned.

I suffered greatly with the use of my powers to perpetuate a greater good. It was the only thing that kept me from suffering too greatly, from ignoring the personal cost – the fact that what I was doing *was* good. The fact that the way I used my powers saved lives, stopped the destruction and pain for others, brought about justice to those who might not otherwise get it.

Still, it *was* at such a great personal cost that I had to stop and wonder to myself if just because I *could*, did that mean I really *should*?

"Blyn?"

I startled somewhat out of my reverie and my eyes flicked up to Jayse's which had revealed themselves in the dim lighting of the cabin earlier that day to be an earthy green.

"Yes?"

"Are you okay?"

"Oh, you know," I said lightly, "still trying my best to stave off a mental and emotional breakdown."

He'd changed, in the corner, behind my hanging clothes, into a pair of thick, warm, flannel pants and a waffle pattern thermal long-sleeved shirt; white above gray and black plaid. He sat down on the edge of the bed and said, "Can I ask you a weird favor?"

"Um, sure..." and I almost felt guilty expecting something weirdly sexual to be asked of me, but that was honestly just the way it was for women nowadays. Although, I didn't especially think it was a particularly *new* phenomenon with the times.

"Can I comb your hair?"

"What?" I asked, taken aback.

"I promise, it's not a perverted sex thing. I just used to comb my sister's hair for her when my mom's hands got too bad to do it anymore, and I was hoping you would let me braid it or something so I didn't end up with it in my mouth in the middle of the night."

"Oh. Yeah, sure... that might be nice, actually."

"Okay."

He got up, found a comb and a rubber band – yes, the awful kind you wouldn't want to use as a ponytail holder, but that should be fine at the end of a braid. He came back to me and said, "No, don't move," when I went to do just that. He climbed up into the bed behind me and settled in, his hands gentle as he gathered up my long hair.

I closed my eyes, knowing he couldn't see my face and relished the contact without my sight to ruin everything.

"What happened to your mother's hands?" I asked quietly when he pulled the comb through my locks for a third time.

"Early onset rheumatoid arthritis. They hurt her so bad, that by the time I was thirteen, I was taking care of most things around the house and my sister."

My heart melted just a little.

"That's a lot for any thirteen-year-old boy to take on."

"Nah," he said unfazed. "I was the man of the house; it was my responsibility to take care of things."

"Your mother raised a good man," I murmured, a wash of tingles sweeping from the crown of my head over my shoulders and down my back at his light and gentle touch. I have to confess, having my hair brushed and played with was a guilty pleasure of mine. I could sit and let my circle sisters do it for hours, but this was the first time I'd ever let a man do it. It was the first time I had ever had a man *want* to do it, *ask* to do it, and I was a bit taken aback but in a pleasant way.

It was nice to be nurtured by a masculine influence for a change. I was so used to the men around me being tough minded and territorial. Such was the life of a freaky witch consultant in the male-dominated field of police work. I'd been doing what I did for the Boston police for going on five years now, and only in the last few months were the police around me in the building I worked in starting to look at me with anything akin to respect.

Jayse combed through my hair for a long time. Much longer than was necessary to free it of any tangles, before he began to weave three sections into a simple single braid down the center of my back.

"There you go," he murmured and set the comb aside on the

rickety wooden chair he'd pulled up beside the bed to act as a night table.

"Thank you," I murmured.

"Thank *you* for not thinking it all weird."

"Not at all," I said, and he chuckled.

"Not sure how you want to do this," he said, easing his leg from around me and moving himself onto his side.

"Just lie on your back," I said, and he looked at me skeptically but did as I asked.

I eased myself onto my side along the narrow strip of bed left behind and fitted myself against his side, pressing my head into the curve of his shoulder, atop the swell of his chest. He sucked in a sharp breath when I draped my leg across his, his hand automatically going to the outside of my knee, palming it. I froze slightly at the contact of his rough palm on my bare skin but eventually slipped easily into the intimate yet still platonic embrace.

Yeah right.

"That's not so bad, is it?" I asked softly.

"Not bad at all," he agreed, although neither of us could really sleep. The lantern had been dimmed to the point it left very little light and the dancing flames of the woodstove was mostly what was left to see anything by.

I closed my eyes, the crackling of the wood and the steady cadence of the howling wind outside lulling me, the shallow but even breaths of Jayse beneath me something to cling to, so I didn't drift so far so fast.

"You okay?" he asked.

"Mm-hmm, you?"

"I'm okay," he said and his voice was a nice timbre, sounding slightly surprised.

I smiled and sank further into the sensation of his arm curved around my back.

"Thank you," I murmured.

"For what?"

"I don't get a lot of human touch, this is nice."

He didn't say anything to that, and the silence sounded thoughtful. Finally, a short time later when I was just on the verge of sleep, he said, "You're welcome, and you're right. It *is* nice."

I smiled as I fell asleep to the sounds of the storm outside, and for once, the storm on the inside was quiet.

ayse...

I felt bad leaving her inside on her own most of the day, but I promised I would make it up to her.

I worked my ass off making sure everything was good. Started the snowmobile, and broke some trail, but there wasn't any getting very far. The snow was still coming down from the sky in hearty amounts that didn't seem like they would let up any time soon, but the wind had slowed down significantly, and the worst of it looked like it'd blown itself out. I should be able to take her back to her cabin tomorrow if the trail wasn't too busted up with fallen trees too big for me to handle on my own.

Shep bounded about in the snow while I restocked some of the firewood we'd burned through, and I was encouraged when the cabin door opened revealing Blyn in my shirt and the thick pair of wool socks I'd put on her feet.

"I raided your stash of canned goods and fixed us some chicken soup," she called out.

"Sounds awesome!" I called back. "Go back inside and sit tight, eat yours up, I'll be in in a minute."

"Okay, I feel bad eating your food. You can restock from the kitchen pantry at my family cabin when you take me there," she called, and I was touched that she would think about me and Shep and our ability to make it through the rest of our stay here.

"Go back inside, don't catch cold," I called. She nodded and went back inside, closing the cabin door.

"I think she likes me," I told Shep. "What do you think?"

He barked at me once and I laughed and nodded.

"Yeah, I think so, too."

Truth was, I didn't speak Husky and I didn't know what my dog had to really say about it, but if it was one thing I did know about Shep, he was an eternal optimist so I took his answer as a good sign.

I went in for lunch and she rose to pour me some soup. I waved her down saying, "You need to stay off of that leg." She winced as she lowered herself back onto the bed, my tattered paperback of one of my favorite Tom Clancy novels turned on its face to hold her spot.

"Hope you don't mind," she said when I chuckled over the book.

"Not at all. Be nice to have somebody to talk about it with."

She smiled and nodded, some wisps of her beautiful dark hair escaping the braid I'd done for her last night.

"I'm getting a little stir crazy," she confessed.

"Should be able to take you in tomorrow barring any big treefalls along the trail I can't get through with my gear."

"Is it sad I'm a little torn about that?" she asked.

"Oh, yeah? How's that?" I asked.

"On the one hand, I really miss indoor plumbing," she said and I laughed. "But on the other…" My breath caught and I really wanted her to say something cheesy along the lines of *I'm really going to miss you.* "The solitude and silence out here have been really nice, and so…" she hesitated and blushing rushed out, "so has the company."

Pretty sure that my heart did a barrel roll in my chest, dropping into my stomach and then soaring back in place on a thermal of sheer, unadulterated joy.

I bowed my head and nodded. "Can't say there's anyone else I would want to be trapped in a blizzard with."

She scoffed. "Please, I'm a hot mess," she said.

"From the sound of it, you've been through a lot," I said.

"Hard to run from your mistakes when they live inside of you, taking up so much headspace, larger than life," she said quietly.

"Our mistakes aren't what defines us," I told her. "It's how we handle them; what we do with them, that does."

She eyed me cautiously, chewing a spoonful of chicken noodle thoughtfully.

"Wow," she said dryly, after swallowing. "You get that out of a fortune cookie?" The twinkle of mischief in her eyes took any insult out of her words. I laughed and shook my head.

"No, just been a philosophy on life I've had for a while."

"It's a good philosophy," she said.

"Feel free to steal it and make good use of it."

She smiled and it held only the slightest edge of sadness.

"You know, nobody knows. We can't suddenly request different partners when everyone knows how well we work together, but that side of us? It's done. We both regret it, and it can't and won't happen again. We both agreed."

I nodded slowly, wondering what she was getting at and not really knowing how to respond, once again.

"That's good," I said. "Sounds like you guys have it all figured out."

She nodded and took a deep breath and let it out in a rush.

"I still feel awful," she said. "And I could really use a shower."

I knew that she felt dirty and unclean about whatever affair she'd had with her partner but…

"I think maybe I can help with that in a few hours."

"What? A shower?"

"If you'd like, something as close to one as I can get you anyway,"

"I would love that, actually," she said wistfully. "You have no idea."

Oh, I did, believe me, and I was surprisingly willing to do just about anything to chase the haunted sorrow out of her dark eyes. If only for just a little while.

"I'll start getting you set up as soon as I finish this, then."

"I owe you my life, now I owe it to you times two."

I chuckled and finished up my soup, had a second bowl and then got to work melting down and heating snow for bathwater.

We bantered as I worked. She wanted to help, I said no. She really needed to stay off her ankle, at least until a doctor could look at it. Finally, I had her all set up, seated on the floor near the concrete corner drain on a sleeping bag. Towels at the ready, a washcloth at hand and a bar of soap; a pail of gently steaming water on the concrete recess in the floor.

"Okay, I think that about does it. I'll be back in to help you up after a while."

"Thank you," she murmured and her eyes were filled with gratitude.

"It's nothing," I said back. "Come on, Shep." My dog bounded to his paws, his tongue lolling out the side of his canine grin, and I opened up the door for us to exit.

I really wanted to stay inside where it was warm, but a promise was a promise.

7

*B*lyn...

The silence was solemn after he'd gone and I closed my eyes, torn between relishing my aloneness for this and missing his company. I plucked at the buttons on the front of his cozy flannel shirt and set it aside and behind me, shimmying awkwardly out of my panties until I rested nude atop the pallet of old sleeping bags and towels he'd laid against the rough, unfinished wood floor.

I sighed, picking up the washcloth and swishing it in the pail of warm water, the fragrant bar of soap set on a plate to one side waiting for me to use it.

It was little better than a whore's bath but it felt absolutely divine to wash my face and to just generally be clean once more. I unwrapped my ankle, baring my teeth at the deep purple and in some areas almost black, coloring of my skin where the trap had bit through my boot and had clamped painfully into my flesh, just below the round bone on the outside. I winced and prodded gently at it with damp fingertips.

I would have to call Miri as soon as my phone had enough charge when I was back at my family's vacation cabin. She would know what to do, surely, but I had a feeling she would be directing me to a doctor versed in modern Western medicine in addition to whatever she could do using the old ways and her hedge witchery.

I listened to the wind pick up outside, the fire warm and crackling cheerily in the grate beside me as I finished up washing, rinsing the washcloth in the warm bucket, wringing it out, the water tinkling hypnotically, the sounds soothing along with the warmth of the cabin with how icy I knew it to be outdoors.

I felt equal parts badly for and grateful to Jayse for braving the freezing temperatures simply to give me privacy.

"Shep, no!" he called out, the shout muffled before the cabin door burst inward as I wrapped myself in the dry and warm towel. Well, not so much as wrapped as pulled it from around my back where it lay folded behind me to clutch it to my chest.

"Godamnit, dog!" Jayse cried, a rueful grin on his lips despite his harsh tone. He sighed, stepping in to snatch Shep by the collar.

"No, it's fine!" I declared. "I was done, just come inside." Jayse hurried in behind his Husky and shut the door against the blowing snow.

"I am so sorry—"

"It's fine," I gently cut him off, turning my head. "Just get warm."

"Thanks," he said, moving into the corner behind my hanging clothes to change into his usual indoor wear.

I sat still, fixing my eyes on the water that I'd spilled seeping across the concrete, trying for the life of me to give him the same courtesy he had been giving me with regard to privacy, unable to help how much I ached to look. To see if he appeared as fit and toned as he'd felt beneath my cheek, under my arm and thigh as I'd lain draped over him the night before.

"Hey, what's wrong," he murmured, settling on the floor behind me, sweeping my hair gently out of my face and draping it over my opposite shoulder. I closed my eyes and realized how strange I must look, frozen to the spot, back exposed, down one flank to my hip. He breathed out, and it swept along my shoulder and back and I trembled with desire.

"Nothing," I said, voice cracking on the lie.

"Tell me what hurts," he said, and I closed my eyes.

"My heart."

"Oh," he whispered, and he didn't sound the least bit surprised. His lips were warm, trembling slightly where they made contact with the skin of my shoulder. I stared hard at the floor, breath escaping me in a shuddering sigh, completely torn.

The attraction was mutual, strong, and becoming stronger by the moment. With every single minute we spent in each other's presence, I felt drawn in further and I wanted so badly to let go, to just allow myself to take refuge in his touch. It left me so at war with myself over whether this was a good idea that I was afraid I gave him the wrong impression.

"Tell me to stop," he whispered, his lips coming back down against my skin and simply resting there, his breath warm, the air rushing across my skin as he breathed me in, a subtle yet erotic current that electrified me.

"I don't want you to." The truth tumbled from my own lips before I could stop it.

"Yeah?" he asked, to be sure.

"I don't want you to stop," I assured him, against my own better judgment.

His hands fell gently to my hips, his beard tickling my skin as he hovered just above it, letting his breath rush over my neck and shoulder, the sensation stealing mine. I was frozen in place, petrified by just how much I wanted this, my heart crying out for some solace and relief, my mind quailing, screaming *bad idea, bad idea, bad idea!*

I was so torn, so confused, and so I tried valiantly to give in to the wishes of my body, my heart, over my mind. Leaning back into his chest, concentrating on the feel of his arms sliding around me, shivering with want as his calloused fingertips slid over my heated skin beneath the cover of the towel.

He committed right back, his mouth pressing against my flesh, his tongue flicking against the side of my neck as he groaned. A man finally allowed to taste nourishment long denied him. His hands splayed flat against my stomach, between my breasts and I reached up, my hand cupping his cheek as he worked his mouth against that sweet spot.

I sucked in a sharp breath, arching, pressing my body into his hands, my head back against his shoulder, my gasp sudden and welcome as he worked that pleasure point in the side of my neck and a wash of ecstasy swept down my opposite side, my brain cross wiring from the rush of sensation.

He moaned appreciatively at my responsiveness, tightening his hold and yet took his time with unraveling my misgivings, pulling the thread that left any thoughts cascading in ribbons of light, spiraling to the floor to dissolve like melting snow.

"Blyn," he murmured, voice light, but tight with a desperation, a need to be as close as two people can be.

I felt it too, needed his hands on me, his body against mine, no barriers, and his cock inside me. I desperately needed this intimacy, this touch, this connection, all without the knowing. Without feeling his feelings, without knowing his guilt, his sorrow, and his anger. Without knowing *everything*. Just me inside my own head and him inside of his yet still sharing this moment. Two people becoming one out of mutual choice, not being stripped of all choice in the matter by rogue magic.

I kneeled up and twisted, walking on my knees, my hands on his shoulders steadying myself as I climbed into his lap, hands traveling over the waffle pattern, a textural delight against my palms and fingertips as I settled to face him. His hazel-green eyes fixed on mine, his light brown hair, almost blond, flopping against his forehead, begged for me to run my fingers through it, so I did.

He put his arms around me, steel bands around my back crushing me to him as I captured his mouth with mine and kissed him desperate for a distraction from my pain, and yes, as awful as it was to admit, for his touch to erase Dax's, to erase my sins and make me new.

He sucked a breath in between gritted teeth, my name leaving his lips like a prayer to the wilderness outside. His hands traveling the sweeps and curves of my body, mapping them, committing every line and landmark to memory as I lifted his thermal shirt over his head.

He let me, pressing his hard body against mine, his skin warm, as I pressed my tits against his chest, my mouth back to his as he practically worshipped me with his eyes and his mouth, his hands traveling to my ass, hauling me up and down, grinding us against each other, my pussy a soaking, wanting ache where his hard length slid against it through his flannel pants.

I reached between us, freeing his erection from the waistband of his pants, shoving them down in front so I could wrap nimble fingers around his scorching length. His eyes closed, his breath coming labored as he choked out, "Oh, fuck." I smiled at his reaction and stroked him with surety, giving a little twist to my wrist action, relishing the feel of him against my palm, his crown slicked with precum.

"Blyn." His voice was strained with warning and I rose up on my knees to fit him at my entrance.

His hands gripped my hips firmly, but tenderly as I lowered myself down over him. His cock was perfect, long but not too thick, pressing out into my walls and giving me a satisfyingly full feeling without stretching me too much. A perfect fit, he bottomed out against my cervix, touching off that slightly spicy glow inside me that traveled along my bloodstream like a favorite melody – sweet and exotic; totally enticing.

We danced to the music the sensation of having him inside me played, and it was pure passion. The silence in my head, the joy in my heart purely my own. I rocked my hips and listened to him moan breathless with desire and longing. He sat up, his arms around me stilling me, one hand buried in the back of my hair the other tight to my ass as he kissed me. His mouth on mine a powerful thing as he devoured my initial doubts and gave me just what I needed.

Closeness, contact, with no expectations. No guilt, no sorrow, no regret.

I buried my fingers in his hair, which was softer than it looked, and kissed him back with fierceness and understanding. He was the shelter from the emotional storm I harbored inside. I was the cure, the key that set him free from his prison of loneliness. We each needed the other for differing reasons but both for valid reasons just the same.

I threw back my head, breath tumbling from my lips in a glorious rush of acceptance as I rocked in his lap not even caring that my ankle hurt, the edge of pain making the pleasure from his touch, his kiss, the depth of his penetration that much sweeter.

God and Goddess if I weren't careful, I could too easily love this man with everything I was for the gift he was giving me right now.

8

*J*ayse...

She was so perfect. So soft and yielding in my arms but so fierce at the same time. She knew what she wanted, wasn't shy about taking it from me, but she gave so much of herself in return. No, I was not sitting here empty handed. My arms were overflowing with this bold and beautiful woman who smelled of wind and starlight, who felt like warmth and gossamer in my arms and whose taste was more intoxicating than anything I'd ever drunk.

She kissed me, moaning quietly into my mouth, her hips swaying in a sensual grind, touching off fireworks behind my eyelids. My cock was seated deep inside her soft and yielding depths, perfectly ensconced in her body, her pussy gripping me with fervor, driving me all sorts of wild until my eyes rolled back in my head and I seriously thought I was going to pass out from the pleasure.

I lay back on the floor and looked up at her, rigid above me, her hands bracing against my chest. I gripped her hips and drove myself up into her and her eyes fluttered shut, her breath coming in an erotic gasp. She stilled to let me do my thing, her voice firm as she praised me, encouraged me, "Oh, Jayse, yes, just like that!"

I thrust up inside her over and over, the sounds of our bodies clapping together underscored by our deep and even panting. She moaned, I groaned and somehow in the midst of it all it came together to make sweet music.

God, she drove me crazy, and as much as I loved her on top, loved to watch her move above me and ride me, it just wasn't quite getting me there and it had to be killing her ankle. I sat up, and wound my arms around her, crushing the perfect globes of her breasts against my chest, and stilling her.

"Hang onto me," I ordered gruffly and her arms went around my neck, holding to me fast. It was awkward as fuck getting my legs up under me to stand up and move us to the bed.

It took a few false starts, and some giggling on her part which was infectious. She said, "Put me down and this will go much—" Which of course, as soon as she said anything at all, I got it and her request was cut off in an adorable girlish squeal that had Shep raising his head off his paws where he'd stretched out on his dog bed opposite the fire to bask in its heat.

"Stay," I said low and even. I couldn't honestly tell you who I had directed it at. Him or her.

The mood tumbled back into the sensual and erotic when I laid her back on the bed and took up place over her, bracing myself on my hands, staring into her eyes as I drove myself deep into her welcoming heat. Her eyes fluttered shut, and I rested my forehead against hers, her fingers running through my hair, her nails lightly scratching against my scalp as I made love to her.

It was a strange thing, sudden, and yet subtle, the way my body responded to hers, the way my heart followed soon after. It was confusing to me but in all the best kinds of ways. I desired her, burned for her, had felt something deep and inexplicable the moment I'd laid eyes on her smooth features, her body laying prone in the pure white snowfall only a couple of days ago.

It could have been a century ago for how I felt for her now.

It was terrifying, in a way. I'd been let down, had been hurt, hell, had been shunned practically my whole life and I was afraid that for how different this felt? It would end the same way... with rejection.

With betrayal. With a hurt beyond measure... but I couldn't take the isolation anymore and for now, I was here with her and she was here with me and both of us were so deep into each other there was no telling where one of us left off and the other began.

It was probably the most pleasurable and united I'd ever been with a woman – not that I'd ever had a whole lot of practice, just two before her and they weren't exactly dalliances that lasted very long. Just long enough to crush me in the end.

"Jayse! Oh, my God!" she cried, arching beneath me, her body pressing into mine, shuddering and taking me to new heights, places I'd never been sexually or otherwise.

It hit me, out of the blue and I came, her pussy throbbing around my shaft, drawing me in deep, holding onto me.

This woman held me in the palm of her hand and I wasn't good with this being a onetime thing. We needed to talk about it. I needed her to stick with me, to want to see me again, and I was afraid that wouldn't happen. Desperately afraid it wouldn't, like I'd never feared anything before.

"God, you're amazing, Blyn," I murmured, placing my lips against hers in a gentle kiss, stealing her breath and replacing it with mine.

"Let's do that again," she gasped, and I smiled, probably the biggest smile I'd ever smiled in my whole life.

"Gimme five or ten minutes."

"Okay."

SHE LAY ACROSS MY CHEST, tracing patterns against my ribs. It tickled, but not in a way that made me want her to stop. She could do whatever she wanted to me. I'd be a liar if I said I wasn't totally infatuated with her.

The firelight from the front grate of the woodstove was reflected in her eyes which were distant, lost in thought.

"What are you thinking?" I asked her gently, smoothing a hand through her hair.

"I was thinking, 'where do we go from here?'" she answered. "I'm not ready for this to end."

"I know, me either, but you have your life and I have to stay out here through the end of the season. I've got a lot riding on having a successful one."

"I know," she murmured. "I can wait until after, if you can."

She sounded hopeful and I smiled to myself. "I definitely can," I said. "I'd keep you one more day if I could, but I really want you to get to a doctor and get that leg checked out."

She chuckled, but it didn't hold much happiness. "Story of my life, find something good and immediately something has to happen to end it all too quickly."

"It ain't over," I whispered. "Not by a long shot." I pressed my lips to her hair in a simple kiss.

She pushed herself up into a sitting position and lowered her mouth to mine. Her lips on my lips was the sweetest sensation and I would be mightily sorry to let her go come tomorrow.

"I want you to restock your food from my cabin's pantry," she said in a tone that would brook no argument and I frowned slightly.

"How'd you know I was starting to really get worried about that?" I asked.

"Common sense," she said with an arched brow, laying herself back down, draped artfully over me.

"Sure you can spare it?" I asked.

She snorted, and laughed at me a little. "Unlike *you*, I can hit the grocery store."

"Okay, yeah. Fair point." I chuckled along with her.

"Is it bad I don't want to go back?" she asked after a time. Her voice held the slightly far away sound of living in a daydream and I could sympathize. I didn't want her to, I wanted her to stay with me. I wanted to explore this new thing with her... but we were adults and that's not how this worked.

I hated being a downer when I said, "No, it's not bad, but we both know there are people out there who are probably worried about you, and we both have our separate lives to go back to. At least for the time being."

"Yeah." She sounded dejected.

I kissed the top of her head again and breathed her in slightly, telling her, "Don't worry about it too much right now. Just enjoy the time we've got left. I promise, we'll reconnect soon."

She cuddled into me and my smile could have lit up the cabin. I held her close, the wind howling through the eaves, the snow pattering wetly against the single cabin window which wasn't glass, but rather a sheet of scuffed acrylic. It wasn't meant to look out of, just to supply some weak daylight.

Shep rose his head off his paws and let out a half yap, half bark. Blyn jumped against my side.

"What is it, boy?"

Shep bobbed his head a few times, made an almost excited whining noise and cocked his shaggy head just as the mournful howl of wolves sounded outside. They were entirely too close for comfort without the walls of the cabin to secure us.

Blyn sucked in a sharp breath and I looked down at her, her deep brown eyes aglow with excitement, her lips curving into a smile as wild as the wolf-song outside.

"It's beautiful," she murmured between howls and I felt myself smile. They were beautiful, and they were also part of the reason I was out here trapping. An effort to thin the pack and protect local live-stock around these parts. Still, I had to agree. There wasn't much out there more beautiful than the wilds around here. Not just the flora but the fauna as well.

There wasn't much that was more beautiful to me than nature, except the woman in my arms right now. Then again, she seemed right at home out here. Part of the wilds I'd so grown to love as a boy and appreciate even more as a man.

I held her close, laughing with her as my dog joined in on the howling.

9

*B*lyn...

It took *hours* to reach my family's vacation cabin with all of its modern luxuries. I can't tell you how much I missed them. The first thing I did upon entering through the kitchen off the wrap-around deck, was plug in my phone. While it was charging, I limped around the kitchen island to put on the kettle to fix us some tea or hot chocolate.

"Please sit down," Jayse pleaded, pulling out one of the stools beneath the granite kitchen island.

"Fine, but only if you kiss me before you raid the pantry," I murmured.

"Deal." He smiled down at me and brought his mouth to mine.

I was going to miss him, which I found odd for hardly having known him for very long. He caressed my cheek with rough fingers and pulled back reluctantly.

"Bittersweet, isn't it?" I asked and he nodded.

"Trapping season only has a few weeks left," he said and I nodded.

"You know where to find me," I said.

"Not if you don't write it down for me." He winked and I grinned. He brought the pad and pen over from the end of the kitchen counter by the door and I set to work writing down my name, phone number, and the address to the Boston police station where I worked.

He set about filling his canvas rucksack with canned goods from the pantry while I did it. We bantered lightly, chatting amicably all while our time together wound down, down, and further down.

"I think this is all I can fit," he said, lifting the sack onto his shoulder.

I sighed and smiled, sad that his departure needed to take place so soon. "Here." I slipped the folded paper with my information and a note into a plastic sandwich bag from the kitchen drawer, sealing it away for safe waterproof keeping.

He smiled at me and tucked it away, and I adored the smile lines around his green eyes, edged in bronze. A truly remarkable pattern of hazel. Deeply moving, reminding me of the coming spring, making me long for longer days and shorter nights where the frozen ground receded and a chance to finally see him again came because once he was gone…

Once he was gone, I didn't know what was going to happen to me.

I didn't know if my powers would come back gradually, or all at once. I almost, selfishly, wished they would be gone forever. In some ways, I wished I could consult the family book, but I didn't know if that was wise. I mean, what if Jayse's anti-magic of being a Null was carried almost like a contagion? I just didn't know if by going to the family book and touching it, if it would dispel some of its magic. There were spells in there, that could be affected or lost – I mean, couldn't there?

Unfortunately, I just didn't know. There wasn't really a way *to* know. Nulls weren't exactly an everyday occurrence. Not since the days of the Spanish Inquisition and those days were *long* gone. Even if a witch could trace their lineage back that far, like the Courtney family could. There wasn't any guarantee there would be any records kept in the family books. A lot of the original grimoires were destroyed back then and a lot of information about the Nulls destroyed along with them.

"I'll walk you out," I murmured, and I was sad that I needed to think about these things. Especially now, when it was time to say goodbye.

"Don't." He traced a gentle thumb along my cheek in a light caress, committing my features to memory. I didn't blame him. I was staring up into those new, spring-green eyes of his, edged in rich, bronze earth.

"I really want to."

"You should stay off that ankle until you can get it looked at."

"Don't argue with me, Jayse Mickelson," I said gravely, and he laughed.

"If you knew my middle name, would you use that against me too?" he asked.

I smiled and bit my bottom lip as I did it. "This is just a first and last offense," I said lightly. Delighted when his gaze fixed itself so solidly on my lip coming free from the gentle bite I'd placed it under. I could see the naked desire all over his handsome face and I liked it. The feeling was definitely mutual.

"Fine," he said, and I slipped onto my good foot, using him to steady myself.

We went out into the light trickle of snowfall. Just a single flake falling from the sky in that way that made you do a double take and wonder if it was actually snowing before you caught sight of the next one falling.

Shep barked a greeting from down by the snowmobile and sled and we went down to him. I petted his shaggy head filled with gladness and wishing that this weren't going on hiatus, knowing that it had to. Still, goodbyes were always so hard for me. Especially given the ones I'd been through as of late.

"I'll call you, come see you, as soon as I get back to the city and get cleaned up."

"Not if I see you first," I murmured, and tipped my face up to his for another kiss. He held me close and it felt so right. Even if I didn't fully understand it from a witch/Null point of view, from a human one, I did. He and I were both lonely souls. His from a lack of people around him, me from feeling like no matter how many surrounded me, I was just lost in the crowd.

The crunching of snow beneath tires had us springing apart and blushing like teenagers caught in the act. I turned just as Shep let out several happy barks at the new company and one of Loving's police SUV's crested the ridge of the driveway and began its perilous trek down its ice- and snow-covered surface until it reached a point that going further would be folly. It's not like anything had been shoveled, I was impressed Kavion even took it that far.

My sister, Miri, was the first out of the car and came running as much as the snow drifts would allow.

"Lord and Lady, thank the Goddess you're okay!" she burst out. I had my back to Jayse and was frantically signaling in front of me to cut it out and not say anything about *anything* magic right now. Miri, knowing me since we were children, stopped short and put her hand up almost as if touching some invisible barrier. Confusion, then fear flitted through her spring-green eyes and she blinked at me.

I wasn't concerned about her saying anything anymore but it broke my heart, her eyes flicking to Jayse and her leaning away from him like there was something *wrong* with him. There wasn't, but I wanted to do my research. I wanted to sit down and explain to him with all the facts, not just stories witch mothers told their witch daughters in the dark and the night to get them to behave, like my mother did.

"Hey, love? What's wrong?" Kavion demanded from behind his driver's side door as he slid his nightstick into the loop on his belt.

"Nothing!" Miri cried. "She's okay!" Then to me, worriedly, she asked, "You're okay, aren't you?"

"I'm fine," I said. "Jayse found me out there and then we got snowed into his trapper cabin. Really, I'm fine." I took a step toward my sister, forgetting myself, my ankle twinging and I gasped, losing my balance.

Jayse caught me by the back of my jacket and pulled me back against him saying, "Easy! I told you, you should have stayed inside."

"It's fine," I said breathless with pain. "I'm okay."

The sound of a third door in the SUV opening brought my attention back up the drive. Kavion was at the back-passenger door and even from here, even beside Jayse, I could feel the menace that was roiling off our new circle-mate Ivan. It rolled out, eating across the frozen distance between us like fire over gasoline and the sheer anger and hostility on his face terrified me.

I knew what Ivan Ivanovich was capable of. I had seen it firsthand close to a year ago. The moment I'd shaken his hand in the hospital. He was a monster, yet his intentions pure... and I simply didn't understand it. What I *did* understand was the lethality and barely suppressed rage flowing down the driveway in Jayse's direction and it made me lean back into him protectively, though with no magic, I wasn't sure how I would stop one such as Ivan.

"What's hurt?" Miri asked, oblivious to the melodrama playing out at her back. Even Kavion was eying Ivan carefully from beneath his Smokey-the-Bear Loving PD uniform hat.

"I, uh, need to get back to the cabin," Jayse said over the low growl of his Husky.

"Yeah," I nodded.

"Please tell me that's not your boyfriend," he said as Ivan and Kavion came down the small hill of the drive.

"No, my brother," I said without thinking.

"I thought you were an only child," he said quizzically and I found myself desperate to get him out of here before Ivan reached us with murderous intent.

"I am! Um, we've been friends since high school, he's chosen family – not blood related," I said, lying and hating myself for it. *I just want all the facts before laying them out,* I told myself for the thousandth time.

"Thank you," Miri said to him, reaching for me. I stepped away from Jayse, limping, my eyes fixed on Ivan whose nostrils flared as he drew himself up to his full height, only the pleading in my eyes staying his hand.

I knew Jayse was safe from Ivan's magic, but I also knew, from my visions, that Ivan was capable of extreme violence without the aid of his magic and fire. I just had no real context for the things I had seen and I hadn't exactly been keen on asking at the time.

Miri gasped softly when she took me by the elbows and I limped away from Jayse, making frivolous introductions.

"Jayse, this is Miri's boyfriend, Kavion, and our... friend, Ivan. Guys, I went for a walk a few days ago and accidently stepped in one of Jayse's traps. The weather was moving in and he didn't know where I had come from so we had to hole up in his cabin for a few nights waiting out the storm. He brought me back here as soon as he could."

"Sounds like a regular hero," Kavion said with a smile, oblivious to any wrong feelings and reaching out to shake Jayse's hand.

"Yeah, except for it was my trap. Should get her to a doctor to look at that ankle, trap chewed it pretty good; even if it didn't break the skin."

"We'll do that, thank you," Miri said, voice soft and grateful, even if it did hold an edge of worry.

"I gotta go," Jayse said. "I'm going to be getting back to the cabin after dark as it is."

"*Da*. That is good. You should go," Ivan agreed and yet still hung back. I was grateful for that.

"Okay..." Jayse mumbled under his breath, clearly weirded out and put off by the big Russian. "Come on, Shep!" He called to his dog which was still standing low, ears back. Shep slunk along the ground back to the sled as Jayse mounted his snowmobile and turned it on.

"I'll see you later," I called out and Ivan grunted and scowled.

"Later, Blyn." He gave a nod to Kavion and a misgiving look to Ivan. With a sharp whistle, Shep jumped onto the sled and Jayse pulled off and down the trail cutting through the woods.

We all stood quiet until Jayse was lost to sight among the trees and the rev of his snowmobile had grown distant. I felt a sadness, almost bereft at his absence but Miri, and especially Ivan had a different take.

"I don't know what to say, Blyn..." Miri said, trailing off a little helplessly and I loved her for it. Miri, who always tried to be understanding of everyone, who didn't judge, who was trying in the face of this new development.

Ivan, however, was a lot less understanding. He hocked a wad of spit and cast it out of his mouth at the ground in disgust.

"We must kill him," he said decisively.

"Whoa, dude, you really gonna say that in front of a cop?" Kavion asked, laughing a little.

"*Da*, you do not know what he is."

"Come on, I'm freezing my nuts off out here. Let's go inside and talk about it where it's warm." Kavion motioned and I winced, but didn't get more than a step or two before Ivan had surged forward and manhandled me up into his arms.

I shouted my indignation but all he did was glower at me and order me, "Be quiet," in his stern Russian accent.

I bit my lips together and we moved through the knee-deep snow to the steps up to the deck and the waiting cabin.

Once inside, Ivan set me in one of the overstuffed, contemporary leather armchairs in the living room. He reached out a hand in the direction of the fireplace and didn't even have to mutter anything, the remnants of the ends of the logs that remained in the grate igniting.

"Guess you didn't get close enough," I said and he scowled at me over his shoulder as he loaded more wood from the pile on the lintel into the maw of the stone fireplace.

"About that…" Miri said gently, her face pinched with her desire not to make waves but her deep concern winning out.

"Somebody gonna fill me in?" Kavion asked.

"I think Jayse is a Null," I said simply.

"And what is that?" Kavion raised his dark eyebrows, confusion on his deep ebony face. He was beautiful, his dark skin rich, a protective shadow at my fair-skinned sister's back. Tall and broad shouldered, he was perfect for Miri, and I loved how he loved her.

"Trouble," Ivan answered succinctly.

"No, he's not," I protested and yipped as Miri pulled my boot off of my injured leg.

"Says you." Ivan sniffed and straightened up, a roaring blaze going in front of him, glinting in his dark eyes and making his hard face seem like something from the depths of Hell with the way the firelight played on it. Of course, that could be my imagination but likely... it wasn't.

I had seen him burn men alive. I had felt his every emotion as he had done it, and I knew that a dark part of him had *liked* what he had done. That it had given him a perverse sense of satisfaction. All of it gleaned within a heartbeat before he'd had the presence of mind to slam shut the connection. I'd gleaned a lot with that single hand-shake, and it was impressive him using his own magic as a shield from mine. Not many could do that. Ivan was just that powerful, though.

"He's not dangerous," I protested.

"He is."

"Okay, Ivan." I rolled my eyes. "Never mind that I just spent the last few days with him snowed into his cabin."

"Means nothing."

"It does too! He doesn't even know!" I argued.

"They are dangerous, his kind." Ivan scowled at me as if that was that and there was no more to it.

"Okay, now I'm *really* lost," Kavion remarked and the sentiment was echoed by Miri.

"I am too. Whatever anti-magic supernova black hole spell that's not a spell he has going on has made it nearly impossible to perform any magic on you to see what's going on. I'm afraid I am going to have to leave the diagnosing to your typical Western medicine, but once I know what it is exactly that you've done to yourself, I should be able to help."

"It will wear off," Ivan said and I felt my shoulders deflate a little in disappointment.

"How soon?" I asked.

"Longer you're with them, longer it takes," he said. "But I do know, the longer you are around them, that eventually things..." he waved his hands in the air and frowned groping for the right word in English. Which, I had to hand it to him. His English, though heavily accented, was getting remarkably better.

"Balance?" Miri suggested.

"Yes, like scales." He nodded and held his hands palm up, juggling them back and forth as if first one was weighted and then the other.

"How do you know all this?" I asked.

"I have seen it before. They are weapon, not people."

"Whoa, that's a pretty hard line, brother. You encounter somebody like him before?"

"*Da*. Kill him. Is better." Ivan gave a sturdy nod and sniffed.

"We are *not* going to kill him, yo." Kavion leaned back and rolled his eyes dramatically. "You gotta leave that old-world shit in the old world, man. Especially in front of me. I'm a fuckin' cop now."

Ivan's forehead wrinkled and he said, "Better him than us."

"Alright, stop!" Miri declared when I opened my mouth to speak. "Ivan," she said in a conciliatory tone. "He hasn't done anything bad yet, Blyn says he doesn't even know about what he is, so let's calm down and first things first, yeah?"

"And that would be?" I asked tiredly. It'd already been a long day and my ankle was throbbing and I wanted a shower, and like a week's worth of sleep in my comfy bed. I'd settle for the shower and for my ankle to stop hurting.

"You, to the hospital for some x-rays of that foot."

I sighed and nodded reluctantly and asked, "Can you at least help me get into some clean clothes first?"

"Sure," she said softly at the same time Ivan scooped me up and said, "*Nyet.*"

Oh, for the love of Lord and Lady...

I got cleaned up and my change of clothes. Ivan sulked, and by the time I was bundled into the back of Kavion's patrol car, I was so frustrated but touched by their doting, I didn't know what to do with myself.

I didn't deserve any of it. I knew that. In fact, my emotions sunk to a whole new low as I stared at the snow piled high to either side of the road as we rolled along carefully in the wake of a snow plow.

I was afraid for Jayse. Afraid of what Ivan might do. It was uncomfortable, sitting back here beside him, and for once I wished I could sense what he was thinking but my powers remained resolutely... I don't know, missing? Shut down? I didn't know how to describe it. I would reach for that part of myself and things just remained comfortably numb but now I was actually missing my abilities. I was almost desperate for them, if only to know my circle-mate's intentions.

"Blyn, are you alright?" Miri asked softly from the front seat.

"Yes and no," I said with a sigh.

"What's wrong?" she asked.

"I don't want to talk about it," I said. "At least, not right now."

"That guy didn't fuck with you at all, did he?" Kavion asked.

I shook my head and looked back from the white outside the window to see his dark eyes staring at me in the rearview mirror.

"No," I said. "Not at all. He took good care of me."

"So, what's got you down?" he asked, and I slid a sideways look to Ivan, shivering when I realized he was staring at me intently.

He turned his head imperiously to stare forward, his chin raised in a sort of defiance, not speaking, but then again, I wasn't either. I didn't know what to say or how to explain things. Especially considering he terrified me so...

We arrived at the nearest urgent care that had any sort of proficiency with non-life-threatening injuries and even though he scared me so, Ivan insisted on helping me. He was a strange man, for sure, and I didn't know *why* he cared so much about what I thought when he clearly paid no attention and had no care for what anyone else thought of him, including the medical staff that was there to care for me.

He stood, a veritable mountain of a man, hulking intimidatingly in the corner of first the waiting room, and then *my* room and would not be dissuaded. Kavion, at least, kept to the waiting room and Miri, thankfully stayed with me, holding my hand.

Still, it was an intense level of awkward when the staff, eyeing Ivan cautiously, asked if I felt comfortable or safe having him stick with me. I smiled and lied, saying it was perfectly fine, but only because I knew he would not be dissuaded and it would cause a bigger scene than it was worth to have him removed.

It both was and wasn't fine, but it was my war to wage, *later*. Right now, I really *did* need to be seen and have my ankle looked at properly. It'd waited long enough.

"And you say you've RICEed it?" the doctor asked, looking at the x-ray on the computer screen.

"Yes, Rest, Ice, Compression, and Elevation." I nodded.

"Good call. In this instance, I don't see anything broken, but there could be some serious soft tissue damage that's above my paygrade to diagnose. I recommend a walking boot for now; we can get you set up here and bill your insurance. I'm also going to recommend you see a specialist in sports medicine. Now, until you can get in to see that specialist, I would stay off of it as much as possible. In fact, I'm going to add some crutches to this order."

I sighed and nodded. I had suspected as much, but I didn't want to say anything. I was given prescription anti-inflammatories, a prescription pain killer, and fitted for a walking boot and handed crutches. Not that I got to use them with Ivan around. He handed the crutches off to Miri and lifted me out of the wheelchair at the exit.

"I can do it, you know," I said crossly, and he simply grunted non-committedly.

"Right, where to?" Kavion asked.

"Back to the cabin, I guess. I still need some time alone to figure some things out."

"*Nyet*," Ivan declared. "Not while he knows where you are."

"By the Lord and Lady!" I snapped, exasperated. "Knock it off!"

He scowled and put me into the back of the car.

"Can we leave him here?" I demanded of Kavion who smiled.

"Nah, but we can drop him off in town on the way out to your cabin if you want."

Ivan made a sound of protest and I scowled.

"*Yes!* I want!"

Kavion laughed, and said, "Sorry, brah, you heard the lady," before he shut the door for me.

Miri wisely got into the back seat with me before Ivan could. Our circle-mate had just been firmly voted off the proverbial island.

It was so late; I didn't make it back to my family's cabin that night.

Instead, after dropping Ivan off at his beachfront little house, Kavion and Miri asked if we could just go back to their place. I'd nodded wearily.

"Yeah, okay," I agreed.

Miri threaded her fingers between mine and gave my hand a squeeze and I felt the slightest spark, her worry and concern swirling in my breast bringing a twinge of my own guilt right on its heels.

I felt like I screwed everything up without even trying, definitely without ever meaning to… it was like I was cursed. Turning everything that I touched to so much bitter broken ash simply by virtue of existing right now.

Not only my relationship with my sisters, but with Dax, and now I couldn't help but feel like I was somehow going to ruin Jayse's life simply by coming into it.

I felt raw, vulnerable, and afraid. What's worse? I felt like I had no real ability to even talk about it without this soul-crushing fear of being horribly judged for *everything*.

Miri sighed and I bowed my head.

"Powers are coming back," I murmured.

"Yeah," she murmured. "I would have thought you would have been relieved but…" she trailed off and I scrunched my face, trying not to wince, trying not to cry, and somehow managing to do both at once. "Oh, honey, no," she soothed. "It's going to be okay; I promise." She hugged me then and as my powers slowly flooded back, all I could see, all I could feel from my sister was empathy and grace… neither of which I felt like I deserved.

"Shields," she whispered. "Come on, you can do it."

I could, and I did, but it was like moving a strained muscle for me. Awkward, painful, and a lot more work than it had ever been before. Eventually, I managed. My powers were still muted somehow, but I knew without a doubt they would be back, the reprieve all too short. I just didn't have a clue how I would manage.

10

*J*ayse...

Shep was barking his head off and I looked up from where I was trying to maintain my snowmobile.

"Shep!" I called out, hands full of grease and a spark plug. He ignored me, which was weird. He was as well trained a companion as any guy could ask for. He just kept on gleefully barking outside the lean-to against the cabin.

"Shep! What in the fuck?" I demanded and then I heard her.

Light laughter and an even lighter murmur, her voice soothing and at once frightening because *she wasn't supposed to be here...* I mean, how did she even get here?

I dropped what I was doing and wiping my hands with a rag went out into the blinding snow, squinting, but sure enough... she was there.

"Blyn?" I asked, just to make sure I was seeing things right. "How did you get out here?"

She shrugged and said, "Kavion brought me, dropped me off just there beyond the trees." She jerked her head behind her at the lone trail of footprints leading back into the woods.

I cocked my head in skepticism.

"I didn't hear a motor," I said and she grinned, standing smoothly but with a bit of a wince from where she'd had her gloved hands buried in the scruff around Shep's neck, massaging my dog into bliss.

He whined when she took her hands off him, and I knew the feeling, poor boy.

"You look like you were pretty engrossed with what you were doing." She faltered a bit. "I mean, I'll need a ride back at some point, I just really wanted to see you…"

I smiled and said, "You're in luck, I have a trapline set out that way. Set it on the way back *this* way. I can take you back in the morning if you're willing to stay the night."

She smiled and it lit up the world, which was already pretty damn bright out here to begin with.

"I brought some goodies with me," she said, hefting a backpack off of her slim shoulders.

"Oh yeah? Can't wait. C'mere, but be careful not to get any grease on you."

She limped forward in an awkward gait and I frowned as she pulled this massive walking boot up out of the snow.

"You came all the way out there in *that?*" I demanded.

She shrugged and with a seductive little smile said, "It's not like I walked."

I smiled in return and leaned down, kissing her firmly.

"Go inside, get warm. I'll be in as soon as I finish out here."

"I'll unpack your presents," she murmured and I grinned.

"Okay." I looked at my dog and said, "Shep, go with her."

He had no problem trotting off after her into the warmth of the cabin with his dorky dog grin plastered all over his loveable dorky dog face.

God, I loved that mutt.

With a grin of my own, I returned to work, determined to get the fouled plug straightened out and me back inside. Her being here was the best surprise, let me tell you.

It wasn't long before I had the snowmobile back up and running and I was able to head in.

She was already divested of her outerwear and cozied up on the end of my bed in front of the fire. She looked up from where she was rooting around in her backpack and with an impish grin, pulled out a deep, flat Tupperware with her first surprise.

"Oh, man. Is that *bread?*" I asked.

"Mm-hm! Baked it myself."

"Oh, wow. I haven't had bread or—" I stopped as she pulled some fresh fruit out of the bag, some apples and oranges also in their own Tupperware.

"You even remembered to keep everything sealed and bearproofed!"

She laughed and nodded and said, "I did!"

"Oh, my God. You gonna share it with me?" I asked.

"If you'd like. Final present," she said and withdrew what looked like homemade chicken soup of some kind loaded with carrots and celery.

"Oh, hell yeah. We need to heat some of that up."

It was a sumptuous feast and with plenty of fruit and these roll things she'd made left over to last me the rest of the week.

After cleaning up, we found ourselves curled up, her head on my shoulder, both of us laying comfortably in bed, staring at the flickering firelight in the woodstove's grate.

"This was a good surprise," I murmured, nose buried in her silken hair, breathing her in a guilty pleasure. There was seriously nothing like the scent of a woman.

"I'm glad you think so," she murmured happily and cuddled tighter to my side.

"Look up at me?" I asked and she did. I placed my lips against hers.

"Mm!" She made a happy, grateful noise and I raised a hand to cup her cheek as we kissed lazily in the firelight.

It was a slow burn, the heat turning up between us, gradually rising, the clothing coming off a piece at a time, hands roaming, gliding over skin, the light touches warm and perfect. She pushed me back, climbing on top of me, straddling my waist once we were nude and the look in her eyes, so deep, so intent, I just lay back and let her take control. I didn't need it.

She rose and fell, her hands braced against my chest, her arms pressing those beautiful breasts of hers together on full display. My hands found her hips, urging her down onto me harder, her pussy slick with her passion and hot with her desire for me which made my own spiral out of control.

God, it was like I *needed her*, like I would die out here without her, and I was so glad she was in my arms, her lush body pressed tight against mine, mouth pressed tight against my own, tongue exquisitely rubbing against my own and exploring the inside of my mouth even as I kept the intense momentum going between us, thrusting up into her silken wet heat from below.

She leaned way back, her perfect tits a work of art above me, begging for my hands. I smoothed my rough hands from her hips up her stomach and flank, her body a modern baroque work of art as she moved sinuously, leaning forward to kiss me as my hands made their way from the globes of her breasts around her back, holding her to me as I took over. I kissed her back, one arm behind her back, stilling her, the other tangling gently in the wild mane of her long hair, holding it back from our faces as I worked my hips up and down, giving her as good as I got.

"God, you're so perfect," I whispered on an impassioned gasp, and I felt her lips curve against mine in a smile of such pleasure at my words.

"You feel so good," she whispered back, and the praise had me lifting her, flipping her in a wild, semi-controlled roll onto her back. I thrust deep, feeling her slick walls close down tight around me, her body arching beneath mine in such a way I was just the merest, scant half an inch from reaching the end to her body. I didn't mind not bottoming out against her cervix when she arched so provocatively.

I clutched her to me, a precious jewel, like a dragon guarding his most valuable treasure and made love to her for God knows how long. Hours.

"You need anything from the pantry?" she asked the next morning.

"Naw, I'm good," I answered. I really wanted to go inside. Really wanted to make love to her all over again, wanted to sip something hot in front of the fireplace on the cushy faux fur rug there, but the season wasn't over and it was a race against time. I had to make the best of it and I had already lost too much time as it was.

Not that I was complaining about that too hard. It was worth taking the time for her. I just had to balance it with my responsibilities not only to myself but to the old-timer who had apprenticed me and who was counting on me to bring in a haul.

"You're sure?" she asked with this charming little half-smile that almost lured me to my demise on the issue.

I grinned back and pulled her to me, pulling down my face shield from the cold and kissing her breathless.

"I have to get back to the line," I said regretfully.

She mock-pouted and nodded slowly.

"I understand. I hope you got what you were looking for, what you needed."

"If the couple of traps I checked on the way in were any indication, it's gonna be a productive trapline," I said. I'd already trapped a couple of martins.

"Okay, I'll let you go," she said, voice husky.

"I'll see you again before you know it, Blyn," I promised, but I tasted the lie of the weeks between us and the end of the trapping season.

She smiled up at me and it was a brittle thing, before she took a step back and with a sigh, let me go.

I instantly felt bereft of her presence.

"Be safe," she intoned and I smiled.

"Always."

I fired up my snow machine and she stepped back under the overhang of her back porch as I wheeled around. With a final look over my shoulder, she raised a gloved hand in farewell and I smiled.

I carried a warm glow in the center of my chest for the rest of the day, pulling up to my trapper's cabin just after dusk.

I fixed Shep and I some food, a well-earned meal, and snacked on one of the oranges she'd left me late that night as I stared into the fire. Missing her warmth, the weight of her body draped over mine, and her slightly sweet, slightly spicy scent.

"Fuck," I muttered. "I got it bad, boy."

Shep whined and rolled his eyes up to me, never taking his head off of his paws in front of him. I smiled at how sympathetic he looked.

"You miss her too, huh?" He whined again and I nodded and turned down the camp lantern.

"Yeah, I feel you," I said and sighed, settling in for another night alone.

The next morning dawned much the same as every other morning. Cold, but clear. I had another trapline to inspect and reset, the one I referred to as my 'short line.' It only took a couple hours to do the loop which would leave me from late morning through the rest of the day to hang my kills and do a few other much-needed things around here. Namely, bring a few in at a time to thaw so I could start the skinning process.

I rode out, grateful to catch a few ermines but the real prize was toward the end.

"Whoa – ho!" I cried at the very obvious snow-dusted furry lump in the snow. "Shep! Come away from there!" I didn't know if it was still alive or aggressive.

I shouldered my rifle and approached with caution. It was still alive. I shot the bobcat and shook my head. He hadn't been trapped for too long, I hoped, but he would fetch a good price.

"Good boy," I said and got to work, loading the big cat onto the sled.

By the time I got back to the cabin, the snow had begun to fall in gentle, big flakes. It was still and silent out in the woods and I parked up under the lean-to against the side of the cabin.

"What do you think, boy? Start with this big bastard?" I asked.

Shep woofed at me and I looked up with a smile, but he wasn't facing me. Instead, he was facing out across the snowfield.

I followed his gaze and was startled to realize that Blyn's friend, Ivan, was lumbering out of the woods in my direction. He wore a big duster coat, a big, olive green, oiled canvas rucksack slung over his broad chest. He had a big floppy black hat on his head, the brim wide and covering his eyes, but his jaw was set and determined and decidedly unfriendly.

"Yo, Shep!" I called. "C'mere, boy!"

Shep didn't immediately obey my command. His head dipped, his hackles raised and he growled in the direction of Ivan who stopped at the edge of the clearing.

"Shep!" I barked and my dog finally obeyed, but he wasn't happy about it. Instead of bounding through the snow in my direction, he slunk my way, ears flat, turning to look at the approaching man and stopping intermittently to growl.

"Shep, what the fuck?" I muttered in disbelief, grabbing a hold of his collar.

I looked up and Ivan had stopped a good distance away, hands out like some old west gunslinger, but there wasn't a gun in sight. I was confused until he opened his mouth and called, "You stay away from sister!" in his thickly accented English.

"What? Why?" I demanded. Glaring.

"You know why! You stay away!"

"Or what, dude?" I took a step in his direction and nearly shit myself. His hands *caught on fire;* and not only that, that fire ringed out around the clearing, melting clean through the snow, to the very ground underneath, steam rising into the air. Shep whined and cowered against my leg and I put up the hand that wasn't holding onto his collar.

"What the fuck, man?" I called, fearful. I hadn't seen anything like it!

"You leave her alone!" he snarled menacingly, and I blinked.

"I don't understand!" I called, genuinely fucking confused, and the fire died down.

Ivan's scowl deepened, and he kept it contained to his hands.

"What is going on?" I demanded.

He raised his hands and the magic flame roared toward me and Shep. I threw myself over my dog who yelped in fear, threw an arm over my head, and waited for the heat, the burning, for my flesh to sear and the stench of burning hair to fill my nose and choke me… but it didn't happen.

I straightened and blinked, the fire licking along an invisible barrier barely a foot from me and my dog.

"Holy shit," I whispered in disbelief. "What the fuck?"

The fire dissipated and Ivan stood, scowling, no different than when he'd been standing before it'd licked around him, blasting from his hands, and he said, "You steal her power, I end you."

Then he took several steps back, the wind blew, and the snow kicked up and he was suddenly gone… the clearing in front of my cabin steaming, the ground scorched and barren, but Shep and I were completely unharmed.

What the fuck just happened… what was that all about?

Was Blyn some sort of a witch?

11

*B*lyn...

My heart sank as I made my way through the snow at the barren landscape outside of Jayse's cabin. He looked up a fair distance from me still, where he was shoveling snow onto the scorched patch, making a trail to his shed so his snowmobile could work. It hadn't snowed in the few days since I'd last been here, so I bet he was really behind.

"What happened?" I called, but I knew. Deep down, I knew. It could only be one thing…

"You would know!" he shouted back sharply.

I stopped in my tracks. I mean, *Ivan…* sure. It could only have been Ivan. I even knew why, sort of but at the same time? I didn't know *why*. I didn't know anything about our new circle-mate really, except for a torrent of disjointed visions from our initial handshake; all of them horrible. I was honestly too scared to go back for more and hadn't touched the giant Russian since that first time when Miri was in the hospital. I was grateful he shielded as hard as he did most of the time.

"Were you ever going to tell me, Blyn?" Jayse demanded and he looked equal parts pissed and hurt with a generous helping of *scared*.

"Tell you what?" I asked defensively, not entirely sure what he was asking. If it was about Ivan or…

"That your *brother* was a complete psycho! That whatever it is about me that weirds people out in general? You know what it is? Don't you? You know what it is, and whatever it is, it scares the hell out of the people closest to you, but not you. Why? Why not?" he demanded.

He leaned on his shovel and breathed heavily.

I stood speechless for a moment, mouth working but no sound coming out. Finally, I said, "You're right, I'm a witch… an Air witch, which means I have the sight of what was and what is, and it can be a burden. A terrible one."

"And me? What am I?" he demanded. I shifted uncomfortably.

"You're a Null," I said. "You're basically anti-magic… you scare them because we're all witches. They're my circle, at least Miri and Ivan are."

He threw the shovel down and gave an inarticulate cry and I took a step forward. "No!" he barked. "No, fuck that! You stay where the hell you are!"

I stopped in my tracks and he shook his head.

"Exactly what is it you do for the police, Blyn?" he demanded.

"I'm a consultant. I use my power to see things from the evidence gathered at a crime scene. To give them new leads and it's awful! Okay?" He put his hands on his knees, panting.

"You should have told me," he said. "He was gonna burn me and my dog *alive!*" he yelled. "He demanded we stay away from you! Why?"

I stared at the too blue sky and felt tears sting the backs of my eyes. I sniffed, the cold making my nose run.

"He's afraid you'll break the circle. That you'll hurt me or take my powers away."

"Then why do you keep coming around me?" he demanded.

"Because it *hurts*, okay?" I said it, knowing. Knowing the consequence if I told him. How horribly I'd used him…

"What? Your powers or whatever?"

"*Yes!*" I broke down, sobbing and he stared at me in disbelief. "I don't want to see anymore! The horrible things that people do to each other! I can't take it anymore!"

"So… was it me?" he asked, mystified. "Or was it just what I could do for you?"

His question seared my soul because… because I didn't have a good answer for him.

"I-I don't know," I said.

"Jesus Fucking Christ," he muttered.

"Jayse, please—"

"No, no, no!" He waved me off and shook his head. Resolute. "I don't want to hear anymore, Blyn. You *lied to me*. Kept things from me for your own personal selfish reasons." He shook his head.

"You don't understand!" I cried.

He nodded, but it was dismissive. "No, I think I get it just fine."

I stared at him, mouth hanging open as my lies by omission wrapped me in a stranglehold.

"Just get the fuck away from me, Blyn," he uttered dispassionately, disgusted, and the tone he used, the look on his face… it cut me to the quick.

You didn't have to be psychic to realize how much I'd fucked up… *again*.

I tried to take a deep breath, but it hitched in my chest. It felt as though I was cracked wide open, the last dregs of me pouring out onto the snow. I couldn't breathe and it was with a heart-wrenching realization I made in that moment.

I'd really begun to love him. To fall for him… and it was over before it had a chance to begin.

Oh, shit. You love him. This is the price you must pay...

God and Goddess, wasn't Karma a bitch?

"I'm sorry," I uttered on a little broken sob, and it was because I loved him that I did what I did next.

I fucked off, back to where I'd come from. Stepping back among the trees, becoming as insubstantial as air, and floating on the wind to coalesce back at the cabin.

Falling to my knees, I held myself as though I could magically hold it all in, but that was a lie I told myself too as the shock wore off and the feelings rushed in like a flood. Utterly destroying me.

12

*B*lyn...

"Hey, Blyn, welcome back!"

Days later, I was back at the precinct in the heart of Boston. Gloves on, designer clothes my only armor against the onslaught of visions that surrounded me, just waiting for the barest touch.

"Thank you, Rollins," I murmured, and tried to give her a smile that felt so very brittle on my lips.

"How was your vacation?" she asked, none the wiser.

"Fine! Fine, it was good," I rushed out.

"Hey, you made it back. When you said cabin in the woods, I thought the movie, you know?" Rollins' partner, Benowitz, was just a few years from retirement and looked it. Gray hair frizzing in a halo around a bald pate, his suit rumpled, tie always askew. A world apart from Rollins who always looked impeccable, her golden wheat colored hair in a perfect French twist, suit crisp and neatly pressed. She always dressed to impress and like me, just about always wore heels.

I'd watched her sprint in those heels and run a suspect to the ground more than once. It was impressive. I certainly couldn't do it. Then again, I wasn't a trained police officer. Just a consultant.

I ignored Benowitz's comment and asked them both, "Have either of you seen Dax?" His desk was empty.

"Conference room," Rollins said, and I nodded.

"Thanks."

I went for the breakroom for some of the swill that passed for coffee, stalling the inevitable. I'd been back for two or three days already, locked in my apartment, riding out the rest of my 'vacation.'

I was still gravely emotionally wounded. Certainly not feeling any better… neither emotionally nor physically.

"Whoa, what did you *do?*" Rollins asked, coming in after me and spotting my walking boot.

"Oh, long story," I said with a brittle laugh.

"Ice on some steps?" she asked.

"Something like that," I answered.

"I've been there."

"The doctor doesn't think it'll need surgery," I said, stirring powdered creamer into my coffee. "I'll be stuck in this for at least the next six weeks."

"Oh, that sucks."

I nodded.

"Well, I hope it heals up fast," she called, and I smiled as I left and she started making up her own cup of Joe.

"Thanks," I said.

I steeled myself and slipped into the conference room. Dax looked up from the file he'd been reading over and frowned over the top of his square, black-framed reading glasses.

"What's wrong?" he asked immediately and I pinched the bridge of my nose and shook my head, taking several deep breaths and sniffing, trying to get myself together before anyone out there saw.

"Nothing," I lied and I knew it was a pitiful attempt.

"Blyn…"

"Nothing I want to talk about," I reiterated sharply. "How much awful is on my docket for today?"

He sighed, shoulders dropping in defeat as his deep brown eyes roamed my face and he raked a hand back through his black hair.

He sighed and tossed the file in my direction and I peeked at the horror show of the crime scene photos within.

"Fun," I said unhappily.

"Yeah, well…" He looked me in the eye and asked, "You sure you should be here? That you're ready to come back?"

No.

"Sure am," I lied, only this time I hoped it was far more convincing.

He looked like he wanted to say something, but wisely, he didn't.

By the end of the day? I'd cried a river and had screamed myself hoarse.

"You need to stop," Dax said gently, sitting at a right angle from me as I pulled my gloves back on and stared numbly at the piece of evidence I'd just handled. I shook. How could I not? I'd just lived one of the most brutal and depraved sexual assaults to date. All from the point of view of the victim this time. The pain, the fear, the devastation… it was all part of me, now. So was her death. The killer had yoked her with the piece of clothesline in front of me and had choked the life out of her while – *shit*.

I felt sick. Shaken to the core, and I'd been on shaky ground before I'd even come in that morning.

"Find something else to do for a while."

"Like what?" I asked and my voice, my tone, sounded cold. Bereft. Forsaken.

"I don't know, Blyn… but you're tearing yourself apart."

I stood up, too fast, and rocked on my feet. Dax reached out to steady me and I cried, "Don't touch me!"

He sighed, and fixed me with a look, shaking his head.

"You need to eat something. Come on, I'm taking you out."

"It's late, your wife…"

"You let me worry about that. I'm worried about *you*."

I shook my head.

"Christ, Blyn. What happened to you out there? You come back and it's like you're falling apart *worse* somehow."

I closed my eyes and bit my lips together and sat back down abruptly.

"Talk to me," he said gently and sank into the seat across from me.

"Everything I touch turns to ashes," I whimpered. "No matter what. It's like I'm poison." I sniffed and Dax tossed the box of nearby tissues at me. I gave him a look, face wet with tears, but he was right. I needed them. I pulled two with my gloved hand and took a deep breath, closing my eyes as though that would keep me from seeing and pressed them to my face.

Immediately, I was flooded with images, just behind my eyelids, the emotions welling up.

Dax. Arguing with Melinda, his wife. Screaming at each other, vase crashing to the floor as she ran her hip painfully into a table behind their couch as she demanded, *Who is she?*

Dax never gave me up. He didn't tell her. His words echoing in my mind…

"Does it really matter? It's over."

"It matters," I whispered, closing my eyes, fresh tears leaking down my cheeks. "It matters to her."

"Things are bad enough," he said, miserably. "And we're not talking about me, we're talking about *you* right now. What happened? What's with the new fashion accessory?"

He tapped the toe of his expensive Italian loafer against the carpeted floor next to the toe of my walking boot.

"I took a walk," I murmured. "Stepped in a god's cursed wolf trap."

He laughed a little, and I laughed too. I mean, it did sound ridiculous.

"Only you, Courtney. Only you."

I laughed slightly again and nodded. "Yeah."

"How'd you get out of that mess?"

I told him. I told him everything. About Jayse. About the trapper's cabin. About the whirlwind romance and about how, like everything else, I fucked it all up.

He listened, let me pour my heart out and heaved a big sigh. "Yeah, that's fucked up," he agreed. "This calls for Maggiano's."

He stood up and plucked my coat off the back of my chair.

"Oh, no… I'm not hungry," I declared.

"Which is precisely why I'm going to drag your ass to dinner. You need to eat. Take care of your body's basic needs. Now come on, let's go. Your sugar's probably low. You know how you get."

"I don't deserve you," I said. "As a partner, or a friend."

He shook his head.

"That's bullshit and you know it."

I sighed and shook my head. That was the problem. I didn't.

We went to dinner, he dropped me off at home, and I went up alone, my heart squeezing tight, the shattered pieces grinding together.

I stayed up most of the night and prayed.

1 3

*J*ayse...

"Hey!" My sister stepped out onto her front porch as I closed the door of my truck, Shep trotting up to greet her.

"Hey, yourself!" I called, hefting my Army surplus duffel out of the back.

"How was it?" she asked, giving Shep all sorts of scritches and scratches as I plodded through the busted front gate and up the cracked walk.

God, Serena was a sight for sore eyes. Her long straight, strawberry blond hair a good dye job, but it worked for her. She had it clipped up in the back, looking comfortable in a pair of hiking boots, jeans, and a waffle patterned, white thermal shirt. Over it, she wore a red and black checkered flannel. Her 'around the house getting things done' outfit.

"You're never going to believe what happened to me out there," I said, as she straightened up and gave me an affectionate half-smile. Her hazel-green eyes, just a shade lighter than mine, lighting up with interest.

"Well, come on in! Tell me all about it."

I went up the sloping front steps, sighing, hoping Mike would have gotten around to fixing some shit while I was gone but… nope. Just because he didn't swing a hammer at his day job didn't mean he didn't know how. There were a lot of things around here that needed his attention that I was more than happy to pitch in or do for them but for his dislike of me. It made him obstinate. Always with the 'I'll get around to it' without actually getting around to it. It annoyed me.

The painted green screen door banged closed behind me, and Shep went over and sprawled in the middle of the living room rug, looking up pitifully, acting like he'd never been fed. I scooched in around my sister and she shut the front door and most of the cold out with it, scooting the draft blocker of some rolled up, raggedy old towels wrapped in duct tape against the bottom of the door.

"I thought Mike was going to fix the front door and the steps," I said casually and Serena blushed a bit and shrugged one shoulder.

"Oh, well, you know… busy," she said. "Tell me about all your grand adventures!" she cried, hugging me tight.

"Uh, can I put this down first?" I asked and she laughed.

"Yeah sure, let's get some of that going, and by 'we' I mean 'you', while I start some tea."

"Sounds good." I looked her over, a sight for sore eyes, and smiled. "You look good," I told her and she smiled and knocked me in the shoulder lightly with her fist. I pulled her into a tight hug and said, "I missed you."

"Missed you too, big brother. Now go on, you reek," she said with a laugh.

"Sorry, sis. Need clean laundry to be able to clean up into."

"Uh-huh, go look at your bed," she said then patted her thigh. "Come on, Shep!" she called. "I got a can of Alpo in here somewhere."

Shep leaped to his feet and went after Serena, tail held high and flagging the air. I went after them, but split off to go down the basement stairs to get some wash going, eyeing the bed over in the curtained-off corner that I called home when I was here. There were some fresh towels and a few packages of thermal shirts and pajama bottoms laying there. I smiled and laughed a little.

Once I had the laundry going, I headed upstairs and asked, "You want I should clean up first or tell stories?"

"Whichever you prefer. I'm good," she said, so I headed over to the kitchen table where Serena had some mugs out and the stuff for tea. I set my clean clothes and towels off to the side on one of the empty chairs and sat down with a gusty sigh as she slid into the seat across from me.

"So, how'd you manage?"

I grinned. "It was a good season, all things considered."

"All things considered?" she asked grinning back. "What does that mean?"

I told her. About all of it. About Blyn and Ivan. The fire and the disappearing acts. About what I was.

She listened, wide-eyed, and said finally…

"Witches? Actual witches?"

"Yep."

"Do you know how *rare* they are?" she asked astonished.

"Uh, yeah. From what I gathered, whatever a Null is? It's partially responsible for that. Nobody said as much, but I have to figure." I shifted uncomfortably in my seat. "We're like kryptonite or some shit for them. Take their powers. Or, like, their powers don't affect us."

"What did Blyn say?"

I felt my ears turn red and gritted my teeth.

"After that thing with Ivan… and Serena, that dude scares the *shit* out of me, I kind of flipped out on Blyn and not in so many words told her to fuck off."

"Jayse!" Serena barked. "How could you?"

"I know, I know!" I pressed fingertips into my eye sockets and rubbed my eyes. "Not my finest hour." The guilt washed over me again.

"Well, at least you know! Jesus, Mom raised you better than to hold someone accountable based on someone else's actions! Do you know how to get a hold of her, at least?" she demanded.

"Look," I said, defensive. "She knew and didn't tell me, she's not entirely blameless."

"Oh, ho ho! No way, buddy. Uh-uh. Did it ever occur to you that in the long history of humankind that judging someone based on them being *other* isn't necessarily the right thing to do? Now, I know you might not be aware, but the comparative religion class I took in college is about to come raring to the fore, or did you forget I got my degree in history?"

"I know you're a history major." I rolled my eyes and she reached out and flicked the tip of my nose. "Ow!" I covered it with both my hands.

"Okay, so listen up. How the fuck do you think the Catholic church managed to burn so many damn witches?" she demanded.

"Uh, by tying them to a stake and lighting the pyre?"

"Funny, you already said you saw this Ivan guy in command of fire." She raised her eyebrows and I sighed.

"Right."

"So, if they even managed to tie the big brute to a stake, what was preventing him from just telling the flames to go away, or making himself fireproof or whatever it is that they do?"

"Oh," I said, sitting back.

"She may not have told you but did it ever get in to your tiny pea brain for even just a second that Ivan was probably *scared of you?* People don't just arbitrarily threaten the fuck out of someone they don't know. They go big against shit that scares the shit out of them, though. This is not rocket science, big brother."

"I feel like an asshole," I said unhappily. "But how was I supposed to know? I didn't even have an answer until, well, you know!"

"I know," she said crossing her arms, but she wasn't about to give an inch here. "So, go get yourself cleaned up, get a good night's sleep, and *go fix it*," she said.

I hung my head and nodded, sighing.

"Hm, it's a good thing I *am* a history major with background in comparative religion, or you might be fucked right now."

I looked up and shook my head asking, "Any luck with that, by the way?"

She shook her head and said, "No. All I can do is keep applying."

My sister's dream job was to work for the Massachusetts Museum of History and Industry. There weren't a lot of positions available, basically she had to wait for someone to quit or retire out.

"Look, big brother. I wouldn't be such a hard case about this but I've known you pretty much our whole lives."

She gave me a meaningful look and I nodded and said, "Yeah," in agreement.

"And in all that time, I've never seen the look on your face as I did when you were talking about this girl."

I nodded slowly, absorbing what she was saying.

"You think it can be fixed?" I asked.

"Only one way to find out," she said. I nodded and got up, grabbing up my clean clothes, clean towel, and toiletry kit.

"I got a lot to think about," I said and she nodded.

"Yeah, you do, and sweep up after yourself. Don't leave my bathroom a damn mess."

I smiled and nodded, taking myself off to get cleaned up.

"And don't you dare clog my sink!" she shouted and I snickered at that.

"Only did it once and I'll never live it down, will I?"

"No, you won't!"

I shut the bathroom door on her proclamation and sighed, looking at myself in the mirror. There wasn't much I could do about my hair, not without my sister's help, but the beard? That was all me.

I set to work really cleaning myself up, and it took a while. By the time I emerged from the bathroom, I'd been in there a while, but felt so much better than when I'd gone in.

I made sure to leave the bathroom as clean if not cleaner than I found it and went out to see if my sister could cut my hair for me. She was in the kitchen making some dinner and looked up when I came through the archway.

"You need a haircut," she said. "Beard is *much* better, though."

"Thank you, Captain Obvious. I was just coming in here to ask."

"I mean, I can try," she said. "I'm no barber or beautician."

"You do just fine," I argued. I didn't want to pay out if I didn't have to. I was stingy like that in some ways. I'd rather use the money on flowers or something. The more I thought about things, the more I felt the need to apologize and try and start from the beginning with Blyn.

I mean, I *missed her*. There hadn't been a day that'd gone by in the intervening weeks since I'd last seen her that I *didn't* think about her.

"Right, not my fault if I fuck it up again," she said.

"You've never fucked it up before," I said laughing.

She rolled her eyes. "That's what you think, you never look at the back."

I laughed harder as she went to find the old bedsheet she used as a drape while I set up the clippers and pulled one of the dining room chairs to the middle of the kitchen.

"Figure out how you're going to grovel, yet?" she asked right before she switched the clippers on.

"No," I said, gritting my teeth. Of course, she would ambush me with a question like that right before starting in on my head. "Whose side are you on, anyway?" I demanded.

"Yours, big brother. *Always* yours," she said, running the clippers with whatever guard number over everything. She'd tighten things up and I'd end up looking good. She'd done this for me a thousand times and *every time* it was the same thing… She wasn't a pro and she was gonna mess up! Angst and woe, angst and woe, rinse and repeat.

I worried about her, sometimes. She was always hard on herself. She was fabulous, dynamic, and awesome. Sometimes it just felt like the only one who could see it was me. I had no idea when she'd started doubting herself so hard, but it sucked and I wished she wouldn't.

"I'm serious," she said, steamrolling her way right over my train of thought and leaving it as flat as a quarter left on the tracks. "I've never heard you talk about anyone the way you talked about her. I'm really hoping you *can* fix it. I dunno, I just have a gut feeling about it."

"A gut feeling?" I asked, a little incredulous.

"Yeah, call it women's intuition, or whatever."

I rolled my eyes. "Did you not hear a word I said?" I asked. "I'm a

Null, psychic powers, witchcraft, magic – *women's intuition*? None of it works around me."

She came around where I could see her, fixed me with a look, and made a great show of shrugging her shoulders.

"Want some unsolicited advice?" she asked.

"If I say 'yes' it wouldn't be unsolicited anymore," I said pointedly.

"Good point." I could hear the shrug in the two words. "Don't call her," she said and I frowned, leaned forward and twisted around to fix her with a look that screamed, 'Don't be stupid.'

She rolled her eyes at me and smacked my head with her fingertips lightly. I turned around and she finished her thought. "What I mean is, this isn't something you fix over the phone. I'm saying, *go see her.*"

"I don't know if that's a good idea," I said dubiously. "She works for the *police*. I show up and shut off her magic or whatever, what if it screws up her case?"

"Duh, go to the station or whatever and say you're there to see her and have someone go tell her you're there. I'm serious, though. *Do the work,* Jayse. *Show up.* Be present. After something like that and weeks of no contact? A phone call doesn't do the trick. If you're really serious, you need to *show up.*"

"Alright," I said, turning the idea of it over in my mind. "Okay," I said. "I'll think about it."

"*Trust me!*" she said. "Have I ever steered you wrong?"

"Yes," I said unequivocally, and she flicked the back of my ear. "Ow!"

"Oh, hush. You did it to yourself," she declared.

"You're so *mean!*" I cried.

God, I missed my sister and our banter.

*B*lyn...

I sat curled on the end of my couch in my thickest, warmest sweater and my equally warm and comfortable leggings, watching the snow fall outside the bank of floor to ceiling windows of my loft apartment. I was home from another mentally and emotionally exhausting day of peeling my eyelids back from the horrors of this world and I felt sick for it. Sick and so fucking *tired*... but there was no one else, and my 'accuracy' was unparalleled within the law enforcement community.

I was no longer the Boston Police Department's best kept secret, and now? Now, the Feds were regularly appearing with evidence bags in hand looking to solve their coldest cases. So far? I'd given them one hundred percent accuracy. It was making me nervous to an extent, after what I had seen Ivan's government do to him.

I didn't want to have to go to the lengths Ivan had gone to just so that he could be free, and I couldn't really say with any certainty that he *was*. I mean, legitimately, his government was *terrified* of him. I think they viewed him as America's problem now. Only thing of it was, he wasn't a problem at all. He had a good heart, deep down underneath all of that rage and pain. He did, and I knew that, too. Just, good luck convincing anyone else of that.

I sighed and sniffed, eyes welling and took a big gulp of the steaming Vin Glögg in my coffee mug, wincing as it was still a touch too hot. The strong, deeply spiced, mulled red wine went down and I felt an almost immediate flush to my cheeks. I worried about becoming dependent on alcohol and the sleep aids I had begun taking, but I just couldn't stop seeing… not by accident and not on purpose, either.

The good I did? It outweighed the thought of my potential downfall or destruction by the debilitating trauma I lived over and over. *A single person could only go through so much lest they go completely mad.*

Of course, my thoughts always drifted back to Jayse when I thought too much about what my overabundance of gift was doing to me. I pressed fingertips to my forehead and rubbed at the headache starting between my eyes.

I wondered how he was doing. I also wondered if I would ever see him again.

I scoffed at myself and downed the ample pour of Vin Glögg in my mug in three big swallows, not caring if it was still too warm. I just wanted to numb the pain away. I felt ravaged from the inside out as much from the hot wine as from my feelings and I sniffed.

Gods, I was so sick of crying, but it was like my eyes had become a leaky faucet. They were constantly misty or spilling over anymore and I just had no control over it. I had no control over *anything* and it was eating away at me, this caustic *thing* and all I could think was… *I deserve it.* As fucked up as that sounded, I couldn't think anything else because *why else would it be happening?*

I dashed uselessly at my tears and stared at the white flakes pattering against the glass of my apartment windows.

I needed to try and close my eyes. I needed to try and sleep. I had to do it all over again tomorrow.

15

*J*ayse...

"Uh hi, yeah, what can I do for you?" The sergeant behind the front desk at the police station Blyn worked out of set his phone back down in the cradle and turned his attention toward me.

"I'm looking for Ms. Blyn Courtney," I said politely. He met my eyes and his blue ones held a certain sort of unease. I couldn't tell you how much just *knowing* what I was made that easier on me. He hesitated. I mean it was *me*, but it wasn't me at the same time. I had no control over what I was or how people picked up on that vibe, or maybe a lack thereof or whatever. Still, knowing was half the battle, so I just smiled and waited patiently while he eyed me up and made whatever decision he was going to make about me.

"Hang on, just a sec," he said and picked up his phone, flipping through a book by it and running his finger down a list of names and short codes. He punched some digits on the key pad and waited.

"Hi, uh, yeah. Got some guy down here for Courtney," he said into the receiver, eyeing me carefully. "What's your name?" he asked me, tilting the mouthpiece below his chin.

"Jayse," I answered. "Jayse Mickelson."

"Uh-huh, yeah, Jayse Mickelson. Uh-huh. Yeah. Okay." He put the phone down and said, "Someone will be right with you. Why don't you go on and have a seat right over there?"

He indicated with a jab of his fingers a line of unoccupied waiting room chairs, their backs up against the precinct's front windows.

I went over and settled onto the one at the end nearest the door, perching nervously on the edge, my forearms on my knees as I waited. There was a secured door to the right of the sergeant's desk. A few minutes went by that felt agonizingly long, and when it popped open, a guy stepped out in a suit.

"Jayse?" he asked me and I stood up, only a little apprehensive.

"Yeah," I said and he leaned way out the door holding out his hand to shake, keeping his leg stuck out so the door wouldn't shut.

"Richard Dax, nice to meet you," he said and I leaned forward and shook his hand. He had a firm grip and looked me over with curious brown eyes. His hair was dark and cropped in a neat, business-like cut.

"Hey, Jerry, you mind hooking up Mr. Mickelson with a visitor's pass for me?"

"Sure thing, Dax."

"Thanks."

"Step over here, please. Sign your name, who you're here to see, and can I see your I.D. please?"

"Sure thing," I murmured and fished my driver's license out of my wallet. He handed me a clip-on visitor's badge and slipped my license into the slot that it belonged in. I filled out the line he indicated on the paperwork and handed the clipboard back.

"Thanks Jer," Dax said and waved me through the door. I went through and he waved at me to follow.

"Blyn's about to do some work for the FBI," he said. "She's told me about you. Truth be told, I'm glad you're here."

"Yeah, uh, she's told me about you, too," I said as he stopped in front of a bank of elevators and punched a button with a grin.

"Yeah? How much did she tell you?" he asked and I shifted a little uncomfortably. Surprise crossed his face and he said, "Wow, that much, huh? Must have made an impression."

The doors swished open and I followed him into the elevator car. "You can't see her right now, for obvious reasons, but when she's done... What you can do, and don't tell anyone I let you do this, is sit with me in observation. The interview rooms are all on the fourth floor. Observation is on the sixth. Think that'll be enough room to keep whatever it is you do," he waved a hand between us, "from fucking up whatever it is *she* does?"

Wow, so apparently, she'd told *him* all about *me*... okay. Not sure how I felt about that. He eyed me and raised his eyebrows. "Well?"

"Uh, yeah." I shook my head to clear it. "Yeah, yeah. Should be fine."

"Look," he said with a sigh, the elevator dinging and bouncing to a stop. "We fucked up, Blyn and I, there's no denying that," he said in a rush before the doors whooshed open. "She's a damn good partner, though. And an even better friend." He took off at a brisk pace and I made long strides to keep up. "So," he said without missing a beat, "I would appreciate it if you treated her good. The fact you're even here says a lot. Not sure *what* it says, yet. That remains to be seen, but it sure says *somethin'*."

He grabbed a lever-like door handle to a gray steel door in a long hall of them and it turned down. "Just stand behind me and don't say *nothin'*," he ordered and I nodded just a little too quickly. I didn't know what to make of Richard Dax, but I did know I was eager. Eager to see Blyn. To know she was okay.

The room was small and dark, with a single office chair in it. There was a bank of monitors and when Dax moved the mouse, they all came alive with a black and white view of an interrogation room. The kind that looked like it had gray painted ceiling tiles for walls. A window set in one of the four walls, a table in the middle and three chairs, two on one side, one on the other. Sturdy, brushed aluminum fixed chairs. None of that cheap folding garbage.

Dax fitted an ear piece around his ear, one of the kind that had the loop that went behind it to keep it on.

"Yeah, yeah, I'm here, Blyn," he said into it and he flipped a switch. Suddenly her voice came through the speaker by one of the monitors.

"Where were you?" she asked.

"Never mind that now, you got the spooks with you?" I frowned slightly. Spooks weren't FBI. They were more like NSA.

"They aren't 'spooks' Dax," Blyn said and I could *hear* her eyes roll.

"You don't know that, Courtney," Dax said bluntly. "This could be some kind of a test."

"Well," she said under her breath, "we'll know soon enough. Here they come."

"Gonna shake hands?" Dax asked, teasing.

"At the end. You know how this works," Blyn said, but she didn't sound happy about it.

"Hi, I'm Blyn Courtney. Right this way," she said, and she was nothing but pure professionalism. Dax looked up and over his shoulder back at me, and put a finger to his lips, eyebrows raised, reminding me not to make a sound. I nodded.

He flipped the switch while Blyn chatted with the FBI and hit another switch before sighing.

"Federal Bureau of Intimidation would have our asses if they knew I was listening in. Blyn will have my ass if she knew you were in here. Don't say a fuckin' word. Just watch and learn," he said, and he flipped the switches and punched keys just as the door opened to the interrogation room and Blyn stepped aside to let two suited figures in past her.

Both were women, one holding a briefcase.

"We appreciate you doing this for us," one of them said and Blyn nodded.

"Of course, Agent Stahl. Please, have a seat." She indicated with a gloved hand the two empty chairs at one side of the table.

She went around to the single empty seat and took it. I looked from one monitor to the other trying to get a good look at her face.

"And you're sure we're alone? No cameras?" the second agent asked, looking around the room and I realized that the audio and video must have been hidden.

"I can appreciate the…" Blyn groped for the right word to use. "Sensitivity, of your case, Agent MacKinnon," she finished finally.

"Right." McKinnon sat down across from Blyn and folded her hands atop the table. "I don't go in much for all this magic witchy woo-woo garbage."

"Ah." Blyn bowed her head slightly with a secret little smile. "Well, seeing is believing, I guess," she said and she put her gloved hands on the desk. "What have you brought me?" she asked and turned to Agent Stahl, as though McKinnon with her severe bun and stark frown didn't exist anymore, thoroughly dismissing her for her rudeness.

"Right," Stahl said, opening her briefcase in her lap and setting out three evidence bags on the table. While McKinnon was probably in her forties, maybe pushing fifties, Stahl looked younger. Maybe thirties. I didn't think the world had gotten to her quite yet. She still wanted to believe. Hell, I was curious, and I kind of wanted to see Blyn in action, myself. Boy was I about to regret that and thoroughly.

Blyn took in a deep breath, closing her eyes. In through her nose and out through her mouth, slowly. McKinnon harrumphed and one of the camera angles showed Stahl kick her under the table. Blyn ignored her.

She opened her eyes and looked grim as she worked her gray kid gloves off of her hands. They were long, like opera gloves, and she set them aside. Not touching anything. Not yet. Holding them out above the table.

"If you could extract the first piece of evidence, please? But try not to touch it. Just let it sit on the evidence bag.

"Okay," Stahl said and did just that, holding the coffee mug out to Blyn in the open mouth of the evidence bag. Blyn closed her eyes, shoulders full of tension beneath her turtle-necked white angora sweater. As soon as she touched the object, her shoulders dropped.

Her deep brown eyes flickered open and she fixed McKinnon with an unfriendly look.

"A coffee mug from the FBI breakroom on your floor isn't going to tell me anything about your kidnapper and killer, Agent McKinnon. However, you really should stop betting on the Celtics with Roman and Chomsky. You're horrible at predicting who will win and he's having entirely too much fun taking your money."

McKinnon's eyes widened and Stahl rounded on her and scowled, sweeping the mug and evidence bag from Blyn's hands. Blyn's eyes widened and she looked at Stahl who was sputtering apologies.

"Don't marry him," Blyn said. "He's cheated on you twice."

Stahl fell mute, shocked, and Dax laughed. "That's my girl," he said. "You get 'em every time."

Blyn sighed and said, "All due respect, of course, I have other cases I could be looking at today. Do you have any real evidence or is this all a test?"

"We do," McKinnon said, high spots of color on her cheeks that were apparent even with the black and white feed.

"Then by all means…" Blyn said, trailing off.

McKinnon opened the next evidence bag and peeled the plastic back from the rope inside it, holding it out like a street vendor would your pretzel you just bought.

Blyn licked her dark lips, and I wished I could see what color she'd painted them. She looked so refined, so put together, and I couldn't decide if I liked it or not. I know that the second she touched that rope; I definitely didn't like what I saw.

Her hands seized it, and her eyes went wide and unseeing. Dax leaned forward in his seat and started talking low and insistent.

"Okay, baby. You hang on. You're okay. Just tell them what you see. Stay with me. You ain't gotta feel this. You just watch. Stay with me, Blyn."

Her mouth dropped open and a strangled sob escaped her lips as her eyes went even wider, welling with tears.

Shit.

"Easy, baby, what is it? Tell us what you see."

"I can't," she moaned and her face crumbled. "Oh, God, I can't."

She took several deep panting breaths and started begging, "No, no, no, no, no…"

"Blyn, baby. You're okay," Dax declared, and his voice had risen an octave. "You're okay. You're not there, you're here. Blyn?"

"No, no, no, no, no!" Blyn shuddered. "No, no, no, no, no!"

"Blyn, you're losing it. Hang on to this reality. Listen to the sound of my voice."

She sucked in a sharp breath, her eyes going impossibly wide, showing way too much white. The two FBI agents exchanged a puzzled look and McKinnon asked her, "What? What is it?"

That's when she started screaming. She stood up abruptly, the chair crashing to the floor, her hands in a white-knuckled grip around the evidence. She tried to take a step backwards and tripped over the chair, her knee-high riding boots scrabbling against the linoleum floor as she cried out in this scared little girl voice through her tears, "Dax! Dax! I don't want to see anymore! I can't see anymore!"

"Shit!" Dax swore with real feeling. "Come on, mountain man! I need your help!"

Blyn was just screaming now. Awful, high-pitched, horrified screams. Over and over and over, ragged and raw, makeup tracking down her face, eyes peeled back wide as whatever she was seeing played out in front of them.

That was the image that was fixed in my head as I tore off after Dax who didn't even fuck with the elevator. We took the stairs, leaping down entire flights and bursting out onto a cubical farm two floors below.

I could hear her screaming real-time now. Long, loud, terrified broken screaming. Everyone halted in what they were doing, looking in the same direction where those animalistic screams were coming from.

"This way!" Dax shouted, and I kept up right behind him as he burst through the interrogation room door.

Both FBI agents were standing to one side, Dax flipping the table out of my way so I could get to Blyn and shut whatever it was off.

"Blyn! Blyn!" I skidded on my jeans-clad knees right up next to her, grabbing her face between my hands. "Blyn, it's me! It's me, Jayse! I got you. I've got you, look at me. Look at me!" I ripped the evidence out of her hands and threw it at the agents.

"I don't want to see anymore! I don't want to see any more!" She was screaming over and over again and sobbing. Just sobbing, so broken. *So fucked up.* I pulled her against me and she clutched at the front of my bomber jacket and sweater and just screamed wordlessly into my front.

"It's okay," I said hushed while Dax grabbed the FBI's shit and stuffed it into the fallen briefcase. "It's okay," I soothed. "You don't have to look. You don't have to see. I'm here. I've got you now."

Shit. I'd had no idea what it'd cost her to walk away from me but I did now.

"Come on," Dax ordered curtly, shoving the briefcase into Stahl's chest. "Come on, get out. Get out of here," he said, grabbing McKinnon by the shoulder of her suit jacket and bodily turning her to the door. He shoved both agents out and shut the door behind him. I could hear them talking outside above Blyn's now much more subdued sobbing. The room suddenly quiet. The talking devolved into shouting and I sighed, kissing the top of Blyn's mussed hair.

"I'm sorry," she whimpered, and I shook my head.

She didn't have anything to be sorry about… but I sure did.

ayse...

We called an ambulance. She was too upset, clinging to me like the last leaf on the branch during a turbulent winter storm. Struggling not to be snatched into the maelstrom, into the dark and the cold.

I held onto her, and when the medics arrived, she shrieked and screamed when they tried to take her from me. I held her hand, walked alongside the stretcher as she gripped my hand with both of hers, twisting her head to keep her face buried, hidden, as we were wheeled out the secured door. The desk sergeant came out, handed me my license and snatched the clip from my collar, giving me a nod.

Blyn was going into shock. Whatever she'd experienced from touching that hank of rope had been that awful, that devastating. Dax was pissed, calling out that he would follow us, that he would be right behind us, all the while Blyn clung to me, freaking out any time I shifted or came near to letting go.

It was confusing, it was loud and urgent, and I just flowed along on the currents, both of us leaves on the wind until the ambulance doors slammed behind us.

The guy back here with us kept asking questions, none of which I had any good answers for. I didn't know Blyn. I didn't know her medical history, I didn't know what she'd seen, or how any of this worked. I didn't know what to say, only what to do and that was *not let go.*

In the ER, it was a lot more of the same, except in the ER they had medicine. Drugs with which to sedate her, getting her traumatized mind to quiet enough that they could maybe get through. Dax found us back there, the curtains drawn around us, Blyn curled on her side, finally settled enough that anyone other than me could touch her if need be without her shrieking and thrashing, trying to skirt their reaching hands.

She still held my one hand with both of hers, curled miserably on her side, shivering, shaking, but definitely not from cold. I was helpless, helpless to do anything but pet her glossy thick hair and to whisper soothing things close to her ear as she gripped my hand through the bed rail.

"How's she doing?" Dax asked, batting the curtain aside and shoving his badge in the nurse's face when she came over to try and kick his ass out.

"Not good," I answered, taking my hand from her hair to rake it through mine.

"What'd they do?" he demanded.

"Sedated her."

"Shit," he swore softly. He went up near her head opposite from me and clutched the bedrail. Blyn cringed when the bed shook finely from Dax gripping the rail and hurt flashed across his face.

"Courtney, it's me, Dax," he said softly, and a tremor went through Blyn as she took a shuddering breath and broke down into quiet sobs.

"Aw, hey. It's okay," he soothed, and I went back to petting her hair. Dax sighed when she wouldn't acknowledge him, or even me really, and let his hands slip from the rail saying, "I'm going to go find the doc, see what the fuck is going on."

I nodded, and he walked away.

"I got you, Blyn," I murmured. "I got you."

She sniffled and kept her eyes shut tight, shuddering beneath my one hand, the grip on my other hand tightening to an almost white-knuckled grip, and I felt like a complete asshole.

"I'm so sorry," I whispered, lips moving against her silken soft hair. "I didn't know. I didn't understand."

"*I'm* sorry," she whined piteously, and I shook my head.

"No, you've got nothing to be sorry about. You can't help who you are…" I mean, neither could I. Wasn't that the bitch of it, though?

Dax came back a little while later and said, "They're waiting for a social worker to free up and assess her. Did she say anything?"

"Yeah," I answered.

"I want to go home," she said.

Dax's face split into a wide grin of total relief. "Hey there, Rockstar. How you doing?"

"I want to go home, Dax. How does it look like I'm doing?" she asked dully, then closed her eyes, swallowing hard and rallying just a bit, her expression visibly displaying her pulling herself together. It was impressive to watch. She murmured, "Sorry," to her partner, and he shook his head.

"Don't mention it," he said. "That was a… well, I don't know what that one was. I've never seen you go that bad."

"I've never seen—" She swallowed hard and gasped, squeezing her eyes shut against whatever, but she couldn't escape what it was she'd seen. It was forever burned into her psyche.

"Shhh," I soothed. "I know it's bad. Just try not to think about it too hard. You're here. You're with me and with Dax, and you're safe. We got you," I said, jostling her hands with mine, giving the one a gentle squeeze.

"Soon as we can, we're getting you out of here," Dax said. "I'll take you home."

That was going to be awhile yet. As soon as the hospital staff figured out Blyn was calm, or at least calmer, they left us to stew for like an hour more. It was starting to feel like they were somehow punishing her for going through something so emotionally traumatic she'd broken clean in two and Dax and I were getting seriously irritated.

"Yah, I *know* you're busy which is why I'm trying to get her some fuckin' attention here so we can get her the fuck outta here and get her home!" Dax said harshly outside the curtain.

Blyn let out a whoosh of air and her shoulders dropped and she struggled to sit up.

"I just want to go home, Jayse. I'm so sorry you had to be there, that you had to see that but—"

"Stop," I cut her off gently. "I'm glad I was there," I said honestly. "That I could be there for you." She sniffed and nodded; her hair tousled on the side she'd been laying on.

"Can you find my coat?" she asked. "Forget these people. I want to go home and they can't stop me from leaving."

"I got your coat right here," Dax said, sweeping back the curtain.

"Sir, you can't just *leave*," the nurse argued.

"The fuck we can't," Dax said, and I lowered the rail on my side and helped Blyn to sit up on the edge of the bed.

"I will call the *police*," the nurse threatened. She was different from the first one Dax had shoved his badge into her face.

"Lady! I *am* the fucking police!" Dax snarled, holding Blyn's winter coat open for her. She shrugged into it, woozy and the doctor decided then was the time to show up with the social worker in tow.

Blyn leaned heavily on me while Dax fed them both the riot act. In the end, a wheelchair was brought because Blyn was on enough tranquilizers to fell an elephant. The strongest shit they could provide to someone her size.

The doctor knew she was a mess, the nurses just didn't seem to care and the social worker? Well, she was only one person in an already stressed system that wasn't equipped to deal with the mental health issues facing the world today.

"Come on, let's go," Dax said curtly and he wheeled Blyn out. She still wouldn't let me go. Had barely let me go to put her coat on and her purse over her shoulder.

I waited with her at the curb for Dax to get the car and pull it around.

"How are you doing?" I asked and she stared sightlessly and said,

"I'm fine..." in this totally unbelievable singsong quality. It was like she was touch and go. Her mind fractured, her psyche shattered. She needed quiet, and rest, as near as I could figure. A real break from whatever psychic or magic abilities she had.

Seemed like it was the least I could do. I felt like I owed her somehow.

I *did* owe her. For not listening. For not hearing her out. For just assuming her motives and what drove her... I'd had no idea.

I held her close in the back seat of Dax's car and she practically curled up in my lap like a kitten, head tucked beneath my chin, arms around me, clinging to me like a baby squirrel to a tree in a gale.

The ride to wherever she lived was a silent one for the most part. The only time Dax spoke was to road rage or voice his irritation at the drivers around us as we moved through Boston's congested streets to wherever it was that Blyn lived.

I didn't know what I expected, but the building we pulled up outside of wasn't it. It was plain, brick, and old but not chic. Not nearly as classy or rich looking as the vacationer's cabin that Blyn had out in the woods up north, outside of Loving.

"Courtney?" Dax called from the front. "Hey, Courtney!"

"It's okay," I said gently. "I've got her."

"K, gimme her purse, Mountain Man. I'll get her keys out and get us inside."

I hated jostling her, the sedatives working on her overtime now, making her pretty unresponsive and a chore to get her purse off of her. I finally settled for unhooking the strap and letting Dax pull it off from around her.

"Gah!" Dax uttered and sighed. "Courtney, baby, you gotta help us out here. Just for a minute," he said gently and I could see plainly, a part of him still loved her. Would always love her. Maybe not as much as his wife, but something was there. Still, it was *me* that Blyn clung to. Me that her grip tightened upon, and while I wished I could say it felt nice to be needed or whatever, I guess I was too nice a guy, because all I felt was a little heartbroken for him.

I wouldn't be able to get rid of the sight or sound of her screaming for a while. It would haunt me, just as whatever she'd seen clearly haunted *her*.

"I've got her," I said and awkwardly got us out of the car, hefting her in my arms. She wasn't too heavy, as small as she was, and I'd lifted dead weight far more awkward in some of the animals I'd trapped. While Blyn wasn't exactly with it, she wasn't exactly dead weight, either. Her arms went about my neck almost reflexively and she held herself up against me.

"Go," I said, indicating Dax should lead the way. I certainly didn't know where I was going.

He swung the car door shut and chirped the alarm, leaving it right there in the load and unload zone in front of her place. He led us into the lobby, the footing outside a bit dangerous, the snow having melted and refrozen on the concrete leading to the lobby door. Inside, we were in a little vestibule, mailboxes opposite the elevator which Dax punched the button for.

We lucked out; the elevator was on the ground floor. He let me go first here, and I stepped into the rickety old car. He stuck a key into a small brass panel and turning it, hit the 'P' for the penthouse. I kind of raised an eyebrow at that. The building wasn't very big and certainly didn't seem like it would even have a penthouse, but I was wrong. The elevator went to the top and the doors behind me opened right into a well-furnished, loft style apartment with a bank of floor to ceiling windows on two sides, along the left wall and right in front of us.

"Take her on over to her bed," he said gently, and I nodded, skirting past the kitchen and around the couches set up in the middle of everything. It was an open floor plan and super modern. Sort of like her cabin had been.

"Jayse, don't leave," she whimpered as I set her on the edge of the bed.

I kneeled down in front of her and sighed, saying, "I'm not going anywhere. I promise."

"Here, we've both seen it all, help me get her changed," Dax murmured, and he went to her dresser against the far back, shorter width of windows and opened a drawer, slipping a satin nightgown off the top of whatever else was in it.

"Uh." I kind of stared at him, flushing, a deer caught in the headlights.

"I've known Courtney a long time. Believe me, she would rather be comfortable," he said, and I nodded, still really uncomfortable with the idea. I touched the side of her face and her eyes flickered open and I murmured, asking if she wanted to change and to sleep for a while. She nodded, out of it, but the consent was given – at least I felt so, and it wasn't sex. It was a change of clothes… although why I felt so weird about it when I hadn't back at my trapper's cabin was beyond me.

Because back at your cabin it was a life or death emergency. Here, she's not going to die if she doesn't get out of her clothes and there's another person here. Like, seriously Jayse, get it together!

I still needed to call my sister, but I could do that when Dax was gone. If he intended on leaving. *Fuck, this was getting all so awkward!*

"Relax, loverboy," Dax said with a kind smile, taking her jacket from me and laying her satin nightgown on the bed nearby. "While I've never seen her this bad, she always bounces back. Things have just been… getting worse, lately."

"How long?" I asked softly.

"A while now," he said with a reluctant sigh. "She tell you her circle-mate, Oaklyn, died?"

I shook my head. "She said her childhood friend died, but I didn't know she was a witch, too. I didn't know *Blyn* was until her brother Ivan showed up."

"That fucking guy," Dax muttered, and I barked a soft laugh as I methodically took one article of clothing from Blyn after the other. It felt like I was unmaking her, like I was stripping away her armor one piece at a time. With every inch of skin that I revealed while she swayed under the influence of whatever they'd given her at the hospital, I felt like I was stripping every last bit of protection she had from the world and seeing what lay beneath it away.

Stop it, I thought savagely. *You're her protection, now. You are. As long as you're here, for whatever reason, she won't have to see a thing.*

"You okay, Blyn?" I murmured, and she nodded, her long, glossy dark hair shrouding her face. She mumbled something incoherently and Dax chuckled.

"They got her on the good shit, that's for sure," he said but I couldn't share his glib attitude about it.

"Anyway, I was saying," he murmured. "Last spring, something happened back home. Her circle sister, Miri, their earth witch, got into some kind of trouble. Oaklyn had been their fire witch, and when she'd died, their circle got busted. Then this Ivan shows up in town, a fire witch, right? Miri had some shit go down and somehow, she threw down with some wild magic and bound them into a new circle with this Ivan guy. Blyn's been having all kinds of trouble with her powers ever since."

"Should you, I don't know, be telling me any of this?" I asked.

Dax shrugged and handed me her nightgown which I slipped over her head. Blyn obediently put her arms through the thin spaghetti straps and I took her hands.

"Up we go," I murmured, and she stood, unsteadily. Dax turned down her neatly made bed, and I whispered, "Okay, sit down."

She did everything I asked, mechanically, without question, and I frowned. I wasn't sure if I liked it or not, then decided that no, I really didn't.

"It's like she's supercharged or something," Dax said, handing me her comforter and sheets to finish tucking her in.

She sighed and I swear she went to sleep the moment her head touched the pillow.

"Is there a way to fix it?" I asked.

"Yeah, but it requires the full cooperation of their circle I guess, and I'll give you one guess who ain't cooperating."

I sighed and nodded.

"Okay," I said.

"Seems like if it's true, you can do what you do simply by existing – maybe you ought to stick around for a bit… if that's not going to affect your busy schedule or anything."

"Yeah, no, I planned on staying," I said. "She and I, we need to talk."

I smoothed some of her hair behind her ear and gazed down at her face which was vulnerable in sleep.

"Yeah." Dax nodded. "I have to get back to the office, and home to my missus."

"Yeah," I said. "Blyn, uh, told me."

Dax twisted his lips and nodded without looking at me.

"She told me, that she told you," he said with a sigh.

"Why do I feel like this is way more awkward for me than it is for you?" I asked.

He chuckled, stuffing his hands into the pockets of his slacks.

"I fucked up," he said. "I own that. I've had long enough to live with it by now, and while it's not comfortable exactly… I don't know…" He looked down at Blyn's sleeping form and a sort of mix of affection and nostalgia crossed his face and he asked softly, "Can you really blame me?"

With a wife at home? I thought to myself. *Yes…* but at the same time…

"No, I guess I can't," I said, bowing my head and shaking it.

Dax chuckled dryly.

"Thanks for saying so, Mr. Mickleson."

"Jayse," I said and he nodded.

"Jayse," he repeated. He heaved a sigh and asked, "You can stay until she wakes up?"

I nodded; my eyes fixed on her.

"Yeah."

"Good deal. Thanks," he said and turned, heading for the elevator. He took Blyn's keys out of his pocket and set them on the kitchen counter next to where he'd deposited her purse on the way in. "Tell her I'll call her, check on her later."

"Okay."

"Nice to meet you, Mountain Man."

"Nice to meet you too, City Boy," I called back and he barked a laugh as the elevator doors whooshed shut.

I sank down onto the edge of the bed and put my hand gently over

Blyn's hip as I felt a lot of whatever had been keeping me up go out of me, sighing and bowing my head, shaking it.

I got up, folded her things neatly and deposited them on the dresser, before I wandered over more toward the living room and looking out her windows over the city of Boston and the harbor. I pulled my phone out of my pocket and called Serena.

"Hello?"

"Yeah, Sis… it's me."

"You've been gone a long time; I hope that mean's things are going well!" she said brightly and I was silent for too long. "Jayse?" she asked. "Jayse, what's the matter, what's wrong?"

"I fucked up, little sister," I said and emotion choked me. "I fucked up big."

*B*lyn...

I woke in my own bed to the click and whir of the central heating coming on. The next thing I was aware of, I was pressed up against something hard, *no not something,* some*one.*

I sucked in a sharp breath, panic seizing in my breast as I pushed against whoever's bare skin in the clutches of the deep dark fear the images, I mean sights and sounds, would start invading my mind any second but there was nothing.

His hold tightened on me in the deep dark of my apartment, and I looked up into Jayse's sleepy face, the nighttime lights of Boston out my windows casting him in bluish shadow.

"Jayse," I gasped and he nodded.

"Yeah, it's me… what time is it?" he asked, sleepily.

"What are you doing here?" I gasped.

He frowned. "You don't remember?"

I thought back and shuddered, trying not to think about it too much. About the blood and the screaming. About the pain and perversion.

Oh, God… he's out there. He's out there and he's going to kill another woman. All of their faces flashed before me. All seventy-two of them and I fought down a wave of nausea.

"I was doing a reading on a piece of evidence for the FBI… a serial killer," I murmured, cutting myself off before I said too much and looking up into Jayse's patient eyes as he held me firmly, but gently in the dark.

"But what were you doing there?" I asked. "Where was Dax?"

"He was there too," Jayse said and he sighed, slightly unhappily. "He intercepted me at the front desk."

I listened as Jayse told me his harrowing part of the tale and praised the Lord and Lady that he had been there. I don't know where I would be right now if he wasn't. Committed, perhaps? I don't know, but his presence saved my mind from irreparable harm, I was sure of it, and the fact that he had stayed, was with me now… *grateful.* I could only be grateful.

"You stayed," I murmured and he nodded again.

"I'm so sorry, Blyn. I feel so guilty—" I placed fingertips against his lips to silence him and shook my head.

"No," I said. "You didn't know."

He pulled my hand away and said, guilt dripping from every word, "I didn't give you the chance to tell me, either. I was so wrapped up in myself and how I was feeling—"

I put both of my hands over his mouth then and shook my head. "It's not your fault."

He pulled my hands away and put my arms around his neck, his arms winding around me and pressing me close to him. I closed my eyes and relished the contact, loving the feel of him warm and alive beneath my touch with no images, no horrors or feelings or sense of anything coming from him. Just… I don't know, something akin to love as he held me tight in the dark. I was certainly cared for, and oh so grateful.

"I thought I deserved it," I confessed quietly, and shuddered, thinking back on that rope. How it'd twisted around his victim's wrists. How I'd felt a savage glee as I undid my belt and I had to swallow back bile. *No one deserves what I just went through.* I knew that. Was keenly aware.

The assault on my senses had been awful. The terror, heartache, and pain of the victim I'd lived fully… but so too had I lived the depraved *joy* the killer had taken in raping and torturing his victim… just one of many, *each of their faces flashing by my mind's eye from the killer's point of view, each one screaming, crying, and in pain as he raped them, mutilated them, and did it all while they wept, screaming.*

"Hey, hey, hey!" Jayse's voice cut through the mental noise of their anguish and his hands cupped my face. "Don't go back there, wherever it is. Stay with me," he implored, and I looked up at him, biting my lips together, sniffing – my nose full and my cheeks wet.

"I'm sorry," I murmured, trembling and he pressed his lips to my forehead. I felt the tension drain from my body.

"Nothing to be sorry about. I'm here, I'm right here. I'm not going anywhere."

I sniffed again and swallowed hard.

"Thank you."

"Don't mention it," he whispered against my hair.

I took solace in his kind and gentle embrace, and though I had been asleep for I don't know how long, I felt as though I could sleep some more, so we cuddled back down beneath the blankets, a chill radiating through the glass window panes that slanted above my bed as the snow pattered against them and melted, frost patterns creeping from the corners in a geometric display of mother nature's brilliance.

"Thank you for staying with me," I whispered and he smiled. I could feel the motion against my temple where he pressed a tender kiss.

"No place I would rather be right now," he said and I believed him.

THE NEXT MORNING, when I woke, Jayse was still in bed with me. He was asleep, and I took the time in the morning light to really look at him.

He cleaned up very nicely. His hair had been cut and his beard trimmed neatly, and the new look suited him. It certainly appealed to me a great deal. I had found him beautiful before but now? Now he was simply breathtaking. Twice now he had saved me from the darkest parts of me and he didn't even know it.

I felt as though I owed him everything. My life as well as my very sanity.

I leaned forward and brushed my lips against his and he startled awake, his hazel-green eyes flickering open, focusing on mine, his chest rising and falling rapidly with his startlement. He looked at me and it wasn't enough. I dipped my head closer to his and went in for another kiss, a better one.

He met me halfway, his mouth crashing against mine, his hand tangling in the back of my hair, not pulling, not hurting, simply cradling the back of my head. His other arm he sent snaking around my waist, pulling me to him. I flattened myself to his body and kissed him with a desperate urgency and I was met, outside all odds, with the same fervency from him.

"I'm so sorry," I whispered.

He looked into my eyes and said, "Me, too." He drew in a shuddering breath and said, "God, I want you."

I smiled and slipped my leg over his hips, my nightgown conveniently already ridden up. I was completely nude beneath the satin and the thought that he had changed me once more made me smile. I knew what a gentleman Jayse was, and I was glad for it.

Now, I could feel his desire through his boxer shorts. He was as hard as frozen steel and yet hotter than a branding iron. I writhed against him, the only thing separating us the thin cotton layer of his underwear.

He kissed me, a hand on my hip, the other holding my hair back from my face as I bent over him. Things were heated, the air between us shimmering with lust and something more. Something not quite definable, at least not yet.

We kissed, hands exploring, lips moving against the others in a beautiful waltz of give and take, our soft moans and the cadence of our breath the music by which we danced. Eventually he arched his hips, sliding his hands beneath my thighs and both of us laughing, awkwardly shimmied his boxers out of the way.

I settled over him once more, and our ardor for one another resumed until with a shuddering breath of relief, he slipped inside of me and I felt... *complete.*

Jayse sucked in a sharp breath of his own, his hands going to the satin over my hips, gripping them firmly to keep me from moving just yet. His hold lessened and I rolled my pelvis, grinding down on him and sighed as pleasure radiated out from my core.

"Oh, *Blyn.*" He somehow both gasped and sighed at once and I smiled, rocking gently, loving him slowly.

The silent hush of my apartment was only disrupted by our heavy breathing and the gentle patter of cold winter flakes against the glass that surrounded us on two sides. His touch was warm, though. Where his hands moved over the satin encasing my body, I felt warmed down to my very soul. I rode him until all sense of time, space, and direction fell away. Until the only thing either of us felt was the mounting urgency to achieve the pleasure that awaited us at the end of this slow climb. A pleasure, that for a while, maddeningly attempted to stay just out of our reach.

It finally became too much, the satin of my nightgown impeding the touch of his hands against my skin, and I lifted it up, off over my head. I let it flutter to the floor at my bedside, the sound of it slipping against itself slick as it pooled on the floor.

"Goddess, Jayse, please *touch me,*" I moaned.

He didn't hesitate, sliding his calloused hands up my body, swiping his thumbs over my nipples which stiffened into peaks at the atten-tion. I bit my bottom lip, rising and falling on my knees, gripping the edge of my modern headboard for support and leverage as I made love to him, gripping him tightly with my core.

We were both on the cusp of that euphoric rush, both of us riding that edge, standing on the precipice hand in hand when the buzzer to my apartment sounded its noxious call.

"Oh, shit!" Jayse jumped beneath me and I startled myself, but *Goddess* he felt good.

I groaned, and the buzzer continued on, and on, and, on, and *on*…

"Whoever it is, isn't going to give up," Jayse said and I closed my eyes and nodded.

"It's Ash, it has to be," I responded. "Better get dressed, looks like you're going to meet the rest of my circle."

Jayse looked amused and drew me down on top of him, pressing his mouth to mine in a lingering kiss.

"To be continued?" he asked against my mouth.

"To be continued," I murmured, and *that* was a promise.

ASH STOOD in my living room, butt leaned up against my couch, arms crossed over her chest, the leather of her jacket and pants creaking as she shifted. She was going back to her natural blonde, at least. Well, she was trying. The black that had been in her hair in the Spring was slowly but surely growing out, the blond out about three or four inches from her scalp. I grimaced slightly as I took her frowning face in. Neither the hair, nor the frown, were a good look.

"A *fucking Null?*" she demanded, then looked past me to Jayse who was making my bed for lack of anything else to do and shot over my shoulder at him, "No offense."

Jayse shook his head and said, "I get it… I think."

I looked back at him over my own satin-clad shoulder, my robe on over my nightgown and sighed along with my apologetic expression. He gave me a pitying look and went to move around the bed to pull things up on the side I was on.

Ash threw up a hand and said, "Nah, ah, ah! You stay right there!"

Jayse froze.

"Ash!" I barked, and Miri, who was hanging back even further away in my kitchen looked up. She was fixing her calming tea.

"I need my powers," Ash snapped. "I have work tonight."

"I get it," I said gently. "I don't know what I'm going to do," I said sighing and Jayse put his hand on my shoulder. I put my arm around his waist and he put his arm around me and sat me on the edge of my bed, still well away from my circle sisters. Not far enough, the apartment while spacious, wasn't quite spacious enough, but we were trying our best here.

"We need to go home," Miri said. "Consult the family books. I looked in mine and found *some* information, but we really could stand to look in the Courtney and Tremblay books."

I shuddered. I did *not* want to talk to my mother… Overbearing was putting it mildly. However, Miri was right.

"What we *need*," Ash spat, "is that big fucking lunk to fucking stop cockblocking our every move!"

Miri laughed slightly and shook her head and I laughed a little too.

"Is she talking about me?" Jayse asked me and I shook my head.

"Ivan," I said.

"Oh, yeah, *that* fucking guy."

Miri looked up sharply from putting my kettle on and frowned. Ash threw her hands up and said, "Thank you! See, it's not only me!"

"Sorry, I'm trying to follow, but you're going to have to catch me up," Jayse said gently.

"When it was our original circle," Miri said. "Me, Blyn, Ash and her twin, Oaklyn, we put a sort of binding on Blyn to help mitigate her power. Sort of turned down the volume if you will."

"Yeah, things were fine, then Oak…" Ash couldn't bring herself to say it.

"Oaklyn died of cancer," I whispered and Ash wouldn't look at any of us, preferring to fixate on the toe of her motorcycle boot as she traced the pattern on the edge of my area rug with it.

"Which wasn't great," Ash said. "But it sort of balanced Blyn out."

"Volume control no longer needed," Miri added gently.

"Then the shit went down this last Spring and Miri accidently on purpose dragged Ivan into the mix. Wild magic happened and bound us into a circle, Ivan taking Oaklyn's place of fire among us," Ash recounted.

"Except Ivan won't agree to binding my powers and we need all four of us for the ritual," I said.

"Why not?" Jayse asked, frowning.

"Ivan comes from a… rough background," Miri said after a long moment where the only sounds that filled the space was the ticking babble of the water in the kettle as it struggled to heat.

"Boy is paranoid as fuck is what you mean," Ash said, dipping her head and turning it toward Miri.

"He has good reason, Ash," I said gently, sighing. On this, I was on Miri's side. Ash threw her hands up and let them fall, slapping her outer thighs, the sound sharp in my otherwise hushed place. The buildup of snow out there only insulated us further, making things seem even quieter in the space we occupied.

"I mean, we've all been there with the shitty upbringings in our own way, Blyn!" Ash cried. I gave her an unfriendly look.

"You don't know, Ash—"

"Only because you won't tell me," she said and gave me a raised lip in distaste. She knew how it was. I didn't share the things I saw. I felt like it was only right. I mean, if I hadn't gotten into crime fighting, I probably would have made one hell of a therapist. Just shake their hand and know all their secrets… know immediately how to help. I'd thought about it. Even had a degree in psychology to prepare for it, for that eventuality… *maybe I should consider it sooner rather than later.* I shuddered and tried closing the door on the vault of what I had seen the day before.

I managed to get it shut, but just barely. Jayse tightening his hold on me, rubbing my satin covered shoulder up and down soothingly, helped me keep my connection with reality to keep the horrors at bay a little longer. Eventually, I would need to confront them. Eventually, I hoped they would lead to getting this monster caught. Locked up or killed, I had no regret in saying I didn't mind either way… some things, some *people*, were just that fucking awful.

You're one of those awful people, Blyn. Just not like this.

I batted the thought away and squared my shoulders.

"Maybe you don't need Ivan to help take it down a notch," Jayse said and shrugged a little. I looked up at him and he looked down at me saying, "I mean, unless you don't want me to stick around. Until you can figure things out, though… I'd like to. I mean—" he blushed furiously and I smiled, raising a hand and gently laying it against his cheek.

"Again, no offense, bro, but *Blyn*, you can't be serious right now!" Ash looked aghast.

"Ash!" Miri cried and the kettle began to whistle sharply. She plucked it from the stovetop and poured out four measures into mugs.

"What?" Ash cried.

"I think the best course of action *is* to go home," I said with a sigh. "Consult the family books."

My buzzer went off and Ash frowned.

"Who could that be?" Miri wondered aloud, going to the plate set next to the elevator and pressing the button.

"Yes?" she called out, her soothing lilting voice the picture of professionalism.

"Agents McKinnon and Stahl for Ms. Blyn Courtney."

Miri looked back at me and I felt my shoulders drop, resigned. I nodded unhappily and she hit the button to buzz them through the door. They got onto the elevator and Miri pressed the button to allow them up to my apartment.

She stepped back into the kitchen and was lifting down two mugs when the doors whooshed open.

The two agents stepped off the elevator glancing around curiously.

"What do you want?" I asked tiredly. The bone weariness soaking into my very soul at the sight of them.

"We need to know what you saw," Agent McKinnon, the rude one, said. "You all maybe mind giving us a minute?"

"Yeah, fuck you," Ash said, and her gaze was stormy. "You all have done enough."

"Ash," I said, warning in my tone.

"No." Ash pushed off from the couch and turned around so she could fully face the two agents. "These fuckers come to you and they take and take and take and take and take, and none of them, not a goddamn one of them, considers the toll it takes on you. Well I'm cutting 'em off!"

"Excuse me, but who are you?" McKinnon demanded.

"Ash…" my tone was low, warning.

"No!" Ash turned back to me and I balled my fists, taking a step away from Jayse.

"Ashlyn Tremblay!" I barked and a subtle breeze swept through the apartment, rustling hair and papers.

"All of you, knock it off!" Miri scolded. She brought a serving tray I kept in with the cookie sheets around and went to the agents. "Have some tea and have a seat," she said gently.

"Was that you?" Agent Stahl asked, a little wide-eyed.

"The wind?" I asked.

"Yeah."

"I think so, I don't know…" I glanced back at Jayse. "It's complicated."

"Yeah." McKinnon eyed Jayse. "Your partner, Detective Dax, explained some of it."

"Have a seat, Agent," Miri urged again. "Let's discuss," she cast a look at Ash, "*civilly*."

"Whoa." Ash turned on Jayse who had moved forward and frowned. "You stay right there."

"Ash, if you're going to be an asshole, you can go," I said tiredly. "My apartment, my rules. Jayse stays near me."

Ash scowled. "Fine," she grated and Miri gave her a look like she swore to the God and Goddess if Ash didn't shape up, she was going to spank her like an unruly child.

We all moved into the living room and took varying seats. Miri handed out her tea and even breathing deep the vapors had a calming effect. Tension eased out of everyone.

"Doctor it how you'd like," Miri said and indicated the milk, sugar, and honey on the tray.

"Who puts milk in their tea?" Agent McKinnon asked, making a face.

"The British," Ash, Miri, and I quipped, with Miri adding, "And everyone else who knows how to drink a proper cup of tea."

"Okay, who are all you people?" McKinnon demanded.

"Agents McKinnon and Stahl, I would like you to meet two of my three circle-mates, Miriam Eilish and Ashlyn Tremblay. Our fourth, Ivan Ivanovich isn't present," I told them.

"Thank the Maiden, Mother, and Crone for that," Ash muttered before sipping her tea.

"This is Jayse," I murmured.

"Hi," he said and added, "I guess I'm a Null." He gave a shrug and smiled and I found it both endearing and charming.

"A what?" McKinnon asked.

"Wow." Ash heaved a sigh. "Come to her for help and don't know a thing about her, do yah?" she asked. She sighed. "Time for a little Magic 101: A Glossary of Terms."

She ran them through it while I got a few sips of my tea in, Miri and I exchanging amused looks and adding details where we thought they were important.

"So, you can't do any magic around him?" Stahl asked.

"No," I said. Then thinking about the bit of witch-wind a moment before said, "At least, I don't think so… enough time away from him it comes back and maybe, enough time with him and things sort of… even out? I'm not sure. That's what we were discussing before you arrived."

"Do what now?" McKinnon asked.

"We were discussing going home, consulting the family spellbooks, trying to figure out how to magic, make everything work," Miri said, smiling.

"Where's home again?" Agent Stahl asked politely.

"The little town of Loving, up the coast," I answered.

"No can do," McKinnon said, shaking her head. "We need you down in DC and Quantico."

"Not gonna happen," Ash said and she gave them a flat, unfriendly look from the arm of the loveseat Jayse and I occupied. Jayse threaded his fingers between mine.

"No, I agree. I do need to help you catch this monster, but I am afraid I am of little to no help to you in my current state," I said miserably.

"Well, you need to get in shape," McKinnon said. "Because this guy already has forty-three kills to his name that we know of."

"Seventy-two," I corrected her softly. She and Stahl exchanged a look, Agent Stahl blanching slightly.

"Excuse me?" Stahl asked gently, wanting to make sure she'd heard me right. I fixed her light green eyes with my own which filled with anguish and sorrow.

"Seventy-two," I said clearing my throat. "And it's going to take all of us to get him, I am afraid."

"Fuck," Ash muttered and shook her head. "Ivan will never go for that."

"Let me try to talk to him," Miri said softly, averting her gaze to the steaming liquid in her cup.

McKinnon took a hard swallow of her tea and made a face. "I don't even like tea," she muttered then looked like she was having second thoughts when she looked down into her cup.

"Give us a few days," I said. "Leave me your card. I'll be in touch."

"We were told to bring you back," Stahl said.

"And you will," I said firmly. "On my timeline. Not yours."

"Trying to force her would be a *really* bad idea," Ash said and her tone was chilly.

Jayse squeezed my hand, and I looked up at him.

"Whatever you need," he said. "I've seen enough. I'm with you," he said.

"Thank you," I murmured.

I was starting to maybe feel like this – whatever this was – was maybe going to work out.

*J*ayse...

She told the FBI agents everything she could remember, which was a lot, from what she'd gathered and seen from touching that cursed hank of rope. After they left, teary and shaking, another cup of whatever Miri had brewed up clutched between her hands, she'd told us the rest.

It was bad. Really bad. She hadn't just *seen* things, she'd *lived them*, simultaneously at points between the killer and the woman he'd been torturing and murdering. My stomach felt sick as she'd recounted the horror of being raped, compounded by the utter satisfaction and glee she'd felt over doing those horrible things to that poor girl from the killer's point of view.

I mean, it was *sick*, the things she'd described. I had no words for it. That was for sure.

After the agents had left, we'd made our plans to go to Loving. Miri and Ash left shortly thereafter – Ash to go pack, Miri to return to Loving ahead of us and to prepare rooms in her house for us to stay in.

Blyn was packing, her phone charging, when it rang.

"Yeah, Dax, hi..." she answered and sighed out harshly. "No, a leave of absence is what I need," she said. "I'm glad the department suggested it. I'm actually getting ready to leave, now…"

She paused as he asked questions.

"No, back to Loving. Yeah, they were here. Yeah, he's right here." She looked surprised. "Hold on a minute." She held out her phone to me with a shrug.

"Yeah, hello?" I answered.

"Hey, yeah, it's Dax."

"I kind of figured."

"You take care of my partner, k?" he said and he sounded worried.

"I will," I said frowning. "You good?"

"Wife packed up and left this morning, but yeah. Yeah, I'm good," he said.

"I'm sorry to hear that," I said and I meant it. I would be lying if I said it didn't make me worry about Blyn. I looked over to her, and she ran a satin something, like a nightgown, through her hands, before putting it in her bag.

"I mean it. Not going to lie, Mountain Man. I think you're the better man for her. I… I gotta sort some shit out on my end. I'm certainly no good."

"I'm honestly not sure what to say to that," I said carefully.

"You ain't gotta say nothing," he said. "Just don't tell Blyn about it. She doesn't need to worry about anything else right now but herself and maybe catching that guy. I've… I've never seen her like that. Whatever it was, it must have been bad."

"The worst, actually."

"Yeah, I kind of figured. Anyway, I just wanted to let you know, we're cool. It's cool. Alright?"

"Yeah, man, yeah. I appreciate it," I said, and he sighed on the other end.

"K, let me talk to Courtney."

I handed the phone back to Blyn and listened to them talk a moment. Finally, she zipped up her suitcase, and ending the call, let out a great big cleansing sigh, her shoulders dropping.

"Okay, I think that's it," she said.

"You okay?" I asked.

She shook her head. "I could hear him, you know… what he said to you through the phone."

"Oh, shit. Yeah?"

She nodded. "Bits and pieces, but it was enough."

"*You* alright?" I asked.

She shook her head and sank down onto the edge of the bed.

"No. Not really," she answered. "I feel like everything I touch turns to shit."

I nodded slowly and went around, sitting down beside her.

"It's not true," I said, gathering her hand in mine. She swallowed hard and sniffed.

"Isn't it, though?" she asked.

"Nope." I shook my head.

"His wife left," she said. "Because of me."

I shook my head. "Because of *him*," I said. "Yeah, you participated, so if you want to push it, because of the *both* of you."

"I feel awful about that. About all of it… I was just…" she put a hand over her mouth and sobbed slightly and I sighed, pulling her into me, wrapping my arms around her and hugging her tight.

"People make mistakes," I said and I was trying not to judge. Truly. I know people got real twisted up inside over cheating, but it *was* true… everybody made mistakes. Sometimes. I could also see, and in some ways feel how broken up Blyn was about it, and it wasn't like she wasn't being honest with me.

Shit.

Everything about all of this was messy, and I wasn't quite sure where to begin on clean up. What I did know? There was something… I know it's funny to say given what I am, but there was something magical about me and Blyn and I wanted to see where this particular rabbit hole took me.

"I'm sorry," she said, pulling herself together. "I'm so sorry."

"It's okay," I told her. "You don't have to be strong all the time, babe."

She sniffed and wiped at the tears getting under her nose and looked up at me with those sable dark eyes.

"Honestly, I would settle for just part of the time right now."

I smoothed a hand over her hair and she hitched a sigh. She'd already showered, dried her hair, and dressed. I'd showered while she'd been drying her hair, and it'd felt… nice. Domestic in a way I had never really gotten to be with a woman.

"Go fix your makeup," I whispered, and pressed a kiss to her forehead.

"Oh, God!" she cried and got up, rushing into the bathroom to look in the mirror. I smiled to myself, standing, picking up her small suitcase and extending the arm on it so it would roll.

I smoothed out her bed and she came out, makeup kit in hand, not a hair out of place; her face perfect and ethereal in its beauty, even without the benefit of powder or whatever shit she put on it.

"Ready for this?" I asked and she nodded.

"Okay." I took her bag in one hand and held out my other. She came to me, slipping her hand in mine, and squared up her shoulders.

We took an Uber to my truck, which was thankfully still down the block from her precinct. It had a ticket on it, but wordlessly, Blyn snatched it from my hand before I could get her door open for her. I stowed her suitcase in the back and went around to the driver's side and got in. She was on her phone, talking to someone, reading off the parking ticket number. Having it fixed, I guess.

"Thanks," I murmured, and she nodded absently. I got my truck started up, the old motor lumbering to life, and I put it in gear and pointed us towards my sister's so I could retrieve my dog and a bag of my own.

When Blyn got off the phone, she crumpled the ticket and stuffed it into the plastic grocery sack I had on the floorboard at her feet to collect any garbage in my truck. I glanced at her and she remained quiet, pensive, for the remainder of the drive across to the other side of the city where my sister's house was located.

I pulled up to the curb in front of Serena's house and Blyn looked up at it, a ghost of a smile on her face. Shep ran along the inside of the three-foot chain-link fence of the front yard, woofing and prancing with excitement.

"It's so normal," Blyn said and she almost sounded relieved. I laughed and nodded.

"I keep forgetting, there are no surprises with you… a single touch on anyone else and you know everything about them."

"Including what they had for breakfast," she murmured. "Yeah."

I nodded, and she smiled at me a little wanly. I picked up her hand and kissed her palm, just as the front door of my sister's place opened up and my sister herself stepped out onto the front porch.

"Come on, I want you to meet Serena."

"Okay," Blyn murmured, and she shifted in her seat.

"Hold on, let me get your door." She smiled and nodded and waited for me. I got out, went around to her side, and opened her door for her. She let me help her out of the truck and we both turned.

"Shep!" my sister cried. "Knock it off!" Shep shut up with the barking but whined.

"Let me go first."

I went through the gate and was nearly bowled over by my boisterous Husky.

"Oh, okay! I missed you too!" I declared. "Hey, Sis," I called up to Serena.

"Hi," she called back down the awkwardly canted steps at me.

"Blyn, I'd like you to meet my sister, Serena. Serena, this is Blyn."

"Hi," Blyn said shyly. "It's so nice to finally meet you."

"Likewise!" Serena called and asked, "Is it safe to shake your hand?"

"Um, with Jayse around, yes," Blyn said, laughing a bit uneasily. She reached up as Serena reached down and shook hands.

"Come on in," Serena said smiling, holding open doors for Blyn. Blyn scooted past her into the house and I followed up, Shep darting in ahead of me to bowl into Blyn for some love.

"Well, hello!" Blyn called, laughing, giving my dog the attention he so desperately craved.

"Come on through to the kitchen," Serena suggested. "I'll put on the kettle, get us all something hot to drink."

"Ah, that would be great," Blyn said straightening.

"We're pretty short on time," I said and sighed.

"Oh?" Serena asked, and we followed her back to the kitchen. "Have a seat, Blyn. Make yourself comfortable," she said.

Blyn took a seat at the kitchen table and put her hands down on it, a slight frown wrinkling her brow before she shook her head slightly and dismissed whatever it was.

"So, what's going on?" Serena asked.

"I'm going to be gone for a few days… maybe longer," I said.

"Okay," Serena said, drawing out the word.

"I'm taking Blyn back up to Loving, sticking around her to nullify her power until she and her sisters can get some shit figured out. I might…" I hesitated and looked to Blyn with a shrug, not sure how much I was allowed to say.

"He might come to Quantico with me, help me keep my power in check so that I can finish helping the FBI with a really… bad case."

"Holy shit, are you serious?" Serena's gaze flicked from Blyn to me and she fixed me with her stare. "You're going to be helping the FBI?"

I laughed a little uneasily and shook my head. "Technically, I'll be helping Blyn so that *she* can help the FBI—"

"Same difference, bro! That's totally cool."

I shook my head.

"Don't say that. Not about this. I'm sorry I can't tell you more, Serena, I just can't but…" I swallowed hard and Blyn and I traded a look. I knew enough now that the look we traded was a haunted one. I breathed in through my nose nice and slow and let an explosive breath out of my mouth.

"Don't worry about Mike," I said. "I'm taking Shep with me so he won't bitch."

"Huh." Serena gave a dubious laugh. "No love lost there."

Shep didn't like Mike as much as Mike didn't like Shep. I'd seen an exchange of growling and yelling that made me uneasy. Serena seemed unfazed, however.

"Okay, I'm going to run down to my room and pack."

Serena nodded. "Okay."

Blyn smiled and nodded, and Serena moved to join her at the kitchen table.

"I won't be long," I assured Blyn and she nodded.

"Okay."

"Come on, Shep!" My dog bounded down the stairs to my basement room ahead of me.

I re-packed my duffel, making sure I had all my urban necessities and my outdoor gear, too. Blyn had said that there might be some time spent outside for rituals and the like, and that we would just have to figure it out as we went along.

I was okay with that. For the first time in a long time, I felt as though I had purpose. Like I wasn't just rattling around in this empty can trying to find something to do. To be good for.

I sighed and looked at my dog, who sat panting, looking up at me, tongue lolling out as I asked, "What do you think, boy? You ready for a road trip?"

He woofed quietly and stood up and I hefted my duffel onto my shoulder. I turned around and found Blyn three quarters of the way down the stairs, hand on the railing, looking around the basement.

"This is where you live, your space..." she murmured and I nodded.

"Yeah, this is my little corner of the world," I said and I tightened my grip on my duffel strap, acutely embarrassed. Shit, why had Serena let her down here?

"You okay?" I asked her.

She nodded. "Um, yeah. I was just getting antsy, I guess. I'm sorry."

"It's okay," I said and I went toward her, gesturing that she should precede me up the stairs.

She turned and went up. Serena stood from the kitchen table, smiling.

"Looks like you guys are set," she said and Blyn's smile for my sister was genuine.

"Thank you so much for your hospitality," Blyn murmured and Serena smiled at her warmly.

"You be safe," she told me and went around the table, coming over to hug me tight.

I hugged her back and said, "Always."

"Okay. Come on, I'll see you out."

She walked us to the door and I called to Blyn casually, "Hey, babe. Can you let Shep in the truck?"

"Sure!" She went down to the truck and called to Shep. He jumped up into the cab and took the seat between us.

"She's…" Serena groped for where to start. "Beautiful. Smart. Funny. Kind… she's wonderful," she said. "I guess I didn't know what to expect but, damn, big brother."

I smiled, relief flooding me.

"I'm really glad you like her," I said and she smiled up at me.

"She likes *you*, so of course I was going to like her."

I rolled my eyes. "That doesn't exactly make sense, Sis."

"Meh." She lifted one of her shoulders into a shrug. "It makes perfect sense when you think about it." She hugged me one more time. "I mean it, you be careful. I love you."

"I love you, too, and I think this is a lot less dangerous than trapping to be honest."

She raised an eyebrow. "Uh, crazy fire Russian?" she asked.

"Got three to his one on my side. I think the deck is a bit stacked against him."

"Well, that's good at least." She waved me off and grinning, I went down the steps and down the cracked concrete path, letting myself out the little gate and tossing my duffel into the back of my truck, wedging it up against Blyn's suitcase.

"I'll call you," I called up to Serena who was smiling and waving at Blyn.

"You better!" she called back and I got back into the driver's seat.

"I like her, she's nice," Blyn said, smiling out the window and waving back.

"That's Serena," I said and started up the truck. Shep wuffed a soft noise, and I put it in gear and pulled smoothly away from the curb. We had a hell of a drive ahead of us.

*B*lyn...

The drive to Loving was both long and exhausting. I was glad Jayse drove for a variety of reasons. One, his truck was made for the weather. Then there was the fact that I still felt as thin and insubstantial as a soap bubble. Completely fragile, my head in too many places at once… then finally, and I felt really awful for thinking it, but I liked having Shep with us, I just wasn't keen on mixing Shep with the interior of my Mercedes.

We stopped around sunset for a late lunch/early dinner at a roadside diner, but pretty quickly got back on the road. By the time we pulled into Miri's driveway, I was beginning to nod off, Shep's back end in my lap, his head on the top of Jayse's thigh.

I was low-key jealous of the Husky. Not going to lie.

Miri and Kavion both stepped out the back door of the wraparound porch as Jayse was grabbing our bags out of the back of the truck. Shep was wasting no time in finding a good spot in the deep snow to relieve himself.

"Hi!" Miri called down cheerfully.

"Hey, stranger!" Jayse called up. I tried to take my suitcase from him but he shook his head and gestured for me to go ahead.

"Ivan?" I asked casually at the melted path through the snow to the door.

"Ah, yeah," Miri said with a nod.

"Hey, your dog ain't gonna have a problem with my black ass, is he?" Kavion called to Jayse and I looked at him like he was crazy.

"Don't look at me like that. Some of these dogs got that shit bred into 'em," he said. "That ain't no lie."

I nodded, the sad reality of it sinking in.

"No, you're right. I didn't think. I'm sorry," I said.

"Don't trip," he said back with a smile and Jayse said, "No, man. Shep's a good boy." He raised his voice. "Aren't you, Shep? C'mon, boy!"

"Well we're happy to have you," Miri said and pulled me in for a hug. "How are you doing?" she asked.

"You mean since this morning?" I countered. I huffed out a plume of breath. "About the same, honestly."

"Aw, well, let's get you both in out of the cold and off the road, yeah?" Kavion waved us through into Miri's kitchen.

"I've been back for a while," she said. "Got everything sorted for you, giving you the Gray Room. I started to go through my books and things…" she paused as Jayse crossed the threshold and both she and I exchanged a look.

"Well, that answers that," she murmured.

"Interesting," I echoed.

Some of her wards had come down, but the oldest and strongest held true, albeit under a tremendous strain.

"What? What is it?" Jayse and Kavion traded looks.

"Don't look at me, brah, I just live here." Kavion held up his hands.

Jayse laughed. "Not magic and just as lost as me, then?" he asked.

"Pretty much," Kavion agreed. "Come on, let them do their girl magic, I'll show you to your room and you can set yourself up." Kavion took Jayse's duffel from him and Jayse nodded.

"Appreciate it."

Miri turned to look at me, shutting the door tightly behind us and the chill out with it.

"So, I've been doing some reading," she said with a gusty sigh. "Your mother wants to see you but she *did* give me the Roth family book. I didn't expect her to give up the Courtney book without seeing you, but I tried."

"Oh, God, where are they?"

"Relax, they're safe down in the basement in my workshop. I figure as long as he doesn't go down there, everything should be okay, but that's not what I'm excited about," she said.

"What are you excited about, then?"

"There's information about Null-Witch relations in the Roth book," she said proudly.

"What?"

"Not a lot, but there's one line that stood out about them."

"What?" I asked with bated breath, feeling like my world had narrowed down to the singular word.

"Nature abhors a vacuum," she said.

I reared back a bit and said, "What?" and confusion tinged my tone.

"Nature and balance, child. Nature and balance," she sang out and just *how many times* had her grandmother said the same thing to us girls?

"Is the Roth book saying what I think it's saying? And where's Ash?"

"To the first, probably. More reading needs to be done. To the second, Ash went on her little bounty hunt and said she would be here tomorrow."

"Oh," I said nodding. We all had to earn a living somehow... even during a crisis of epic proportions.

"Jayse was telling me on the drive up, that his sister might have some information on Nulls to help piece things together," I told Miri, sliding out of my coat and handing it to her. She hung it on a set of hooks by the back door and my purse along with it.

Miri frowned slightly. "Is she one, too?" she asked.

"No, they grew up near here, and I guess she's always been this really big history buff. She was telling me that's what she went into when she went to college. History with a focus on comparative religion. Specifically focusing on witchcraft and Christianity and the clashes that resulted in the 15th century; being famous for its Spanish Inquisition."

"Oh…" Miri looked a little green around the gills. "And which side of those clashes is she on?" she asked carefully.

I smiled warmly. "I met her today. She's on our side as any modern woke person typically is. She was trying so hard not to ask, it was cute."

"Wait, what was that?" Miri asked when my face gave me away.

"I saw something, when I touched her kitchen table," I said.

"Wait, with Jayse there with you?"

"Yeah, I don't know if it was real…" I said. "I mean, it was like one of my visions but like you said, Jayse was with me and it was, I don't know. Like a distant dream."

"Like when you very first started to see?" she asked and Lord and Lady that was a long, long, *long*, way back.

"Maybe? It's been so long."

"Hm." She looked thoughtful a moment then asked, "Hungry?"

"Yeah, actually. I am."

"Fresh baked bread with some butter and honey will fix you right up," she declared and I smiled.

"Add a hot cup of tea and you're on."

"Pfft! Always! You just have a seat."

Miri was going about her kitchen when the men returned. I moved over in the breakfast nook, and Jayse slid into the seat beside mine. Kavion slid in across from us and Miri happily doted on the lot of us.

"It's been a while since Eilish House has had guests," she said beaming, setting a bread board with a freshly baked loaf of country white bread, warmed in the oven between us. Some earthenware plates, fresh churned butter and honey, and our evening was almost complete. As soon as the tea hit the table, we were pretty much all united in relaxing and talking about some more pleasant things than murderers and haywire power situations.

The night wore on until the wee hours of the morning and sometime between one and two during an opportune lull in the conversation, Jayse gently gathered my hand in his and with a tired smile said, "I think it's time I get Cinderella here to bed."

I snorted. "You lose a shoe at midnight..." Miri finished with me, "You're not a princess, you're drunk!"

"Ha, ha, ha," Kavion said with an eye roll and put his hand on Miri's back. She smiled at him, and the love that radiated from both of them was beautiful. Like something akin to sunlight filled her kitchen coming from them.

I sighed and smiled, happy for them, and Jayse stood. Shep raised his head up off his paws and I slid into Jayse's seat and then stood up, myself.

"Come on, you," he said and the gentleness in his tone, the kindness in his touch? Well, it just melted me some.

"Goodnight, you guys," Kavion declared and I smiled.

"Goodnight," I said.

"I love you," Miri said to me and I hugged her.

"I love you, too."

The room Jayse led me to was the first door off the stairs on the second floor. He keyed open the lock with the old-fashioned but still functioning skeleton key and let us in, Shep trotting in ahead of us and sniffing around the room.

The bedside lamp was on, but the rest of the Gray Room was cast in muted shadow. It was soothing to the eyes and restful in here. I always liked the Gray Room.

It was as the name implied, done in varying shades of cool, soothing gray. The wallpaper gray with giant, light pink cabbage roses on it. The wingback chair, also a silvery gray velvet. The coverlet on the bed, a rich dove gray velvet. The sheets? A cool slate gray. The carpet, gray, the area rug, gray with big pink cabbage roses... even the curtains that hung from the giant, four-poster canopy bed were a sheer gray.

It was lovely.

This room also had a bathroom attached directly to it, which was nice. I went in and smiled. Jayse had unpacked a few things, our toothbrushes side by side in the holder on the old-fashioned Victorian white porcelain pedestal sink.

"Thank you," I murmured, and he nodded.

"Take your time," he said, and I nodded and shut the door. I used the bathroom, washed the makeup from my face, and brushed my teeth. When I went out, Jayse had the bed turned down, his pajamas on, and mine laid out on the foot of the bed for me. He kissed me gently and went into the bathroom, leaving me to change in solitude.

I did so swiftly and got into bed.

When he came out, I was rubbing some of Miri's sensual rose lotion into my hands and arms from the bedside table. The stuff was magic for dry winter skin and I was so stealing the little jar when we left here.

"Smells nice," Jayse murmured. He looked good in his flannel, blue, plaid print pajama bottoms and his soft white cotton tee. I almost felt overdressed in my slinky satin nightgown, but it wasn't for him. My sexy sleepwear was for me. After a long day of slogging through the worst that humanity had to offer, I liked to treat myself with soft things, finer things, things that comforted me and made me feel good...

I realized, in a flash of clarity and insight into myself, that that was likely why I had so easily fallen into Dax's arms and he into mine. *Comfort...* both of us inundated on a daily and only one another to understand... by no means was it an excuse for our awful behavior but it *was* a reason. I smiled wanly at Jayse as he got into bed beside me and thought to myself, *he deserves so much better than you, Blyn Courtney... so much better.*

"Hey, what's this?" he asked, thumbing the moisture from the tear that fell on my cheek away.

"I feel so guilty," I confessed.

"About what, baby?" he asked me.

"About Dax. About his wife, and what we did. About how I am *such* a shitty person for it, and how you deserve *so much better...* and how I don't deserve you here, helping me."

"Oh, shit. Oh, baby, *no...* No, no, no..." He sighed and pulled me against him, holding me tight. "Look, I can't say anything about the whole Dax situation. I mean, it happened, and we all make mistakes in our life. Big ones, little ones... the question is, did you *learn* from those mistakes?"

I shook my head and said miserably, "I don't know. I mean, how can I know?"

"Shh," he soothed and hugged me tight. "I'll admit," he murmured, "things are moving lightning fast in some ways. Still, it's not like we have a choice. I feel like we're being swept along on this current, you know? It's both thrilling and exciting, but it has its downsides. It's scary, too."

I nodded, smoothing my hair behind my ears, saying nothing. I mean, what was there that I could say?

"There's no punishment any god or goddess, or whatever you believe in can mete out that you haven't already put yourself through ten times over," he said and I nodded. I mean, he wasn't exactly wrong about that.

"Come here," he said firmly and slid down in the bed. I went to him, grateful beyond measure for his presence, for his willingness to comfort me and hold me despite the awful thing I'd done.

"You need to go easier on yourself, babe," he whispered and held me tight.

"I don't... I can't," I whispered brokenly and he nodded and tucked me against him. Shep thumped down onto the floor and let out a snuffling doggy sigh and I had to smile at that.

"Wow," Jayse murmured, chuckling. "Way to be dramatic, dog."

I chuckled too and closed my eyes.

Despite the stress that rode me and was eroding me from the inside out, it wasn't long before I started to fade. Jayse reached up and shut off the lamp, immediately returning to hold me and I thought to myself hazily as sleep dragged at me, *I don't deserve him...* It was my last thought before I fell into a deep and dreamless sleep... at least I thought it was.

J ayse...

"You look troubled," Miri said and set a cup of coffee in front of me at the breakfast bar.

"I am," I said with a sigh. "I'm worried about Blyn."

"What's wrong?" she asked, genuinely confused.

I fidgeted, not knowing how much to say and finally with a frustrated sigh asked, "How much do you know about her and Dax, her partner?"

Miri's green eyes widened slightly and she took a deep breath and let it out in a whoosh. "Nothing, really... is... is there something there?" she asked.

"There *was*," I said, hating myself. "His wife left him. Blyn is tearing herself up over it, but I mean, I get it. I don't condone it, like at all, but I *understand*, if that makes sense."

"Oh, no, poor Blyn," Miri whimpered and looked out her kitchen window at the stark blinding white blanket of snow outside disrupted by my goofy dog, bounding through it, grinning his huge doggie grin.

"I feel awful for outing her like this without her here," I said. She'd gone to her mom's, Kavion driving her over there to fetch her family book. She'd hated herself so much for asking me to stay behind but I guess she and her mother didn't have the best relationship to begin with. I guess there was a lot of judgment there coming from her mom and the last thing she needed was more stress and drama by pitching up on her mother's doorstep with a Null; the boogeyman of all witchkind, at her heel.

No, I'd stayed here, and she'd gone to her mom's and I felt maddeningly helpless being here rather than there, which I honestly had such a maddening urge and drive to stay glued to her at all times. At least for now.

"Everything will be alright," Miri declared. "It's just going to take a little hard work and ingenuity and maybe just a little magic to get us all there. As for feeling like you've tattled on her?" Miri put a hand on mine and I jumped slightly. The contact surprising me. "Don't worry too much. When you're in a circle, you tend to be inextricably linked to your circle-mates. During times of great stress, things tend to bleed out, and we get a sense of what is going on with one another through overwhelming emotion and even in our dreams. For politeness' sake, we don't talk about those things or really acknowledge how much each of us really knows, but… we know, you know?"

Her bright smile dimmed with a little heartache and I nodded.

"Which is why you got so freaked out when Blyn just sort of dropped off the radar," I said. "Because of me. Because of what I am."

"Precisely," she said, taking back her hand and shaking it out without thinking. "You can't know how grateful we are when it happened at the apex of her being swept up by her power yesterday."

I blinked. "Shit, that really was only yesterday, wasn't it?" I asked.

Miri nodded. "It happens like that sometimes. So much happening so close together that it all blurs together and you start losing sense of time. It happened last spring for me. Starting with the Matchmaker's Festival."

And that was how I learned all about her and Kavion and how they got together. I have to say, it was a nice way to pass the time.

*B*lyn...

I stepped out of my mother's house clutching the family book to my chest, grateful to have escaped any more of her scathing tongue.

Kavion looked up from his phone and through the windshield of his Loving Police Department SUV. He frowned and I took in a deep, cleansing breath and let it out, bounding down the steps of Courtney House and over to the passenger side of the vehicle.

Kavion leaned way over and opened the door for me from the inside.

"Thank you," I said breathlessly, getting up into the warm interior, holding my family's book to my chest like it was a lifeline.

"You okay?" he asked.

"Nope," I answered. "Just drive, please? Back to Miri's, away from here."

"Sure, sure thing. Anything illegal go down in there?" he asked.

"What?" I asked.

"Like, you kill your mom?" He winked at me and grinned and I laughed nervously.

"Don't think I haven't thought about it," I said. "Maiden, Mother, and Crone; our relationship is… difficult on a good day."

"I've met her a few times," Kavion confessed. "Seems like a real ol' battle axe as my dad would call her."

"She is that," I agreed, nodding slowly.

I fell silent. My mother seemed to think I needed to be doing something more respectable with my powers. She didn't agree with my chosen profession and she especially hadn't liked us girls binding ourselves to that weirdo… meaning Ivan… like any of us had had the choice.

All three of us were shielding pretty hard from him, and I was almost certain he was shielding from the rest of us just as hard. I was surprised he wasn't flipping his shit knowing I was close with Jayse again.

He *really* didn't like Nulls, but there was a reason for that. I just wasn't completely clear on it. I'd seen a lot when it came to our Russian comrade, but there were still a series of jumbled visions and sounds that hadn't made sense. He was, in essence, like an incomplete jigsaw puzzle, only half of the remaining pieces were missing altogether.

"Can you check and make sure Jayse moves off so I can get this to the basement?" I asked and Kavion nodded.

"Sure, just a sec. Wait right here."

He got out and went to the back door and into the kitchen, knocking the snow off his boots before he entered. Shep came out and started frolicking in the snow and *that* made me smile.

"Uh, Chief?" squeaked over the radio. "I think some witch just walked out of the harbor. Chief, are you there?" I rolled my eyes and Kavion came over the radio.

"You serious? It's cold as… it's… it's *cold* out there. I'm on my way!"

I laughed and shook my head. Ash. It had to be. She always did know how to make an entrance. I got out of the car and Kavion came out the back door.

"That bitch be *crazy!*" he shouted and I laughed.

"I don't disagree. You better hurry, she's going to need a warmup and a ride the rest of the way."

"I'm on it," he said, throwing himself into the driver's seat and starting the vehicle up. Lights and siren on as soon as he hit the end of the drive and turned out onto the road. I went to the back door, Miri holding it open.

"I hate it when she does that," she said.

I shook my head. "Me too."

Ash always had been... more liberal with the use of her powers.

There's a cost for everything and everything has its cost... I thought to myself.

"How was your mom?" Miri asked.

"My mother," I grated, and she gave me a sympathetic look and ushered me in the back door and right to the door leading down into the basement.

I went down the stairs and turned into her workshop space.

She had the workbench cleared, the Eilish and Roth books as well as several history books open on its surface.

I brought over the Courtney book and heaved the heavy thing up onto the table. It was stuffed full of things and I was *really* hoping there would be some kind of an entry to it.

"Jayse okay?" I asked.

"He's fine," Miri assured me. "Reading through some non-magic historical tomes up in the library."

"I miss him, is that weird?" I asked.

"No," Miri said with a smile. "He's your rock at the moment, your security."

"I already feel my powers coming back," I said with a sigh. "Like an itch inside the back of my skull."

"It's happening faster now, interesting," Miri declared.

She went to the fireplace and ladled out some tea from the cauldron there. She handed me the cup.

"Might as well get started," I said, shrugging out of my jacket after taking a cautious sip and setting the cup aside.

"No time like the present," Miri agreed, taking my coat from me and going to a nail jutting out of the post at the bottom of the stairs. She hung it there and came back, slipping into her seat. I closed my eyes, muttered a small prayer and a spell for clarity and opened the Courtney family book to begin searching.

"Magic is definitely coming back online," I said sighing as I opened the family book directly to a page containing information about the histories of the family and Nulls in specific.

An hour or more after settling in, Ash came clattering down the basement steps with the Tremblay book, hoisting it up onto the workbench.

"Enjoy your swim?" Miri asked, casually bemused.

"It's not really *swimming*, per se. I walk into the water in Boston, close my eyes, take a few steps and walk out of it here in Loving. No swimming involved; my feet never leave the bottom. It's cold as fuck, though," Ash declared.

Miri and I laughed and Ash smiled, settling on the stool at the head of the workbench as Miri slid off her stool and went for the hearth.

"Anything yet?" Ash asked.

"A few scraps of information," I answered, checking my notes.

She took my legal pad from me and looked them over, nodding.

"Let's dive in," she said with a gusty sigh. "Thank you." She took the tea from Miri and sipped it.

"Ah, that's good."

We settled back in and a half hour later Ash perked up.

"Holy shit, I think I found it."

We both looked over as Ash's eyes skimmed the page, then she looked up smiling and went back skimming the page again. Miri and I slipped off our stools and went around to look.

"What?" I asked, whispering in astonishment.

"It makes sense when you think about it," Miri said with a sniff.

"Only the Christians can twist something this natural and pure of intention into something so fucked up," Ash said dryly.

"*Ash*," Miri admonished.

"What?" Ash demanded. "It's true. You know it's true."

Miri sighed. We knew it was pointless arguing the point with Ash, too many of the Tremblays had died in the Inquisition. Their family line had gone from riches to rags and had nearly been wiped out completely. Which, now that I thought about it, with the Tremblay book being the oldest among the four, it *did* stand to reason that it would have more in it about the Null's than any of the rest.

"So how you feel about it?" Ash asked, looking sympathetic for once in her life.

I pinched the bridge of my nose and winced.

I didn't know. All I did know was that this was, once again, all my fault…

"I prayed for him, I think," I confessed. "I mean, not him specifically, but I did pray to the Goddess for aid. Begged for it, actually…"

"And what happened?" Miri asked.

I threw up my hands. "I wound up miles from my family cabin in an obscure part of the woods and stepped in one of Jayse's wolf traps."

"She does have her flair for the dramatic sometimes," Ash said, a charmed little smile on her lips. "Wonder if it was her time of the month."

"Could you *be* any more irreverent?" Miri demanded. Even the most patient of the sisters had her limits, so it would seem. I smiled at both of them, grateful.

"I can't tell you how much I've missed this," I said and Ash and Miri each looked at me and slightly startled in turn.

"Me too," Ash declared.

"Me three," Miri said softly.

It went unspoken that we *all* wished Oaklyn were here, and shortly thereafter, that despite his stubbornness, we wished for Ivan, too.

We were still so incomplete, being at odds with him.

"What do you think?" Ash asked. "Should we give it a go?"

She meant contacting Ivan; we all knew that's what she meant through the ties that bound us.

Miri and I nodded in unison and we all stood up, and went to the hearth, kneeling in front of it. Miri stopped at the bank of apothecary drawers and jars behind her workbench for the requisite herbs for the fire.

We settled in a semi-circle around the hearth and Miri cast herb to flame. Ash spit, the saliva sizzling, and I waved a hand gently, stirring the smoke. We closed our eyes and reached out through our bonds into the fire, calling to Ivan's element.

"What do you want?" he growled in his imperious Russian accent. I opened my eyes and met his in the burning coals of the flames.

"Help us," I whispered. "Help *me*…"

"*Nyet*," he said and scowled.

"Ivan." Miri tried to reason and he turned his head in her direction, the flame roaring up the flue and the chimney beyond as he roared again, "*Nyet!*"

"You do not listen!" he added a moment later when we didn't speak.

"No, *you* listen, Sparky!" Ash, snapped. "Like it or not, you're part of this circle, and sucks to be you but majority fucking rules, here. You can go back to being a sulky bastard when this shit is done, but what's going down? It's bad juju, motherfucker. This guy has already killed seventy-two women and girls!"

"Not my problem," he growled. "Ask your—" What he said was in pure Russian and I couldn't catch it but it sounded a lot like zetch-ee-nee-noll. The meaning was pretty freaking apparent, though. He was demanding we ask Jayse for help with the magic required to locate and apprehend the Savage Torture Killer. Apt name, right?

"Ivan," Miri pleaded but the fire just burned higher and he said in clear English, "No," and the fire completely went out.

"Wow, he is *really* butthurt about Jayse," Ash said with a sigh.

I scrubbed my face with my hands.

Jayse… how to tell Jayse? How to tell him what we had found…

"I'm going to go up," I murmured. "I need to talk to him."

"Well clean up down here," Miri said softly.

"Fuck that, if boyo isn't going to hook his sisters up, we have more homework to do. I hate feeling like the only one putting in the work when it comes to the group project," Ash griped.

"I'm *sorry*," I said. "You're right." I let out a frustrated sigh. "Jayse can wait, I'll stay."

"No." Ash slapped a hand over her face. "Not what I meant. That was *not* a dig at you. It was meant for Ivan."

"Still, I *should* stay. I'm the one asking for your help in all of this."

"No, you got us here," Ash said. "Let us do some of the heavy lifting for a minute. Go talk to your fated man," she said with a chuckle and I sighed.

"Ash," Miri said sadly as my feelings rippled out over the three of us.

"Oh." Ash leaned back from them. "Sorry, I'm just going to shut up now." Her light embarrassment washed back down the line.

"It's okay," I whispered. "We'll either figure this out or we won't."

Miri threw more wood on the coals, the candle and indirect lamplight soft around us.

"Go," Miri urged and I got up.

I went… and I didn't know anything of what I was going to say to Jayse.

I found him in the house's library, the windows dark outside which sort of surprised me. I mean, I hadn't thought we had been at it that long, but apparently it was a lot longer than I had thought.

"Hey." He sat up sharply when I appeared in the archway, Shep's shaggy head rising up off his paws. Miri's Raven familiar cawed in his cage in the corner.

"Hey," I murmured back, hugging myself.

"What's the matter?" he asked and got up, coming to me. Blessedly, my magic blunted with every step in my direction he took. Although, when he reached me, when he touched me, this time, I could still feel it. Like a blush of breeze across my back, whispering that it was still there.

"We found something, about witches and Nulls," I said softly, and I sniffed.

"Oh, hey," he said. "What is it?" He got up and came to me and gripped my upper arms, massaging them through my sweater. Shep whined and got up, coming over to me.

"Um, do you know when Kavion is supposed to be home?" I asked.

"No," he said gently. "You want to take this to the bedroom?"

I both really did for privacy but did *not* by the same token. I finally nodded and he took my hand and led me gently out of the library to the bottom of the stairs.

Once in the Gray Room, he shut the door behind us, Shep standing around looking a little lost before Jayse told him to go lay down.

"So, what's up?" he asked softly.

I shrugged and told him the news. "We're sort of soulmates," I said and looked at him. His grin was *not* what I was expecting.

"I'm sorry, what?" he asked.

I sat down on the bed and he came over, sitting down with me and looking to me to explain.

I told him what was in the Tremblay book. About how, historically speaking from a witch's point of view, the purpose of Nulls was to restore balance. How nature abhorred a vacuum indeed, and how sometimes, a witch was born under circumstances that made her so powerful, *too* powerful, and when that happened, a Null was simply just there to negate that power. To balance the witch out.

Traditionally, these relationships took many forms, from best friends, to lovers. Some became marriages, some same-sex couples, that part didn't matter… what mattered was a witch and a Null were meant to be inseparable from that point on.

Fate intervened… nature found a way…

"I am really failing to see the downside to this, Blyn," Jayse said gently, tipping my chin up with a light touch. I met his eyes and sniffed, eyes welling.

"You mean that?" I asked, my voice warbling.

"Oh, baby girl… yeah. I mean that with every fiber of my being. You *have* to stop beating yourself up." He pulled me into a tight hug and brought his mouth to mine, kissing me.

My blood immediately ignited under his touch, the air stirring in the room a touch as my power whispered through it, ruffling his hair lightly as desperately, I clung to him. I wound my fingers in his so soft light brown hair and pressed my mouth to his, as his arms went around me and crushed me to him.

"What is that?" he gasped softly and I asked him, "You can feel it?"

"Yeah."

I nodded and begged him, "Kiss me again," and he did, his hand sliding beneath my sweater, caressing my ribs. I moaned into his mouth, needing more of that, more of *him*. As the whispers started, a feminine and masculine sound sweeping through the room as though in conversation, the words indistinct and far away, no matter how I tried to follow what they were saying, it was always indiscernible.

Jayse didn't seem to notice that part, but I was aware. Aware that wild magic rode the air and that whatever this was between me and Jayse, it was a real and tangible thing and that if we did this, if we made love right now, it would be more than just bumping uglies. This moment held a weight and promise, a consequence to it, but whatever that consequence may be? I felt no fear. In fact, I was *eager* for it.

"Get these off," I begged, tugging at his belt loops of his jeans.

"Naked," he ordered. "Get naked."

We tore our clothes off as quickly as possible, our mouths locked, sometimes paying attention only to our own garments, at other points working on each other's but all with a fervency born of a need to be close to one another.

The whispering intensified, sometimes accompanied by sweet laughter, and I asked Jayse through a kiss as we pressed our nude upper bodies together, "Do you hear that?"

"Yeah, don't care," he said gruffly, and swept my leggings and panties down my body, shoving me back with a spirited laugh from me.

Joy surged through me and my sorrows and doubts fell from me in tattered ruins.

I am here my daughter, you do wonderful by me... this, my gift to you, you have earned well.

The Goddesses voice echoed throughout my heart and mind and I gave myself over to the wild magic of her will completely.

Jayse shoved his pants off and climbed over the top of me, and I reached for him, pulling him to my breast, his mouth to mine, as the light currents of air swept over our skins, cooling the sudden fever that had overtaken us.

"Love me," I begged.

"You and no other," Jayse swore. "So long as you love me back."

"Maiden, Mother, and Crone!" I gasped. "I love you, *so much*. For everything that you are, for being here with me... *oh, God, too!*"

He slid inside of me, and it was thus that he truly did complete me.

I gasped and writhed to get closer to him as he drew back and surged forward again, his girth playing against the walls of my pussy which I tightened around him.

"Oh, *fuck*, Blyn!" he cried.

"Oh, Jayse, harder!" I clung to him and he complied with my wish, driving into me that much harder, touching off waves of pure, shining pleasure within me, the flame of our lovemaking causing me to rise, slowly, steadily, into an almost out-of-body experience.

I rode the thermal high, high, and higher still as he kissed the side of my neck, holding me close with one hand on my ass, the other on my breast, squeezing, the sensation of his rough palm against my nipple pleasing beyond words.

"Oh, God, oh, Blyn..." he panted, and I was with him, riding high, wings outstretched.

"Just a little more," I begged, and he nodded, and kept his pace even and fierce. I climbed high and higher still until I couldn't quite *breathe* and then I held him to me tight, so tightly, jamming my tongue past his lips, stroking it along his as we both *plunged*, the sensations whipping past and through us both, into the pure ecstasy that awaited us in the abyss of orgasm below...

22

*J*ayse...

There was this loud, bass sound when we both came. Like a sonic boom, only quieter, and the whole house shook. Just once, fast, back and forth, the glass rattling in the window-panes, things shifting slightly on the surface of the dresser. I was vaguely aware of Ash and Miri crying out and laughing somewhere down below as I lost myself completely in Blyn and in whatever had been building between us since the moment we'd met each other.

It was like the lid popped off, and our essences, the very fiber of who we were *mingled*, weaving into each other and locking tight and it felt so *right*.

I don't think I had ever come so hard or so much in my life. She and I were sticky with it, practically glued to each other from the waist down, but by some miracle, had missed the coverlet completely. I stood up swiftly, dragging her up and off the bed completely with a yip of surprise, her arms and legs going around me as I kissed her deeply. Standing there, holding us both up.

"What was that?" I asked.

"Wild magic," she whispered against my lips, giving them a gentle peck.

"What does that mean?"

"I… I don't know yet," she said and I believed her.

"Should I be scared?" I asked with a smile, but I didn't feel scared. Not one bit, not at all, if anything… I felt more centered, more down to earth and *normal* than I ever had at any point in my life before.

"No," she said and sighed in satisfaction. "No, I don't think we should be scared."

She slid down my body and put her feet to the plush carpet and I sort of helped her toward the bathroom.

"I do think we should clean up, though." I chuckled.

"It's like you read my mind."

She froze slightly and looked at her hand where it touched my skin. We looked at each other and I cocked my head. "You didn't, did you?" I asked and she shook her head.

"I don't think so," she said.

She let me go and I felt the loss of her hands on my skin keenly, but I wasn't going to say anything about it.

"Do things feel…" she trailed off.

"Different?" I asked.

"Yeah," she murmured.

I nodded. "Yeah. But I can't tell you what it is."

She shook her head. "Me either."

"Wanna touch me again?" I asked and she smiled and reached out. I twined my fingers with hers and her smile grew.

"All quiet on the Western front?" I asked and she nodded.

"North, South, and East, too, I think."

"I don't get it," I said. "What changed?"

"Are you worried about it?" she asked and I was, but at the same time, it was… muted somehow. Not exactly a priority, even though it felt like it *should* be.

"Yes and no." I reached into the tub and turned on the water.

"Take a bath with me?" she asked and I nodded.

"That was my intention."

Weird, maybe we were inside each other's heads?

"Wait…" she went to the little end table in the corner, between the pedestal sink and the clawfoot tub. There were candles perched on a silver mirror tray on its tops and she bent at the waist, gripping the edges of the table and puckering her lips blew gently as though she were blowing out the tallest candle.

Except that's not what happened. What happened, was a spark appeared at the tip of the wick, then a light curl of smoke, before a lick of firelight leaped up to perch on the candle's top.

"Whoa," I uttered and Blyn smiled wholesomely and repeated the trick on the rest of the pillar candles.

She opened the drawer, fished out what looked like a bath bomb, and dropped it into the bath.

"Turn out the light and you go first," she said. "You're bigger."

"Yes, ma'am," I said, and I switched out the bathroom light and got into the tub first, the candlelight lending a nice ambience, the fragrance rising from the water an herbal, earthy delight.

Blyn got in, in front of me and leaned back against my chest. My arms automatically went around her, and she laced her fingers between mine, my hands laying over the backs of hers, swallowing them completely.

She cuddled back into me and I asked, "So, what happened?"

"I think," she murmured, "balance has been restored."

"Wait, like, so… I'm not a Null anymore?" I asked.

"I don't know that I would go that far," she said.

"Okay." I shook my head slightly. "This is all so confusing."

"It is," she agreed. "I don't know exactly what this means, but I know that I no longer fear my power. It's at a level that I can control… despite being with you like this. Like, you can be close to me now, and it still works. I don't know if that will be true of my sisters or any other witch who approaches you, though. We just don't know enough about any of this."

"I see," I said. "So a lot of this is like, trial and error…"

"Yeah," she said and didn't sound terribly happy about it.

"But this," I said, lifting her hands and waving them with mine like a bit of a puppeteer. "This is good news, right? The fact you can magic things near me without it being all scary overpowering."

She nodded slowly. "It's a relief… yes."

I hugged her tight, the water sloshing a bit as we shifted and she waved her hand, the faucet turning itself off. The sudden quiet was nearly deafening.

"I'm sorry," she said. "I'm not usually so petty in my uses of my power, but I am really feeling the need to take the temperature of the room, so-to-speak."

"Test the waters?" I asked. She smiled, leaning her head all the way back to look at me with her lovely dark eyes.

"That's Ash," she said and I chuckled.

"Ah." I nodded.

"Are you okay?" she asked and I nodded.

"Yeah," I said, a little disbelieving myself. "I mean, I feel different, but it's *good*, you know?"

"Good how?" she asked and I smiled.

"Like, *connected* in a way I haven't ever been before," I said, and I kissed the rounded cap of her shoulder.

She smiled, turning her head and cuddling back into me as the hot water played against our skins.

"That's good," she said and sighed out, a pleased, tranquil sound I'd never heard from her before. Before, her sighs held the weight of sadness and worry, of deep anxiety and dread. This one was, well, lighter than air.

"Best part," I said and she perked up. "I still love you, and like crazy, too." I nipped the side of her neck gently and made growling snuffling noises into the crook of her shoulder. She giggled and jerked in my arms as I tickled her and the sound of her laughter was everything right in my world.

23

*B*lyn...

I woke safe and warm in the circle of Jayse's arms the next morning. He rubbed his hands over my nude back, kneading along the spine, smiling down at me to gently wake me... and wake I did, a smile of my own gracing my lips.

"Good morning," I murmured.

"Good morning," he murmured back, his smile growing.

"What is it?" I asked, and he put a finger to his lips and cocked his head slightly. I listened, ears straining curiously, and heard Miri and Ash outside laughing and shrieking.

"Snowball fight?" I asked excitedly, and Jayse laughed and nodded.

"I think so."

"You do understand we *have* to get in on this," I said, and he nodded.

"Race you getting dressed."

We did just that, and he beat me by a narrow margin. To be fair, he had a lot fewer clothes than I did! I mean, I had a bra. That already put me at a wild disadvantage.

We thundered down the stairs, Shep bounding and leaping around us excitedly and pulling on our coats, hats, and gloves, which we found hanging from the hooks just inside the front door, we went out, Shep racing ahead of us and bounding through the snow.

"Ambush!" Jayse cried and picked up handfuls of snow and launched them at my shrieking sisters.

I haven't felt so light, or played so hard, since Oaklyn had died and it honestly felt *good*.

"Wait, wait, wait!" Ash cried, laughing, and we all stopped. "Miri, do you feel that?"

Miri stopped and cocked her head. "Yeah. Blyn, how do *you* feel?"

"Fine!" I declared, and we all stood in the yard and looked at each other.

Jayse looked from one to the next to the next of us and asked, "What?"

"Our magic's back," Ash said.

"I mean, we don't feel any different around you," Miri declared.

"I mean, cool… I guess?" Jayse shrugged and smiled, panting and out of breath and Shep ambushed him from behind, going up on his hind legs and pushing Jayse forward and onto his knees into the snow. We all burst out laughing.

"Like, does that mean he's not a Null anymore?" Ash asked and Miri shrugged.

"Or is it just because we're in the same circle?" I asked.

"That could be, too," Miri said.

"Think we ought to figure it out," Ash said with a shrug as Jayse listened but played with Shep, running him around the yard, stopping suddenly to psych his little doggie brain out and pick another random direction.

"We need to figure it out *fast*," I said with a gusty sigh. "Killer's still out there."

"Yeah, we were thinking about that, too, this morning," Ash declared.

Miri looked troubled and I felt it, too. The underlying urgency was creeping back in. Our playtime was short lived, the reprieve over.

"Back to the books," Ash declared.

Jayse nodded and got Shep to calm down, some.

"Let's get you two breakfast, first," Miri declared.

"I'd love that, actually," I said and we went back into the house to do just that.

Miri dished us all up some oatmeal from the electric pressure cooker on her counter and poured coffee from her coffeemaker nearby. We doctored the oatmeal with honey, brown sugar, some nuts and a little cinnamon before we all took seats at the breakfast nook.

Kavion came in the back door midway through the meal and joined us looking tired.

"Are you just getting in?" I asked.

"Yeah, twenty-four-hour shift," he said. "I do 'em sometimes so I can spend more time with my girl." He bent down and kissed Miri who swooned against his chest. I smiled and Jayse took my hand under the table, giving it a squeeze.

We all agreed we did *not* want to risk the family books, not knowing exactly what was going on with the wild magic of the night before and whether Jayse was still a Null or if something had happened to balance things so completely, he and I were just witch and a regular person… I mean, there wasn't anything *inhuman* about being a witch. We were all still humans, we were just a bit extra.

We hit the books, Kavion hit the rack, going up to his and Miri's room for some much-deserved sleep. However, as the day wore on, he joined Jayse in poring over the non-magic books. Jayse called his sister with the new information that we'd found and she'd told him that she was on her way to the library at Boston University, her alma mater. She said she would see if there was anything she could find in some of the history books of the decidedly Christian persuasion.

Stranger things have happened.

"You know what sucks?" Kavion asked at dinner.

"What?" Miri asked.

"All those Nulls and Witches that were like meant to be together. Could you imagine?" he asked. "Killing your *soulmate* without even knowing it?"

"Talk about instant Karma," Ash said. "Living your whole life without that other part of you because you were too bigoted?"

"That's one way to look at it," Miri said softly, threading her fingers through Kavion's.

"Yeah, but how tragic is that bullshit?" Kavion asked.

"I don't want to think about it, to be honest," Jayse said, giving my knee a squeeze under the table.

"Luckily, we don't have to," I said softly, looking up at him. He smiled and gave a nod, and the warmth radiating from his hazel eyes as he looked at me melted me to my core.

We didn't get any further when it came to the conundrum *of how safe was it to have magic around Jayse?* Short of finding a random witch outside of our circle to volunteer as tribute to get near him and have his or her powers swept away for a time, we might never know. It wasn't something we wanted to do to anyone, as there were reports throughout history that some lower-level witches never managed to regain their powers having once come in contact with a Null, even for a short time.

Of course, those had come from the witch side of things *after* the Nulls had been widely used as a weapon by the Catholic church, so we didn't know the actual veracity of the claims.

My phone rang as we had gone back to looking over the books in the library after dinner and I answered it without looking.

"This is Blyn," I said.

"Ms. Courtney, this is Agent Stahl," she said and I sat up.

"Yes, Agent Stahl. What can I do for you?"

"I'm afraid it's what you can do for us..." she said. "A young woman's gone missing in the Savage Torture Killer's area... she's only seventeen."

"Oh..." I licked suddenly dry lips and took a deep breath. "Seventeen, you say?" Everyone around me stilled. "Are you sure that she's been taken by *him?*" I asked.

"Only one way to know, her knapsack was found. It's waiting here at Quantico for you. What is your location?"

"I'm in Loving at the Eilish House Bed-and-Breakfast, but Agent Stahl?"

"Yes?"

"If you're sending transportation to fetch us? You're going to have to pick up four."

"Four?" she asked.

"Yes, I need Mr. Mickelson and my circle sisters with me."

Everyone nodded grimly.

"I gotta stay here," Kavion said. "Shep's good to stay here with me," he said to Jayse and Jayse looked troubled for only a fraction of a second before he nodded.

"I appreciate that, bro," he said and Kavion smiled and nodded.

"We'll have agents there from the airfield within the hour and a helicopter or plane waiting," Agent Stahl declared.

"Very good," I said and ended the call. To the rest of the people in the room I sighed and said, "To Quantico we go."

WE WERE PICKED up in a black SUV by men in suits an hour and a half later. We packed the family books and consecrated and sealed the bag with magic. We did the same with a regular old book in a satchel and brought it near Jayse as a test. Our magic seals against harm held, and so we felt relief in bringing the actual family books around him.

I could tell Jayse felt bad about the extra measures we had to take, but that he also understood. *Something* had definitely happened the night before when he and I had been swept up by the wild magic of the Goddess, but we were still trying to piece together and figure out exactly what. There was just so much happening in such a short amount of time for all of us, there was no tracking *everything,* you know?

We rode from Eilish House to the small airfield outside of Loving. From there, we took the waiting helicopter to another, bigger airfield and boarded a small plane which then took us to *another* airfield where we were airlifted *again* by *another* helicopter to the grounds at Quantico.

It was a harrowing few hours on the plane, hitting a lot of turbulence and being the butt of several jokes from Ash complaining about my not smoothing the ride. There were certain things you, as a witch, did *not* mess with and nature occurring in its natural form at its most powerful, was one of them.

It was one thing for Miri to force growth on a little sapling, but it was another for her to try and stop an earthquake.

Likewise, it was one thing for me to call up a fierce but distracting wind, it was another for me to stop a storm or tornado or whatever in its tracks. It just wasn't something you did. We were small and paltry things as compared to the will of the God and Goddess. I wasn't that arrogant to presume to tell them what to do. Neither was Ash, but what Ash *was*, was irreverent enough to kid about it. Sometimes too far.

I hated flying and her jokes about the turbulence were not helping. Jayse's hand in mine, however, was helping marginally.

I was grateful to touch down at our final destination.

Agents McKinnon and Stahl were waiting off to the side of the helipad when we landed. It was dark, growing late, but there wasn't anything for it. There were things that needed discussed and a knapsack to touch and a seventeen-year-old girl's terror to live real-time knowing that it was just the beginning for her… knowing that far worse could be happening to her at this very moment.

I steeled myself, took the suitcase with the family books from Ash and stepped out under the whirring rotors of the helicopter, my power pushing out at the artificial wind from the blades, not a hair stirring on my head. I didn't want the lashing snow against the family books. Warded and protected as they were, I was paranoid. They were invaluable and to my knowledge, this was the first time they had ever been taken outside the town of Loving since their arrival so many long years ago with the town's Originals.

McKinnon and Stahl looked gobsmacked as Jayse took my hand, his duffel over his shoulder, and Miri followed us up with both her carryon-sized suitcase and mine. Ash followed Miri with her backpack and gym bag of retrieved clothing from her original home at Tremblay house.

"I would ask how you do that but we don't have time," McKinnon called. "Come on!"

We were ushered into an institutional-like hallway of plain white walls and flat, gray, business-like carpet.

"Where precisely is this douchebag operating out of?" Ash asked as we moved up the hallway, her bounty hunting instincts at the fore, her tracker ways adapting to the new parameters of hunting an 'unknown quantity.' Her words on the grueling flights down.

"The Midwest," I answered without thinking. "I saw cornstalks in my vision from the rope. An old barn… blades and tractor parts… he may be a farmer or attached to a farm."

"That's right," Stahl said soberly. "The kidnappings, rapes, and murders have all been occurring in Iowa."

"That's great," Ash muttered.

We were led into a conference room and McKinnon gestured at a corner for our bags. "You can put those there," she said. "For now. We have accommodations being set up for you in the dorms."

"Housing us along with the recruits?" Ash asked curiously. "That's gonna be a trip for them."

"It's still a trip for me," McKinnon admitted.

"Where is it?" I asked curiously, and I couldn't shake the nerves rattling my confidence that I could do this. My shoulders tightened, all along my spine locking up painfully.

"First, let's get out the books," Ash said. "See if we can't boost the signal and you and I work in concert.

"What is and what was, what is and what could be," I agreed.

It was our powers of sight… I could see what is and what was, while Ash could see what is and what could be. Simply put, I saw past and present while Ash could see the present and sometimes glimpse the future. Handy trait for a bounty hunter, yeah? It was why she had gotten into the business. Well, that and the adrenaline rush.

Ash had always been the wild child of the lot of us.

"Okay, I'm gonna need a bowl of water, the bigger the bowl the more surface, the better. Tap water will do just fine."

"Some smaller bowls with rice or salt to hold these candles will be of benefit, too," Miri said gently.

Stahl was noting it all down as we spoke while Jayse asked, "Should I find someplace else to be?"

"No," I said. "I think that as long as we are together, balance has been restored. I think I need you as a means to siphon off or nullify my excess power. I think that's why, for all intents and purposes, you aren't nullifying everything around you anymore. You're acting as a sort of…" I didn't want to say familiar out loud as that would sound *really* rude non-magic or not.

Miri came to the rescue. "Focus; I think the word you're looking for is 'Focus.'" She raised her copper eyebrows at me and I nodded, sending my gratitude through the magic that bound us. Miri was the only one of us with an actual familiar, so she knew exactly the thought I'd had regarding it all.

"Yes, precisely," I said. "Jayse, would you mind?" I turned to him and he came over and hoisted the heavy full-sized suitcase onto the boardroom table.

"Let's get rid of some of these chairs," Ash said to Agent Stahl. "Move 'em out into the hallway."

"Should I get some recruits in here to help with all this?" she asked.

"It's the middle of the night," Miri said. "Let them sleep. We are strong, capable women." She smiled and pulled a chair out from under the table and sent it rolling to Ash. Jayse, without being asked or prompted, pitched in.

I smiled and whispered the incantation that sent the wards and magical locks falling away from the suitcase containing the family books. Miri whispered her word of power and then Ash came by and did the same.

"I don't get it," McKinnon said as Stahl was speaking into her phone asking for the things Miri had requested. "Nothing's happening."

I smiled. "For the most part, magic is a subtle and unseen thing. It's not always flash and pomp."

"Huh." She took a chair from Ash and rolled it out into the hallway. Miri and I got into the suitcase and took out the family books.

"Might need to conjure some items," she said. I nodded.

"Your workshop has everything?"

"If it doesn't, my storefront does," she said. She'd taken over the *Wick & Stone*, the little metaphysical book and tea shop in the heart of Loving. It required enough attention that she switched to running it full time and closed down her B&B. Closing the B&B was also to give herself and Kavion some much-needed privacy as they established their new lives together.

I smiled at her, proud of her beyond measure. She'd been through it and rather than wilting, she'd *thrived* and continued to. I was grateful beyond measure that she was here.

We spent the next hour setting up for the first round of spells to conjure what we would need for the big round. I was afraid that McKinnon and Stahl would be disappointed as the three of us, without Ivan, would need a rest before we could do anything to help with their serial killer.

We conjured the right candles and the proper herbs for what we planned and with it passing the witching hour, which was actually three in the morning and not midnight like most mundane thought it was, we called it quits.

"What, that's it?" McKinnon asked. "You didn't even touch the girl's backpack."

It was true, the backpack still sat at one end of the conference table in its evidence bag.

"You're right, I didn't."

"Blyn…" Ash's tone held warning.

"What?" McKinnon demanded.

"She's pushing herself too hard for you," Miri said softly.

"It's okay," I said. "She's right." I looked to my healing sister and asked, "Do you have anything with which to give me a boost?" She looked at me with misgivings and finally nodded, holding out her hand. I held out mine and closed my eyes, opening myself up. There was a green flash of light on the inside of my eyelids and energy and vibrancy poured through my connection with her. It was like a triple shot of caffeine only better.

I perked up noticeably and Miri's hand fell away. I opened my eyes and Jayse slid in front of me, his hands falling to my shoulders and gripping them firmly.

"I'm worried about you," he said and his brow crumpled into a frown of that very same concern.

"I know," I murmured. "It's just this one, small thing," I said. "Then I'm done for tonight. I promise."

"Blyn…" His voice held pleading.

"She in some kind of danger if she does this now?" Stahl asked.

"No," I said.

"Yes," Miri, Ash, and Jayse chorused.

"Then we wait until tomorrow night," Stahl said and then directed her attention to McKinnon. "And I don't want to hear a thing about it!" she snapped at her partner.

"Fine," McKinnon grumbled but didn't look happy about it.

"And spare us the coming guilt trip," Ash told her, eyeing her without compassion.

McKinnon, to her credit, kept her mouth shut.

We warded the shit out of that conference room and left everything there, where it needed to be.

"This would be so much easier if we had Ivan," Miri said tiredly.

"Right?" Ash said as we were being led to quarters where we would be allowed to sleep, dragging our luggage with our clothes and things behind us. "We could seriously have him just ask the victims, get all kinds of information from beyond the veil. Stubborn asshole."

"Wait, you can seriously do that?" McKinnon asked.

"Ivan can, he's a fire witch," Miri said.

"I'm so sick of his shit," Ash declared.

"He has good reasons," I told her for the millionth time. "His government royally fucked him over. He's afraid it will happen again here."

"He's not American?" Stahl asked.

"Russian," Ash grunted.

"You *guys*…" Miri admonished and Ash and I traded somewhat guilty looks.

"I'm sorry, we shouldn't have said anything. You're right," I told my earth witch sister.

"He's here illegally," McKinnon guessed.

Miri scowled at the both of us.

"Look," I said tiredly. "If you have any compunction whatsoever to try and leverage that either with us or against him, we not only walk but you will never see, hear from, or *find* any of us ever again. You won't even remember we existed…"

"Are you threatening me?" McKinnon asked, outraged.

"Only if you threaten us first," Ash said and she meant it.

I felt a shift within myself and realized that Ivan was watching, listening… that he just couldn't help himself. I tentatively reached down the thin-stretched line, over the many miles between us, and tentatively touched, asked without words, one more time for him to help us… it felt as though iron doors were slammed on that line, severing it for the time being.

"I think his resolve is weakening," Miri said. "He really is a good man, you guys. It just… it just takes more time to convince him and sometimes he doesn't need convincing at all. It's all very strange."

"Let's sleep on it," Ash suggested. "Let the big dude marinate on it."

"All the same," Miri said. "You might want to build a big bonfire somewhere on the property, have it ready to light. I believe in Ivan and I think we're going to need it."

Strange thing was, even though I had no reason to, I believed in Ivan, too.

"Come on, dorms are this way," McKinnon grated and pushed open a door to the outside. We walked through the silent snow-covered dark to another building and were escorted to a suite of rooms with a central living room and shared bathroom.

"Thank you," I murmured as they left and Miri shut the door and then Jayse was there, taking me into his arms and holding me tight. All the stress, tension, and even some of the mountain of exhaustion falling away as I leaned into him heavily.

"Let's get some sleep, huh?" he murmured and I nodded.

"Sounds wonderful," I conceded.

*J*ayse...

She was so sleepy by the time I got us both out of our clothes and into the narrow bed, we didn't bother with pajamas; we didn't even think to take separate rooms. All we wanted was to sleep and to do it holding each other close.

Her world was amazing to me, mind-blowing in ways and in other ways heartbreaking. She took so much on herself and selflessly at that... and it seemed like it was only me, her sisters, and maybe Dax that really saw it. What she put herself through in order to serve a population that had no care or thought toward the cost or the toll it took on her.

We lay beneath the thin blanket and sheet, her back to my front, and slept solidly without moving an inch for however long.

I woke, sometime in the afternoon if I had to guess, with Blyn moaning softly in my arms, her rear grinding back against my cock which was happy as fuck for the attention. I moaned softly and pressed my lips to the curve of her neck where it met her shoulder.

She gasped as I kneaded one of her breasts with my hand, nipping at the sweet spot in the side of her neck.

"Jayse…" she whispered and I smiled, my name on her lips sounding like a plea.

It felt naughty, angling her, slipping inside her, but it also felt oh, so, good.

I pressed into her warm, wet, grasping tight pussy and it damn sure felt like coming home. No magic, no mysticism about it. She guided my hand down, pressing my fingers to the front of her body and I cupped her pussy, pressing my fingers into her clit as she writhed to get more motion out of me.

We had to be careful. The bed we were on was *super* narrow, meant for one person, and I wasn't about to fall into a heap on an FBI dorm room floor. What I *was* about to do was get my woman off in spectacular fashion.

I drove into her at a steady and sedate pace, my balls tightening, that tingling sensation that threatened I was going to come any minute ever-present in my body. I was going to be pissed if I lost this battle and came before my Blyn, so I focused extra hard on getting her there.

It wasn't lost on me that we'd been together so few times and yet I already knew the exact combination to her lock. I slowed my thrusting pace, concentrating on slicking her wetness over her clit, making small circles over that sweet bundle of nerves while maintaining an even pressure. She gasped, and I had my hand at the ready to quiet her if need be, laying my opposite hand against her throat, not squeezing, just drawing her back and down onto my cock, holding her body to mine, the thrill of control and the delicious dirtiness of that hand on her throat thrilling us *both*, I think.

She gasped, her breath coming quick in these short pants that thrilled me all the more. I rotated my hips *just so* for a better angle and with a sharp cry, her nails bit into my hip, her other hand going to cover her mouth as she shuddered against me.

Her pussy throbbed around my cock, putting it in a stranglehold that tipped me over my own edge and we gasped, choking on our cries in unison as we shivered with delight against each other's bodies.

"Oh, *Jayse*," she hissed and I smiled against the back of her shoulder, pressing a reverent kiss against her skin.

"This hand was okay?" I asked, softly stroking her long and perfect neck with my thumb.

"Oh, Gods, yes," she said with a slight laugh. "You could have gripped a little harder even."

"I'll remember that," I said. "It's not my usual thing, but you… you do things to me," I confessed. I jolted as she wriggled against me, my limp dick, still oversensitive, slipping out of her body and sending wild sensations through me. She turned over so she could face me, looking up at me with those wide, beautiful brown eyes of hers.

"You do things to me too," she whispered and pressed her lips to mine. We kissed. Long, slow, and darkly sweet, like a rich deep chocolate slow to melt on the tongue.

"Is it bad I just want all this part to be over?" I asked roughly. "That I just want to spirit you away, spend like a week or two making love to you, and work on getting on with the rest of our lives?"

She looked up at me and touched my bottom lip with her fingertips gently, sighing out like I had just said the sweetest things to her rather than the selfish shit that had actually just spilled from my trash mouth.

"It's not *bad*," she murmured. "It's *human*, and I don't think for a minute that those wants and desires come from a dark place, Jayse. That's not you. I one hundred percent believe those wishes come from a place of love and concern for me and for my sisters… and I share them. I want this to be done, too. I want justice for those women and girls, and I want to send this monster straight back to whatever dark plane of existence he was spawned from."

"So, what's the plan?" I asked. "How can I help?"

She sighed and smiled, closing her eyes and cuddling in close.

"Just keep doing what you're doing, please… and know that I love you so very much for it."

I gathered her up tight in my arms and kissed the top of her head, the slight jealousy and frustration I felt over her situation and focus being locked up tight elsewhere fading into oblivion.

I felt her love; I loved her fiercely in return, and there would be time. There had to be. This was just one small facet of our lives. A chapter in a book and I was hoping not a very long one at that.

I wanted to show this woman peace. I wanted to hold her tight every night. I wanted to kiss her tears away and bring her joy. I had never felt so fiercely over anyone else, ever… except maybe my sister, but that was by no means the same as this. A pale imitation, in fact.

"So, what's next?" I asked softly, changing the subject.

"Um, a shower and some food. Take care of some basic needs, then time to reevaluate the game plan with Miri and Ash.

"Okay."

We heard voices out in the main area of the suite and Blyn drew in a long, fortifying breath.

"Let's do this," she murmured and I steadied her as she climbed awkwardly out of the bed we were in. She went out into the main area as naked as the day she was born, leaving me laughing slightly to myself, the sheet pooled in my lap as she shut the door softly behind her to preserve my modesty.

THE CAFETERIA at Quantico was like every other corporate, hospital, or college cafeteria you ever laid eyes on. It had about the same variety on offer, too; just maybe a little healthier and a little more upscale – with things like quinoa salad on the menu, which I took a hard pass on that one, alongside your typical fare of cold-cut sandwiches and cheap imitation fast-food burgers.

None of it looked particularly appetizing, but I had to eat. Miri was just ahead of me, and she practically squealed in delight over the quinoa. I turned to Blyn who raised her eyebrows amused at her earth witch sister who paused at every houseplant in every corner and hallway to check on its wellbeing.

It was funny at first, then curious when a couple of the plants had actually reached out for Miri as she went to leave them.

The recruits all looked on at us curiously. I think it was the lack of uniform; gray polos over khaki five-eleven brand tactical pants. It felt odd that everyone around us was open carry, their standard issue Glocks hanging on their waistbands.

We took up a four-top table over by the windows. The snow was falling again, the vegetation outside already buried under a pretty damn thick layer of white. Finally, one of the recruits at a neighboring table turned in his seat in our direction.

He was a black kid with an easy smile, his hair neatly clipped close against his scalp with crisp lines around his face and mimicking a part down one side.

"Hey, yo," he called out. "You guys the witches everybody seems to be talking about?"

Ash lowered her spoon across from me and glanced over. Miri who sat beside her muttered, "Ash…" in a warning tone.

I spoke up before Ash could smart off and make any new enemies. She seemed to have a knack for pissing people off and rubbing them the wrong way.

"I'm not a witch," I said simply.

"Oh, you're not?" The guy gestured past me. "But they are."

"Astute observation," Blyn said, wiping her mouth with her napkin. She leaned back in her seat and fixed the table of agents-in-training with her appraising dark eyes.

"I suppose you would like us to do some parlor tricks for you, now?" she asked.

The kid, smug, looked back at the rest of the recruits at his table that all kind of exchanged glances and shrugs, a few of them giving him a chin thrust, to egg him on.

"Nah, I would like to see some real magic," he said.

"Sorry to disappoint you," Ash said, dipping her spoon back in her soup. "We aren't trained monkeys to perform on command."

Miri looked at the kid who seemed to be the table's mouthpiece and frowned saying, "You know, I have a tea to help lower the risks of having an attack," she said. "I know you only have a mild case as compared to others, but still."

One of the guys at the table laughed and asked, "You implying he's got herpes or something?"

The black kid was starting to look pissed.

"No, I'm sorry, I didn't even think about that… I was talking about your sickle cell anemia."

The table went quiet and the black kid's face went blank with shock; I think.

"How'd you…"

He sat back in his chair and the guy next to him said, "Dude, how the hell would she know about that?"

"Ah, so not a secret, then." Miri smiled. "Of course, I'm a witch, not a doctor, so I'm not *technically* bound by HIPAA."

"You serious right now?" the guy asked. "You got a *tea* for that?" He shook his head. "I don't know nothin' on how something like that could even exist."

"Excuse me," Miri murmured and Ash laughed as she got up out of her seat.

"Doctor Miri is in the house," Ash muttered as Miri took her tray over and the recruits made room for her to sit and talk with the kid who'd spoken up first.

Blyn smiled and shook her head. "She always was a miracle worker at catching more flies with honey."

"Sometimes, I think she's *too* nice," Ash complained.

"Not possible with her," Blyn responded.

"Oh, yeah?" Ash asked slyly. "What about Ivan?"

Blyn rolled her eyes. "Not going to get any backup from me on that one, sister," she told Ash. "I'm on her side. I've got insider information, though. Ivan's *really* a good man under it all. He's just had to do some really terrible things and his conscience can't abide them. I understand his reasoning… he'll never admit it, but he's scared."

Ash looked pensive for a moment then hummed in thoughtfulness before turning back into herself and her soup.

"What's after this?" I asked.

"Homework," Blyn said with a long-suffering sigh. "Always with the homework…"

She wasn't lying. They pored over the family books and tried their best to strategize for just about every eventuality for what Blyn might uncover once she touched the knapsack. We were waiting on McKinnon and Stahl to join us before she got into that. I guess they'd been called on the carpet with the brass over all of this. I mean, they were going all out.

Finally, just as dark was starting to overtake dusk, they arrived. It wasn't *that* late, still being on the tail end of winter, but you know.

Miri and Ash were lighting candles. Someone had found an earthenware wide, shallow bowl and had filled it with water at Ash's request. Miri sprinkled it with herbs and Ash had dropped a few drops of oil from a tiny vial from inside her jacket pocket.

"What is all this?" McKinnon asked. "Last time she just touched the object and freaked out."

"This," Ash explained, leaning over the table to set a candle in a salt base, "is so you can see too."

"What?" Stahl asked. "Is that really possible?"

"Yes," Miri responded.

"Well, let me get a camera crew—"

"Pointless," Ash quipped as I leaned up against a wall and crossed my arms, well out of their way.

"Why?" McKinnon demanded.

"Cameras will pick up an object moving, or something physical happening," Miri explained.

"But it won't pick up the magic, it will just see a sitting bowl of water," Blyn said.

"Such is the nature of things," Miri said.

"The will of the Goddess," Ash affirmed.

"Okay. What can we expect?" McKinnon demanded.

"Watch and find out," Ash declared and held her hand over the Tremblay book, the pages flipping of their own accord and landing on the one she apparently needed.

"Let us begin," Miri said and I steeled myself, eyes riveted to Blyn, for whatever was about to happen.

*B*lyn...

Ivan was watching. I could sense it. I chanted along with Ash and Miri, each of us with our own part to the spell, the words intertwining a crown of woven vines circling above us. The knapsack was out, resting on top of the evidence bag, my hands hovering above it.

I glanced from one sister to another. We all had our parts. Mine was to see, Miri's was to protect our hearts and minds from the evil we were about to witness and Ash's was to channel what was into the scrying pool, revealing all for all to see.

At the nods from my sisters, I lowered my hands and made contact with the well-worn canvas of the teen's backpack.

"Addison! Addison Jane, you get back here!"

I turned and looked up the porch steps at my father and gave him double shots of my middle finger.

Fuck him! How dare he tell me what to do with my own body! I wasn't taking the birth control for birth control, it really was all about my cramps. Anyway, I needed to get to school. I walked for the street outside our farm and the school bus pulling up at the end of our driveway.

"Too far back," Ashlyn intoned and I nodded carefully. My power flowed over the bag beneath my hands. I went through the day, images flitting amorphously past my gaze. *The packed halls between classes, science class, history – Mr. Phelps droning on and on about the storming of the Bastille.*

Football practice, going over to my friend Jayne's after school to get ready for the game. It was the final game of the season... we lost. We lost badly. Arguing with my boyfriend, Eric. He left. He left me in the school parking lot, everyone else had gone. My dad had taken my phone... I was forced to walk.

Walking home. It's cold, so cold, stopping at the quick mart at the edge of town for some hot coffee to warm up. I barely had enough change. Stepping outside.

"Need a ride?"

Startling, coffee sloshing over my gloved hand, soaking it. Dammit! I looked to the speaker; his hands stuffed into his Carhartt jacket. Jeans and cowboy boots. Typical attire for just about every farmhand out here, his upper body and face cast in deep shadow.

"No, I'm good... thanks."

Creepy. I didn't like him. Super creepy vibes. I start walking, the bag slung over my shoulder. A truck goes by me. A pickup, old like from the sixties, yellow, bed rusted. Iowa plates...

"Get the plate number!" Agent McKinnon yelled.

"Shh!" Agent Stahl said.

"I *know!*" Agent McKinnon said again.

"Hush, now," Miri ordered them both.

I keep walking, the taillights fade over the slight rise in the road, fade into the distance. I keep walking. I have at least a mile, mile and a half to go. Cold, so cold... one foot in front of the other. I start counting the steps. One, two, three, four, five, six, seven, eight. One, two, three, four, five, six, seven, eight.

Eight is my number. My magic number according to Jayne's numerology charts or whatever. So I count to eight, over and over... One, two, three, four, five, six, seven, eight. One, two, three, four, five, six, seven, eight. One, two, three, four, five, six, seven, eight.

Headlights, coming at me, blinding, he switches on his brights – what an asshole! I put up my hand to shade my eyes and the truck screeches to a stop in front of me. I take a breath to yell but the door flies open and he gets out. Something in his hand, I can't see, I scream.

"You don't tell me, 'no' you little bitch!"

My bag slips, falls into the ditch. I try to throw myself along with it but he grabs my arm and raises whatever is in his other hand. The blow to my head hurts but knocks me out.

I'm vaguely aware of Ivan's roar of anger, his rage pulsing down the line that connects us as I sever my link to the bag beneath my hands.

Addison Jane's name haunting me, how frightened, how scared…

Summon me…

"Well, looks like Ivan's finally on board," Ash said dryly as I take a deep breath.

"You got that too?" I asked softly.

"Yeah, me too," Miri declared.

"So, what now?" Stahl asked as Jayse's hands fall to my shoulders, massaging, kneading out the tension.

"Now, we're going to need that bonfire," I said and Ash and Miri, capturing my gaze, nodded in unison.

OUTSIDE IT WAS COLD. The bonfire had been built to specification along what the FBI agents and recruits called the 'physical conditioning route.' Several agents and recruits alike had gathered at windows in the dorms overlooking the wilderness running path, watching through the trees as my sisters and I gathered around the pyre with our books and candles, herbs and anointing oils, ready to undertake our second Greater working of the night.

It was actually nice out here. Woods, a small clearing and field sloping gently from the buildings in the direction of a deep pond that was frozen over with ice.

The moon hung high in the sky, full, which only helped us in our endeavor. The Mother watching over us as we stood ready.

"Jayse?" I called and he came over with a torch and lit the pyre for us before backing off to where Agents McKinnon and Stahl stood with some of their bosses and some of the braver trainees.

"Miri?" I asked when the fire had climbed sufficiently and Miri nodded and started, her arms upraised.

"Over cracked earth and rocky shale, Fire! Walk with me!"

Ash went next, "Through murky waters and over rivers, Fire! Walk with me!"

"Through dense air, cold and winter, Fire! Walk with me!" I intoned.

All of us in unison called to our brother using the same chant, "Fire! Walk with me!"

Over and over until the magic and our intentions were set, "Fire! Walk with me!"

The floodgates of our connection to our fourth opened wide, we called to him, "Fire! Walk with me!"

"Fire! Walk with me!"

"Fire! Walk with me!"

"Fire! Walk with me!"

I whispered, "By the power of three times three, Fire, walk with me…"

The air began to stir, the fire climbing high and higher into the night and we chanted, "Fire! Walk with me!"

The flames began to twist, to distort, and we chanted, "Fire! Walk with me!"

Our very beings hummed and thrummed with the magic we called and through gritted teeth we called, "Fire! Walk with me!"

I was vaguely aware of Ivan on the distant shores of Loving, far to the north and east of us, a fire built before him, reflecting in his dark eyes. I reached out metaphysically over time and space, through love and grief and called to him, "Fire! Walk with me!"

He reached out the same time I reached into the flames here and took my hand. I grabbed onto him, a very physical touch, gritting my teeth as the fire licked at my fingers and *pulled* with every ounce of my strength both physical and unseen and Ivan stepped from the flames, walked from his reality there, into my reality here, looking down his nose imperiously at me while people gasped and shouted off to the side.

I looked up at him in his black duster coat and said, the plea in my voice clear, "Fire, walk *with me...*"

He grunted and let go of my hand, eyes unreadable as the fire died and the cold rushed in.

"Where is this man?" Ivan demanded a moment later.

"We don't know," Miri said. "In the Midwest, maybe? Somewhere?"

"We were hoping you could help us with that, big guy," Ash said, standing up from over near the water's edge, connecting with her element. "Only you have the hookup with the other side," she said with a shrug.

He grunted and frowned.

"Please," I begged. "Don't let this girl, Addison Jane, die."

Jayse stepped up behind me carefully and put his hands on my shoulders, lending me some emotional strength. Only I had seen what this evil prick had done, and what he would do to Addison if we didn't get to her first.

Only I knew firsthand the evil in this particular man's heart... had lived it through his eyes as he had done unspeakable things.

"You have object?" Ivan demanded.

"Evidence, you mean?" Stahl asked.

"Body would be better," he said and Stahl blanched.

"We have things belonging to some of the dead girls," McKinnon said and muttered something about Ivan being a creepy fuck under her breath. Ivan didn't so much as flinch... at least not with his body. His eyes which were fixed on mine told a different story, however. Miri reached out and took Ivan's hand and I reached out and took the other.

"Oh, we doing this?" Ash asked and took mine and Miri's free hands.

We were at once swallowed with the bond between us.

They don't understand, I whispered through our connection.

Let them be ignorant, Miri added.

They're right. It's not your job to correct or teach them. It's just our job to save the girl and stop this sick fuck.

I'm here, his voice echoed through my mind in Russian, but for all that I didn't speak the language, here we understood each other. Here, language nor accent was a barrier to understanding.

What do you need? I asked him.

THE THINGS that we asked for were brought. The pyre was refueled and rebuilt atop the embers, lit with a wave of Ivan's hand.

The balance had tipped in regard to this man, and evil walked the earth in his skin. We were sure of it at this point, and it was another balance in need of correction.

Ivan ignored Jayse now that he no longer deemed him a threat, and I hoped that someday it would go beyond indifference and that someday maybe even a friendship could be born. It was probably wishful thinking, but whatever the case, I had faith in Ivan even though he didn't seem to have much faith in himself.

I held open the evidence bag for him and he dipped his thick-fingered, big hand into it groping for the chain of the locket it held and fishing it out.

We took our positions at North, East, South, and West... raising our arms in supplication to our Goddess.

Ivan called to the sky in the language most comfortable for him, his native Russian, though through our circle we understood him perfectly.

"Giselle Montrose, I call beyond the veil, through fire and blood I would speak with thee!" He withdrew his athame from within his coat and nicked his thumb, pressing it to the body of her locket and raising knife and tribute to the sky.

"Giselle Montrose, I call beyond the veil, through fire and blood I would speak with thee!"

We barely dared to breathe, the beating of our hearts against the cage of our ribs an almost painful thing...

"Giselle Montrose, I call beyond the veil, through fire and blood I would speak with thee!"

The flames of the pyre twisted, forming a column, almost a fire-nado, twisting high and higher still before resolving into an almost braided rope of flame, twisting, amorphous, struggling to resolve further as the night held its breath and *something* pressed from the other side outward.

"Giselle Montrose, I call beyond the veil, through fire and blood I would speak with thee!"

Miri, Ash, and I's lips moved, as we murmured our spells of healing, of support, and of containment. It was a dangerous thing standing on the edge between life and death like this. It wasn't always guaranteed that the one you called would hear. It wasn't always sure that something darker with malintent wouldn't try to answer that call instead. It took a full circle to do this and even then, it could be dicey.

"Giselle Montrose, I call beyond the veil, through fire and blood I would speak with thee!"

That rope of flame finally gave a final twist, bowing in almost deference to Ivan as it folded itself in half and bowed outward from within, like blowing glass, the form it took instead of a vessel or amphora, rendering into that of a willowy girl, her long hair blown back from her face into licking flame.

"I heed your call, but why?" she asked.

"Ask your questions," Ivan said in his roughly accented English. Stahl and McKinnon stared speechless, Stahl gathering her wits first and stepping forward.

"We're looking for the man that hurt you, the one that killed you… can you help us?" she asked and I winced.

Giselle looked stricken for a moment, her expression twisting as she raised those hands of flame and covered her face, shrieking… We'd forgotten to tell Stahl not to remind her spirit of how she died. It could be traumatic, especially if the person died violently, which Giselle had.

"Why are you doing this to me?" she demanded. "Why would you make me go through such nightmares and horrors all over again?"

Ivan spoke to her, and she turned her attention back to him.

"To stop him. To ensure no more must join you... please. Answer our questions."

Stahl made short clinical work of the Q & A session that followed. Giselle, to her credit, was brave in death. From my touch of her locket earlier, I had known she was both brave and stubborn in life and in her death too. Which is why I had chosen her among those we had articles for. She had hissed, spit, and cursed her killer even as he'd hurt her, even as he'd murdered her.

She was formidable, that one. Strong.

"Go, be at rest. Peace be with you in death as it never was in life."

She turned back to Ivan and nodded. "Catch the son of a bitch," she said with venom. Her final words haunting… "Send him to me."

Ivan gestured, and she reached up to the stars the fire twisting and burning down. Stahl was on her phone reading off details.

"There's only one farmstead within a fifty-mile radius that meets all of those details," the male voice on the other end of the phone said.

"We go..." Ivan declared through our bond.

"We go..." Ash, Miri, and I echoed.

"I will lead the way..." I murmured.

I turned to Stahl, Jayse, and McKinnon…

"We're going."

"What?" McKinnon asked.

"There's no stopping us," I said. "We owe it to that girl, and all that have gone before."

"Babe…" Jayse met my eyes and something was there, something unspoken passing between our unique bond. He nodded, and I could see there wasn't a precise, full understanding in his eyes, but there was the ghost of one.

"I love you," I murmured.

"You come back to me," he ordered. I nodded.

"So mote it be," I whispered and let the wind carry me far afield, stepping through the air and into it.

*J*ayse...

"So mote it be," she murmured with deft certainty and closed her eyes. I don't know how to explain what happened next. She just became clear, as insubstantial as smoke, and disappeared. Drawn to a place we had no name for. I felt it, somewhere in the center of my chest, the distance growing between us.

"What the fuck?" someone shouted. "Where the fuck did she go?"

"Iowa, I think," I said.

There was a mad scramble after that. Moments went by and Miri walked back slowly, first one step then two, a soft smile painting her lips.

"Don't you move!" one of the senior agents, a man yelled at her. She took several more steps and turned, walking in among the trees and stepping behind one, disappearing too, although the tree was thin, too thin, she should have been visible on the other side after half a step, but she was just gone.

"Hey!" McKinnon barked and I turned.

Ash was walking toward the pond and called out, "Ivan, you mind?" Ivan raised his arms high, brought them down, swinging them at Ash – no not *at* her, *past* her and the fire went with his motions as he directed it at the pond's frozen surface. The heat was immense, incredible, as it jetted over the pond's frozen surface, clearing a path into the water's frozen depths.

"You better warm my ass up on the other side," Ash said.

"You stop right there!" the same man yelled as Ash stepped down into the chilly water. She kept walking, the water climbing to her knees, then hitting her mid-thigh.

"I said, *stop!*" the man yelled at her and Ash threw up two middle fingers, gasping as the water hit her chest. One more step and she sank below the surface, the water reflecting the moon and firelight and nothing… not even so much as a few bubbles. She was just gone.

The man pulled out his gun and leveled it at Ivan. I stepped between them and called over my shoulder, "Go!"

I looked back; Ivan nodded at me once, then stepped into the flames. They whooshed, a great gout of them rising into the sky and then they settled… the four of them gone.

"What the fuck was that?" the guy demanded, and I turned back to him.

"Pretty sure my girlfriend and the rest of her circle are in Iowa. Also, pretty sure she'll call you." I didn't know why I had the sense that she would, like some other things, I just knew.

"Might want to be ready when she does," I said and I looked back at where the four of them had been.

I huffed a bit of an incredulous laugh and shook my head.

Not only was I in love with an incredibly powerful witch, I couldn't *wait* to tell my sister Serena all about it. I put a hand over my beard and rubbed back and forth over my mouth. I almost couldn't believe any of what I'd just seen was *real*, but then Stahl's phone rang.

"Yeah, hello?" She put it on speaker. "Where the fuck *are* you?"

"A farm outside the town Addison Jane disappeared from. I'm pinging you the location now. We'll wait for your men."

I smiled and turned back to the man who I think was Stahl and McKinnon's boss.

"See, I told you," I said.

He turned and stalked back toward the main building and Stahl and McKinnon turned to me. "You'd better follow us. We need to set up a command and get eyes on this situation."

"We aren't here to stop you," I said, raising my hands. "We're here to help you. We've always been here to help you."

"I'm really beginning to regret calling you freaks in on this," McKinnon snarled and Stahl rolled her eyes behind her partner.

I wisely didn't say anything. I didn't want to be uninvited. I was worried about Blyn.

We went into one of the buildings and into a room that looked like it could be a control room for NASA. I put my hands in my pockets and hung back against one of the rear walls. I settled there and just hoped I would be ignored as I observed what was happening.

There were several men and women bustling about, putting on headsets, booting up computers, talking on cell phones and getting connected with whoever was on the ground out in Iowa.

They tuned in to body cameras, dash cameras, and got communication established with the lead agent in charge out there in farm country. A face flickered onto the screen, a man in his thirties, maybe forties. He wore black glasses frames with a camera on the rim.

"Yeah, can you see and hear me?" he demanded. He was in the passenger seat of a car hurtling down the highway, lights flashing, but no sirens. Not yet.

"Yeah, we've got you, Cliff," the upset boss man from outside said. "These sons of bitches witches went fuckin' rogue on us. I think they're there. Some freaky shit watching them disappear like that."

"Yeah," Cliff said. "I saw the video."

"I want them all in handcuffs," the boss declared and someone said, "Sir, I don't think that's a good idea."

"That was your first problem," the boss snapped. "You, thinking. That's *my* job."

Wow, okay, what an asshole.

"We'll have to deal with that later. What I need to know, is the intelligence they're providing legitimate?"

"It is," I said without thinking.

"Who said that?"

"I did," I said, stepping out of the shadows at the back of the room.

"And who are you?" Cliff asked the camera, squinting like he could see me through it.

"Name is Jayse," I said. "Jayse Mickelson."

"And why should I listen to you, Jayse Mickelson?"

"Well, my girlfriend is the special witch in charge of this little party of yours out there and she's probably the best chance you have at catching this killer alive."

"Oh yeah? How's that?" he demanded.

"Sir, it's the next turn, hang on."

"Well, you'll find out soon enough," I said, thinking about Ivan.

They turned down a dirt drive, fields on either side and stopped at the end. The breath whooshed out of my lungs in relief when they got out of the vehicles and we saw Blyn, her circle spread out behind her.

"What the fuck?" someone said incredulous at their keyboard.

"Those four, arrest them!" the boss said.

"Try and I'll pull the air from your lungs until you pass out, and we'll be gone," Blyn declared and Ivan stood a little taller behind her.

"If I do not scorch you from face of earth first." His fists lit up in a corona of flame.

"Alright! Everybody calm the fuck down!" Ash said. "You really have to listen to that douche?" she demanded.

"No, not really," Cliff said. *Smart man.*

"What?" dude barked outraged, and a more important man slid into the room behind him as he went *off.*

"Miguel!" the more important man barked. "You can leave."

Miguel turned ashen and left the room.

"Agent Gates, this is Arthur Higgins, Director of the FBI. Would you care to fill me in on the situation at hand?" he asked.

"Well Director Higgins, I honestly have no idea what's going on. I just got here."

"Good man," Higgins said shrewdly. "Someone who does know what's happening, get me up to speed."

Work fast, I thought to Blyn even though she couldn't hear me, and I settled back down back against the wall, glad to go back to some semblance of obscurity.

*B*lyn...

I opened my eyes in a clearing. There was an irrigation ditch filled with water nearby and I sucked in a sharp breath as a thatch of dead cornstalks behind me whispered. Miri stepped out of them and whispered, "It's okay, it's just me."

"Ash and Ivan?" I asked.

The water below us in the irrigation ditch rippled and Ash rose from the murky runoff like a creature straight from Hell.

"Ivan better hurry up and get is ass here," she complained, shivering.

"Hard to when he has no fire," I whisper-shouted harshly.

"Nothing for it," Ash said and pulled a stick from her pocket and snapped it. The cornstalks next to us went up in a whoosh and Ivan stepped from them. He reached out a hand and Ash was enveloped in fire, the flames licking at her skin and clothes, but not touching. She sighed in relief and with a motion from her hand, the water leaped from the irrigation ditch and extinguished the burning stalks.

"I hope no one saw that," I uttered as I pulled out my phone and called Agent Stahl. I pinged her the location of the farm and ended the call.

"Right," Miri murmured. "Now what?"

"Now we find the main drive and wait for backup."

"Watch out for traps," Ivan rumbled.

"Oh, you think?" Miri asked.

"The ghosts, they know," he said and Miri nodded, closing her eyes.

"I'll ask the earth then, shall I?" she whispered and said, "Follow me." We followed my earth witch sister single file, me, then Ash then Ivan bringing up the rear. He could see over all of us anyway.

"How long do you think it will take for the FBI to get here," Miri asked nervously.

Ash snorted. "Too long. Law enforcement is a joke."

"I thought you *were* law enforcement," Miri whispered back.

"Nah, I'm a bounty hunter. Big difference."

I rolled my eyes. "Not *that* big of a difference," I muttered.

"Huge difference," Ash shot back and I had to somewhat concede the point. I mean, bounty hunters weren't exactly a branch of known law enforcement. They did, however, fill a niche that was needed, otherwise, why else would they exist?

We hid in the shadows, waiting and Ash kneeled down by a puddle of water in the dark, dropping oil onto the surface and chanting softly. Images resolved on the water's surface, like a reflection but not. Big SUV's, red and blue lights, I was arguing with one of the men in charge.

That was all, though.

"Fuck," Ash muttered.

"We go now, we kill him," Ivan said judiciously.

"Nobody is dying unless it's absolutely necessary," I snapped. "Ash, try again after I'm done arguing with whatever special agent in charge, alright?"

"Yeah, alright," she said.

We heard the crunch of gravel beneath tires and stepped out of the shadows as the FBI pulled up several minutes later.

They arrived, someone in Quantico ordered our arrests. Things devolved and then, divine intervention... the director himself stepped into the room in Quantico and diffused the situation.

"Which one of you is Blyn Courtney?" Agent Gates demanded, and I stepped forward.

"I am. This is Miriam Eilish, Ashlyn Tremblay, and Ivan Ivanovich. The rest of my circle," I said. "We're here so no one else has to die."

"Except killer," Ivan grated, and I looked over my shoulder at him.

"Only if we have to," I murmured.

"Problem, folks. We don't even know where he is."

"Not true," Ash said stepping up. "Let's take a new peek at the future, shall we?"

I nodded, and she stepped over to another murky puddle in the gravel closer to the FBI men. She dropped her oil, said her incantation, and the image resolved. The stainless-steel building on the edge of the property, men lined up, breeched the door, went in and *boom!*

"Right, so fuck door number one," she said.

The water clouded over and a new image coalesced. This one of Ivan in a pit somewhere, the killer between him and the victim, the girl in her underwear, arms above her head, tied at the wrist. Dirty, cold, afraid... the killer held a knife out at Ivan and Ivan threw flame at him, burned him alive, when he turned, Ash lay sightless and staring, her chest a red ruin.

"*Definitely* fuck door number two," she said and sniffed.

Door number three was a *slim* margin of success. It didn't look like anyone died at least. Same underground room, roots tangling everything, the victim bleeding this time, the wound not fatal. We all stood around grim.

"But *where* is the room?" Agent Gates asked.

Miri closed her eyes and held her hand above the earth, questing with her magic.

"It's the storm cellar," she murmured, gesturing behind the house, and frowned. "He knows we're here." Her eyes snapped open. "We have to go; we have to move now."

"You're sure it's the storm cellar?" I asked.

"Positive," Miri said.

Goddess forgive me, God protect me, I thought to myself and my sisters cries were lost as I shifted and slid through the air to coalesce in front of our victim, my back to her. The killer turned from his monitor and I drew the air from his lungs. Still, we all could hold our breath, and some people for a long time at that. He lunged for me, and I sidestepped him, but barely. Holding onto my power, stealing his air as he grabbed for me.

He wasn't panicking nearly as much as I wanted him to. I just had to buy us time. I just had to dance with him until my people got here because fuck all three doors... I wasn't about to risk my circle or *anyone* else.

He slashed at me with a knife he pulled from his leather apron and I pulled the line on the shotgun he had trained up at the doors. It went off, the roar deafening in the small space and my ears started ringing. I coughed, the stench of gunpowder stuffing itself right up my nose, but the trap was negated, a hole blown clean through the storm doors up the stairs but *not* through any of my people.

He lunged for me and I barely skirted the blade, in fact, technically, I didn't as it bit into my coat, some of the goose down stuffing going flying. I kept a hold on my magic, and he was starting to slow, using up whatever reserves of oxygen he had in his blood with his frenetic motions.

"Blyn!" I heard Ash scream up top, but I couldn't allow myself to be distracted. He tried to draw air, but I denied him. He fell to his knees and I slipped behind Addison, and I still denied him.

"It's alright," I told her as she screamed through her gag. "I'm here to help you."

"Fire!" I heard Ivan snarl and spun from where I was behind our victim, putting myself between her and the doorway up the stairs. I put up a buffer of wind just in front of myself and the girl, trying to include our attacker as all oxygen was sucked from the room and flame whooshed down the stairs at us, engulfing *everything* in its path.

I had known Ivan's intentions, just as my circle had known everything that had gone on down here, our conduits open wide between us.

"Blyn!" Miri cried and I called back. "I'm alright! We're alright! Just get down here!"

There was a clatter on the scorched stairs as FBI men in their SWAT team regalia rushed in, their flashlights bouncing, the lights having gone out down here when the fire raged. I guess I hadn't done too well in protecting the killer who gasped, choking and sputtering, half burned at our feet. The FBI pulled his arms behind his back, burns or no and zip tied his hand as Addison sobbed and put her arms around me, falling to her knees and nearly taking me to the floor with her.

"Ivan," I gasped, and he came to me, lifting the girl in his arms and taking her up the stairs to Miri and her healing arts. Agent Gates stopped next to me and put a hand on my arm as I breathed in the stench of burning hair and flesh, closing my eyes against the images it evoked from Ivan and a distant past I care not to ask him about... *ever...* I had seen enough.

"You alright?" Gates asked, panting. They had run full tilt in my direction.

"Just get me outside," I gasped, and he helped get me to Ash who helped get me up the rest of the stairs.

"You crazy bitch!" she screamed at me hysterically, pulling me in tight against her once we broke the surface of the storm cellar of horrors. "I'm the only one that's supposed to do crazy shit like that! What is *wrong* with you!?"

I didn't know. I shook my head. I threw up.

I leaned over on my knees and threw up. Shaking my head, I told my sister honestly, "I don't know. It was the only thing I could think of. I was the only one who could do it."

"Well don't ever do that again!" she shrieked and pulled me back in tightly.

I hugged her back just as tightly, as Miri put Addison into a healing sleep.

"Killer's burned pretty bad," I said for Miri's benefit, but her green eyes rose to meet mine and whatever she'd sensed from Addison, though she was physically whole by all outward appearances caused my loving sister, so full of grace, to say, "Goddess help me, but *fuck him.*"

Okay, Miri… I thought to myself.

A gunshot went off and we all jumped. Agent Gates came up the steps and sniffed. "Make you a deal," he said with a sniff. "I'll keep your secrets in the official report if you keep ours."

I stared at him wide-eyed and slightly aghast. He shook his head.

"He lunged, pulled the rope on that shotgun when y'all heard us approaching. One of my men fired down the steps, took him out and your boy rained fire into the storm cellar. After seventy-two women, there wasn't any way I was going to risk that bastard getting off on a technicality."

"I'm single, wanna fuck?" Ash asked. "Because you're straight speakin' my language."

"Ash!" Miri and I cried in unison.

"Take deal," Ivan said quietly. "Break deal, and I will come for you," he said to Gates.

"I ain't got no interest in any of that," Gates said, shaking his head.

"I know how to keep a secret," I said and we looked to Miri who smoothed some of Addison's hair with her hand, my sister's pale, freckled cheeks wet with tears.

"Who would I tell?" she asked. "I just want to go home."

"We'll get you on the first plane back to Quantico to debrief."

"Do you guys mind if I go ahead?" I asked softly, Jayse's soul calling to mine.

"No," Ash said tiredly, letting my arm go and sitting on the ground.

"*Nyet,* go," Ivan declared with a sniff.

"You have it in you?" Miri asked, worriedly.

I nodded.

"I have it in me," I declared.

"Then goddess see you swiftly on your way," she murmured. "Your work is done."

I nodded, shrugged out of my ruined coat and let it fall to the ground. I didn't want to scare Jayse.

"Blessed be, my circle," I said.

"Blessed be," they all chorused in unison and I closed my eyes and swirled into nothing on a surprised exclamation from Gates.

I materialized near Jayse, using him as my anchor point, and gasped, staggering slightly in my exhaustion. I would likely sleep for an entire day. Maybe more at this rate.

"Blyn!" Jayse caught me in his arms.

"I'm alright," I murmured, clinging to him and barely to consciousness. "I'm okay. I just need… sleep…"

I don't remember a thing after that.

*J*ayse...

The cleanup from whatever had gone down in Iowa was swift and so efficient it reeked of cover-up, but I didn't care. Blyn was home. I'd filled with dread when she'd disappeared, watching the cameras bounce as they ran full tilt around the house.

When she'd appeared beside me in the control room, when she'd reached for me, soot stained, cold, *but alive* and physically unhurt, I praised whatever powers that be, that were out there. I didn't even care what was what. God, Goddess, whatever... Blyn was *home* and in my arms and that was all that mattered.

Medics were called when she passed out and she was rushed to the infirmary. They couldn't find anything wrong with her.

Those were some really dark hours for me, sitting by her bedside. The hours while we waited for her circle to return by plane. The hours of wondering what could be wrong – if anything was wrong. Miri came to us before she went back to the dorm and hugged me tight.

"She'll be fine. Magic has its price, and she'll pay it in sleep, as must we all."

I was so relieved. Less so when I was shooed off to sleep by myself back in our dorm room.

She slept harder and longer than the rest of her circle. While they all slept for a full day and night, Blyn slept for three. Miri explained it was because Blyn had used more magic than any of them.

It was one of the longest three days of my life. Watching. Waiting. Holding her hand and reading to her some of the history on witches and Nulls that my sister had found from my phone. When Blyn finally did stir, I was there with Miri and Ash. Ivan refused to leave the close quarters of the dorm room he had been provided until it was time to go home.

On the third day, as the day wore on into evening, her eyes flickered open and she took in a sharp breath. Miri looked up from where she had her family book perched in her lap, looking for ways to help Addison, and I stuttered to a stop reading from my sister's latest email.

"Don't stop," Blyn murmured. "I like listening."

I laughed and stood up, leaning over her and kissing her soundly.

"You scared the crap out of me," I murmured against her lips and she smiled.

"I'm sorry. I just didn't want to wait for a plane ride back. I just wanted to be here, with you."

"I should have figured you didn't have enough after… well, after everything," Miri said, taking her sister's other hand.

Blyn smiled at us both.

"I love you both so much," she said.

"Aww," Miri declared. "We love you, too!"

I would have loved everything a lot more if I could have Blyn to myself, but that wasn't about to come out of my mouth. Instead, what I said, was "I love you, too," and I brought her hand to my lips, kissing the back of it softly, reverently. My beautiful, brave woman.

THE FBI's hospitality ran out pretty quick. They had us packed off to the airport on regular plane tickets back to Boston practically the next morning. We were all okay with it. We couldn't wait to be away from them. To put the whole thing behind us.

Ivan didn't like flying commercial. Too many people. It took everything Miri had to keep him calm. From the Boston airport, Kavion picked us up. Blyn and I were basically where we needed to be, but she had to escort the family book home, so rather than stay in Boston, we went back to Loving. My truck and my dog were both in the small town and I missed my dog like crazy, so I was okay with skipping through the big city.

Ash, however, was not. She parted ways with us at the airport, opting for an Uber back to her apartment.

We dropped Ivan off first as a mercy, even though we had to pass Eilish House first. He turned to me and gave me a nod before leaving the SUV and Blyn cuddled into my side.

"That guy is forever going to hate me," I said and Blyn and Miri laughed.

"He doesn't hate you," Miri said.

"He respects you, but Ivan is… Ivan. I don't think he thinks he's deserving of friendship," Blyn said and she looked after the giant Russian with worry in her eyes.

"He'll find his way," Miri said softly. "But it has to be *his* way."

Blyn nodded but didn't look all that convinced.

When we got back to Miri's, I could hear Shep howling in the locked kitchen. I got out of the truck and was like, "Awww, buddy! Can somebody let him out?"

Miri spoke a word to her house and the back door unlocked and opened, my dog flying over the back steps and bounding through the snow which had finally begun to melt around here into my arms.

"Hey!" I cried, laughing, and I hugged him tight, taking the time, no matter how tired I was, to play with him. He was *not* used to me being gone for a long period of time like that.

"Go on get inside, I got this," Kavion told the girls, and I called up to him from flat on my back in the melting snow, from under like fifty-six pounds of dog, "I'll help in a sec."

"Naw, you good, playa." He grinned down at me and hefted the suitcase full of the family books, carrying its bulk in with him first.

I took a couple bags once I got Shep to calm down, and he passed me going out for the last one. I set down Miri's bag inside the door and took Blyn's, my duffel already over my shoulder.

"Go on up, Blyn has. I'll bring you guys some tea."

"Thanks," I murmured, and I did go up, Shep on my heels.

Blyn was in the shower in the small bathroom and I thought that sounded like a *great* idea. I ditched our bags, got rid of my clothes and went in, pulling back the curtain and stepping in behind her.

"Hmm," she hummed out happily as I folded her into my arms.

"Finally feels like just us," I murmured and she nodded. We were both tired from our journey, but we were home, sort of, and it felt good to be here.

"Feels like home," she murmured, and looked up to me. "Is that weird?" I shook my head and stared into her beautiful face.

"I was just thinking the same thing," I said. "Is *that* weird?"

She shook her head no and sighed.

"What now?" she asked.

"That's a good question," I said. "You wanna keep going with the crime and punishment thing?"

She tipped her head back and let the steaming water from the showerhead wet it.

"I've been thinking about that," she murmured. "I do," she said finally. "But I would like to scale things back."

"Yeah?" I asked.

"Yeah."

"This is a pretty big talk," she murmured.

"Scared of it?" I asked.

"Yeah," she confessed.

I smiled down at her and bowed my head, bringing my lips to hers. "Then we don't have to talk about it," I whispered against them. "We don't have to talk about anything right now."

"Kiss me," she begged, and I obliged.

God, this woman had the softest lips I'd ever tasted. Everything about her, the way she tasted, the way she smelled, the way she felt tight up against me like this. Every bit of it was insanely intoxicating. All I knew was that I was willing to compromise on *any*thing for her. It didn't matter, big or small. We would magic make it work. We had to, because she was, indeed, my soulmate and there wasn't anything I wouldn't do to keep her in my life.

"Jayse," she whispered, my name a plea on her lips.

"Yeah?" I asked quietly.

She looked up at me, her arms twined around my neck and begged me, "Make love to me?"

"Here in the shower?" I asked her softly. "Or out there, on the bed?"

"Both," she murmured mischievously. "Both is good."

I chuckled and brought my mouth back down to hers and plunged my tongue past her lips, sweeping it against the velvet sweetness of her own.

She moaned in my mouth and it was a sound that was thick, like the old-fashioned molasses chews that were a fond favorite around here.

I held her tightly to me, my hands on her ass, my cock growing in firmness and length pressed against her tight little body. Yeah, I would do anything to stay with this woman. Anything at all. I would hold her, kiss away her tears. I would laugh with her and hug her every time she asked. It was to the point, that even after knowing her for so short a time, it didn't matter. I was certain. I was sure. This was the woman I was going to ask to marry me.

I kissed along her jaw, down to the side of her throat, exploiting that sweet spot, making her gasp, her flesh pebbling under the touch, those goose bumps sweeping out over her shoulder and down her arm as she delighted in my touch, her hands sweeping over my body, my skin, causing the same sort of rush and reaction.

She slipped to her knees in front of me, and looking up through the fall of water, she took me into her mouth without a second thought.

I choked on my surprise, closing my eyes as she swallowed me whole, that velvet pink tongue of hers playing along the underside of my shaft and making me weak in the knees.

"Gah!" I shuddered and shook my head and said, "Baby, we gotta move this to the bedroom. I'm not gonna be able to stand through this."

She laughed evilly around me and I let out another strangled cry.

"Don't make me beg for mercy," I muttered and she let my dick pop delightfully from her mouth, standing and offering her sweet candy lips up to me. How could I refuse?

I kissed her, we showered for real, then dried one another sensually, and it was on.

She led me into the bedroom, crooking a finger at me, bidding me to follow and I did. Like Shep on a lead.

She scooted up on the bed, and I went to prowl up there after her, but then I had a better idea. I backed off, planting a kiss first on the top of one foot then the other. I hadn't feasted on her in a minute, and I wanted the taste of her sweetness on my tongue. I alternated kisses, first one shin then the other, climbing her leg slow, so slowly, the love and lust turning her already sinfully dark gaze smoky, hazy with desire.

I worked my way up her body so tantalizingly slowly until I reached the apex of her thighs, then pulling her roughly to the edge of the high bed, I kneeled, prepared to worship.

I captured her waist in my hands, holding her against my mouth as I kissed her pussy, plunging my tongue into her opening and raking it up through her folds. She collapsed back onto the bed with a guttural sigh and gripped the coverlet at either hip as I lavished her cunt with attention from my lips and tongue. I smiled to myself and closed my eyes, breathing her in, tasting her, loving her with my mouth.

If heaven were real and had a taste, it would taste just as Blyn Courtney did against my tongue.

God, Goddess, whatever… I just couldn't get enough of her.

*B*lyn...

Maiden, Mother, and Crone! Jayse had me at his mercy. I closed my eyes and breathed deeply and evenly as he teased me to heights I hadn't even considered could exist! I swallowed hard, my mouth suddenly dry, my sawing breath not helping matters in that department, as he worked me with his mouth.

Good, it felt so good... but it was missing something, and that missing something was maddeningly keeping me firmly on this side of that edge we all craved to ride for as long as possible before toppling over into that shining fall.

I arched my hips slightly and whimpered and Jayse laughed at me, darkly, conniving, *teasing*. He knew just what to do and he chose to deny me for now. I was okay with that. I *had* started it after all.

"Jayse, *please*," I begged a moment or two later and I swear the sigh that emanated from him was one of pure satisfaction. The satisfaction of a man who was listening to the most pleasing music to the ear.

It struck me that *I* was the thing that made that sound for him. That just one sigh from my lips could please this man so thoroughly. That he ached for me, burned for me, just as much as I did for him. I gasped as he introduced one of his long fingers inside of me, questing with that damnably sweet come-hither motion for that spot that he knew would let me take flight.

It was that motion, the even sweeter play of his lips and tongue from the outside that had the celestial bodies calling to me, calling me home among the stars. With every stroke of his fingers, every swish of his tongue, I rose high and higher still among those stars, until glimpses of silver light flitted at the edges of my vision and I started to see without seeing the play of color and light of our mixing auras, like a nebula or brilliant galaxy painting around us. Those blues, purples, and pinks shot through with specks of silver starlight. As though he and I were cut from the same cloth as space and time itself.

"Oh, Jayse!" I breathed and shut my eyes, the swirling starlight playing inside my eyelids, my hands traveling to his hair, gripping it as I ground my pelvis against his mouth. He moaned against my body and it was that last little bit, that last little thing needed to push me into the fall and fall I did. I plummeted, shrieking back toward earth, the sensation of falling through the pleasure so real, I put my hands out to the bed on either side of me to somehow break my fall.

I was drifting in that fall, both plummeting so very fast and supported by the drift of wind and warmth that I felt lighter than a feather. Only vaguely aware of Jayse standing above me, licking his palm, slicking it against the head of his cock as I twitched with wave after wave of sensation, sprawled out before him.

He wasted no time, thrusting inside of me, deep, to the hilt. I half gasped, half cried out at the full sensation, my pussy rippling around him, causing him to bow his head and still his hips, groaning at the sensation.

He stood, panting, rooted inside me for several seconds while we *both* regained ourselves and then, without missing a single other beat, he began to move. Sweetly, surely, *carefully* inside me. Stroking in and out, adding a gentle roll to his hips that pushed him up against the roof of my cunt and made me squeeze down on him that much tighter.

He raised my legs against his chest, hugging them to him as he stood at the side of the bed, pushing into me, thrusting sweetly, driving me wild, working me up all over again. I held onto anything I could to convince me this was real. The velvet fibers of the coverlet digging into my palms as he rooted around inside me with his cock looking for that winning combination that would drag me mercilessly back up through the atmosphere, to dance with him among the stars before we both lost our footing and were sent hurtling back to earth.

I don't know how long he fucked me like that. It could have been minutes; it could have been hours. I didn't know. I didn't care. I was just grateful to be completely lost in him.

He closed his eyes, turned his head and laid a reverent kiss against my calf and with a shudder, lost his rhythm and pushed just that last little bit further into my body. I gasped and fell all over again, plunging with him down, down, and further still down, until it felt as though we fell impossibly long, impossibly hard, through the earth's crust, further down still through the heat of her blood, to splash down into a river of pure, unadulterated *bliss*.

I don't remember moving. I don't remember him slipping from my pussy, or when he climbed up onto the bed. I don't remember straightening out on the bed, or when he pulled the blankets up over us both. I don't remember cuddling into his chest or him switching out the light. I don't remember him petting my hair or kissing my forehead.

I don't remember any of those things in the way that you should remember them; I just know that they happened. They happened, and I liked it, and I wouldn't trade a night like this one for anything. Not gold, not power, not even to end world hunger at this point.

Call me selfish… but I drank Jayse's attentions in this night and I hoarded them away like a dragon sleeping on its treasure in the center of my heart.

*J*ayse...

"I have to return the family book to Courtney House before we can go back to Boston," Blyn murmured at the breakfast table the next morning and she didn't look happy about it.

"I can do it for you if you want," Miri said and I shook my head.

"Has to be me. That was the deal," she said with a heavy sigh.

"Do you want me to go with you?" I asked carefully.

"You don't read as a Null anymore," Miri said. "At least not to me."

"No one looks at me funny anymore," I agreed. "At least none of the recruits did, and I haven't noticed anyone around town do it."

We'd decided to stay the weekend, and Blyn showed me around Loving. It was nice. Wonderful in a way seeing the place she grew up through her eyes.

Miri had taken us to her shop, formerly the *Wick & Stone*, she'd renamed it after it'd been willed to her and now, it was *Away with Herbs*, a metaphysical body care shop, with tea, bath bombs, salt, and herbal soaks, and everything in between. It was doing well enough that Miri had help, a couple of girls to run the counter when she had to do things like run off for almost a week and help her circle help the FBI.

Blyn looked apprehensive, and I didn't think it had anything to do with my status as a Null.

"My mother can be... difficult," Blyn said and I glanced at Miri who nodded.

"Then it's decided," I said. "I'm coming with you. No way am I letting you walk into any more lion's dens alone." I covered my lady's hand with my own where it rested on the table and she smiled up at me.

"She has a habit of making underhanded biting remarks," she warned.

"I can take it," I said with a shrug, and it was true. I'd taken shit my whole life. This certainly wouldn't be anything new.

"That's my problem with the whole thing," Blyn said with a sigh. "You shouldn't have to."

I hooked a hand behind her neck and dragged her forehead to my lips, kissing it, and saying against the warm skin and her silken hairline, "You let me worry about me and my feelings. Huh? You worry about so much already."

She smiled and huffed a bit of a laugh and nodded.

"Mm, alright."

We finished breakfast, I loaded the truck, and with her family book clutched against her chest, the damn thing almost as big as she was, she stood on Miri's porch and wished her sister a temporary farewell. Kavion was off at work, and we had gotten to say a quick goodbye the night before along with our goodnight wishes.

Miri hugged Blyn, big damn spellbook and all and both of them sighed in unison, laughing as their breaths plumed the air.

"Drive careful!" Miri called to me and I raised my hand and waved.

"You know I will!" I called back to her. "Shep!" I called to my dog and dropped the tailgate of my truck. "Come on, boy!"

He made the running leap up into the back of my truck and I raised the gate to secure him. It would only be for the ride over to Blyn's mom's house. I didn't want anything to happen to her book.

"You ready?" I murmured.

"As I'll ever be," she said dubiously, rolling her eyes. I smiled and kissed her before opening her door for her.

She held out the book to me, and I was touched. That she would have so much faith in me; that she would trust me so completely. I took the book from her and she climbed into the cab of the truck reaching so I could hand it back once she was settled.

I shut her inside carefully and went around to my side and got in.

As soon as I started the truck, got us backed out of our parking spot, and put it into gear to give us some forward motion, she reached for my hand. She radiated nerves, and I almost wanted to say that she was more afraid of talking with her mother than she was about touching any evidence anymore. That was saying something... to me at least.

I gripped her hand in mine and followed her directions, the truck warming up slow and being a bit stubborn about it. We pulled up in front of a big old Gothic-looking Victorian painted lady. Unlike Miri's house which was painted in earthy autumn tones, this one was done in bejeweled royal purples with deep fuchsia accents and black trim. It worked with the building's architecture but still in some ways managed to be ostentatious. I wasn't quite sure how to feel about it, even as I threw my truck into 'park' and Blyn let out what sounded like a long, suffering sigh.

"Here we go," she murmured unenthusiastically, unbuckling her seatbelt.

The front door to the house opened and a woman, tall and imperious, stepped out onto the front porch. She looked like she'd stepped right out of time with the way she was dressed – from her old-fashioned granny boots, to her deep purple and black Victorian tea dress, to the black beaded piano shawl around her shoulders, the fringe swinging. Even her hair was up in a bun, and I know this sounds bad, but with the iron in her hair, she looked just like the wicked stepmother from the original Disney *Cinderella* animated movie. Like, the resemblance was uncanny.

I could see hints of Blyn in her mother, but it looked like she had *seriously* taken after her father. I wondered if that was where her mother derived some of the utter disdain; she was looking down her nose at Blyn with as we went up the walk.

"Mother," Blyn said as she reached the top step and her 'I' turned into a yelp as her mother lashed out with one hand, gripping Blyn's arm and reeling her in, crushing her daughter into a hug.

"What *happened*?" her mother demanded. "What did you *do*? Honestly, Blyn! You could have been killed!"

Her mother sniffed and the tears started immediately and I looked from her to Blyn who was struggling a bit in her grasp.

"Mother! Lord and Lady, let me go! I can explain—"

"Yes, well I'm going to need you to."

"I can't believe you were *spying* on me!" Blyn cried and I just sort of hung back not sure what was going on.

"Oh, I wasn't! I *dreamed* it. A mother always knows!" her mother cried and then the other shoe dropped. "How could you do this to me?" her mother demanded.

Blyn thrust her family book away from herself and into her mother's arms. Either her mother took it or it was going to get dropped. Predictably so, her mother took it from her. Blyn took a stumbling step back and I reached up a hand. She took it and her mother seemingly just realized I was even there.

"Who are you?" she demanded.

"You just lost your chance to find out," I answered. "Come on, baby. Let's get you home," I said to my woman.

"Excuse me! I am her mother and *this* is her home?"

"Exactly," I snapped at her. "Excuse you!"

I lit into her selfish ass and didn't exactly hold back. Blyn was trembling against my side and I could tell, of everything she'd ever been through with and for *anyone* else… this right here, her mother, hurt her the most.

It was too bad the woman just couldn't seem to see the forest for the trees. Her daughter was incredible, selfless, brave, and kind. I wasn't sure how she turned out so well when *clearly,* she was raised around and by a narcissist.

It all came down to that one phrase – *how could you do this to me?*

Blyn didn't do anything to her mother. She'd done it all for *other* people. Most notably, a person she didn't even know – Addison Jane.

I got my lady out of there and I was hoping against hope we would never have to look back. I mean, at least not for a while, anyway. Who knew what the future held? Well, except maybe Ash… a little bit.

"Thank you," Blyn said hollowly, and to her credit, she didn't cry.

"The blood of the covenant is thicker than the water of the womb," I told her. "That's the original phrase they bastardized 'blood is thicker than water' out of."

She sniffed and nodded. "You've got family, babe. In Ash and Miri, and even Ivan, I think."

"Would you mind if we stopped one more place?" she asked and I nodded.

"You just name it," I said.

"Ivan's. He's out on the coastal road just outside Loving. A row of beach houses. Mostly dilapidated, but some of them still have people living in them. Not usually year-round. Mostly, they're just summer homes, but yeah… I'd like to check on him if that's okay."

"You just lead the way," I said, scooping up her hand and pressing a kiss to the back of it.

And so that's what we did. We went down through town, hanging a left at the main drag and cruising the strip of touristy businesses on one side and the docks on the other. Fishermen were working their nets and it was as idyllic as small-town life could get, really. I liked it out here. It was simple, but I didn't know if there would ever be convincing Blyn to leave the fast pace of city life and the front lines of helping the voiceless behind.

It was her calling.

Her suggestion of scaling things back was appealing. I was thinking, if she were inclined, of wintering here so that we could sort of have the best of both of our worlds. We seemed to be doing this thing where we were thinking along the same lines and voicing the same things and I wondered if that were part of whatever our magic was or if it was a soulmate thing.

"I'll smooth things out with my mother later," Blyn said as the wide expanse of beach and gray-swept sea beyond it passed by her window. I steered the truck out of town along the cracked two-lane ribbon of road toward a line of houses in the distance.

"Only if you want to," I said. "I know the type, baby. She's a real Karen. Ask for the manager, everything is all about her all the time."

Blyn snorted a laugh and nodded slightly. "That's my mom," she agreed.

"You ever think about kids?" I asked softly and she looked up at me.

"Yeah," she said. "You?"

"Yeah."

We were silent for a time and she said, "Do you want to start working on them now, or?"

"In a year or two," I said. "I would really like to marry you first."

"Mm." She smiled. "Typically, we do a handfasting first," she said. "It's that one, just up here. The brown one. Yes, this one."

I rolled to a stop in front of a brown house that looked like it could use some love.

"To be continued," I said, pulling forward on the gear selector and shoving it up into 'park.'

"Absolutely to be continued," she said smiling and pulled on the door handle, popping her passenger side door.

She climbed down out of the truck and Shep paced back and forth in the bed, whining excitedly.

"You can bring him," she said and I dropped the gate on my way around so he could jump down.

"Come on, boy," I said and he jumped down, talking in that Husky kind of way.

Blyn let us through the low gate in the low wood fence surrounding the place, the wood weathered and gray with salt and improper sealing. The front door to the house opened and Ivan ducked out the door onto the front porch.

"Hey," Blyn called softly and went up to him, hugging him as he impassively stood there. He bowed his head and grunted and after a moment, returned the hug.

"How are you doing?" she looked up at him and asked.

"Good," he said with a nod.

"We wanted to come by before we left town," I said and Shep stopped short of the porch and looked up, bowing low and whining. I'd never seen him do that. He laid down, tail tucked and Ivan nodded.

"Come, drink with me," the big man ordered and he went back inside.

Blyn and I exchanged a look and followed.

His place had no furniture in it that didn't have a white dust cloth over it. Like he didn't use these rooms at all. In fact, he bypassed the kitchen completely and took us out back into what looked like an old carport refashioned into a garage. It was warm in there, despite the lack of garage door or anything and it being open to the wind coming off the Atlantic.

I looked around at all of the forging equipment and felt a sort of nostalgia. I'd done some forging for a while, part of learning how to rough it and homestead. I didn't have the means to do it at my sister's place or the cabin but could use the facilities at my mentor's place if need be.

I asked a few questions as Ivan pulled a kettle from near the forge and poured some hot tea into three old-school Russian tea glasses. Like some original shit, the red glass held by tarnish silver holders. He took the one from the set of four that was cracked at the rim and gave us the whole ones as I asked, "So, what are you working on?"

He looked over at me as I took a sip of what could only be tea from Miri while I eyed the scraps of steel sorted in barrels along one wall.

"Knives," he said simply and I kicked one of the barrels.

"Got some good high carbon steel here, looks like leaf springs from an old Ford, am I right?"

He raised his chin and looked me over quizzically for a moment before saying, "*Da*."

I smiled. "Been a long time since I pounded anything out, I kind of miss it."

"You forge?" he asked, and I nodded.

"I learned a thing or two," I said. "Bet I could learn a lot from you if you'd be willing to teach me. Could stand to use some help maintaining my traps."

"Traps?" he asked.

"That's what I do, I'm a fur trapper."

"Ah." He nodded. "Yes."

It was an awkward visit, but I had to hand it to Ivan, he was trying. Blyn and I hated to cut it short, but it was going to be late by the time we made it back to Boston as it was. Ivan held out his hand to me and I shook it.

"I misjudged you," he said, and I nodded.

"That's okay," I said back, and it was. I think that was the closest thing I would get to an apology from the man, and that was okay. I would take it.

"You stay safe," he told Blyn. "Away from spooks."

Blyn smiled and nodded and said, "I will. Love and light, brother," before hugging him farewell.

Ivan's face twisted at the word 'brother' but only for a second, faster than a flicker of lighting through the clouds.

Shep was pacing the front yard when we got back through that way and I let him up into the cab of the truck first. I tucked Blyn in beside him and went around to the driver's seat.

"Your place?" I asked, and she nodded.

"Feels like I am leaving home rather than going back to it," she observed.

"Same," I told her.

Same...

$\mathscr{B}$lyn...

I wasn't supposed to have a dog in my apartment, but I didn't care. Shep made the ride up with us in the elevator and as soon as the doors shushed open, he trotted into my space. It made me smile.

Jayse let me go first and I sighed, hanging my purse and sweater on the coat-tree just to the right of the elevator.

"Here," I murmured, taking my suitcase from him and wheeling it into the laundry room beneath the stairs up to the loft. The loft was *technically* supposed to be the bedroom, but I preferred to keep it as my office, library, and ritual space.

Jayce followed me and helped me lift the case onto the dryer so that I could open it up and dump my dirty things directly into the wash basin.

I laughed gently as he started to strip me and dropped those things in as well. Then suddenly we were kissing, my hands tugging at his clothing as his duffel dropped to the tile floor.

Our lips moved against each other's urgently, our hands pulling at clothes, the chill of the vacant apartment caressing our skins. It would warm up in here, soon. The sensors tripped; the thermostat engaged.

"I want you nude and writhing underneath me," Jayse murmured against my ear. He nipped at the lobe and confessed, "I can't get enough of you."

I moaned and swooned into his embrace, too tired for coherent thought, ready to let my body do all the talking.

"Come here, baby," he murmured, and I leaped, twining my legs around his lean hips. He carried me out and around to the bed, laying me on it.

I closed my eyes and twined my fingers through his soft hair as he kissed his way down my nude body, moaning when he took one of the stiff peaks of my nipples into his mouth. He teased it with his tongue, his sharp hazel eyes looking up at me, gauging my reaction.

I writhed for him, my body dancing as he pulled the strings of my nerves so beautifully, like a puppeteer. He knew just what to do to me, and I loved that. I absolutely loved being at his tender mercy. The torture he wrought upon me exquisite.

I loved the way he loved me. I just wished we weren't always so *exhausted* when we got to share one another like this.

He smoothed his hands over every inch of my skin, laying butterfly kisses in their wake and I melted into the cloud of my bed, breasts heaving as he kissed lower and lower, nestling his mouth against my cunt and lavishing my pussy with attention.

I arched beneath him and he settled the backs of my thighs over his shoulders, his hands gripping my waist, pulling me to his mouth so he could feast on me, tongue lapping at my core, teasing my clit, taking me on that tight spiraling thermal high into the late winter sky up through the heavy clouds, pregnant with rain until I could be sat on the crescent of the moon.

And still he teased me, withholding that last touch that would send me over the edge, listening to me cry out, moan, and beg for it with a wicked curve to his lips as he listened to me languish in this exquisite agony he'd created.

"Oh, *damn* you, Jayse!" I cried laughing and panting at once.

"You want it?" he murmured, before flicking his tongue against the already tremendously sensitive nub of my clit.

"Yes!"

"You love me?" he asked again with that teasing edge to his tone.

"With everything!" I confessed.

"With everything?" he asked, and I could tell that had probably caught him slightly off guard.

"Yes!"

"Hmm," he hummed, sounding quite pleased with himself and slid his middle finger inside me, gliding through my wetness, finding that trigger point easily and exploiting it until I shuddered involuntarily and cried out. My hips bucked as electric pleasure zipped along every nerve as though I'd been struck by lightning and I plunged, falling back to earth, Jayse's arms wide to catch me.

I came back to myself, gasping. Panting. The starbursts of light dissolving from my vision in time to watch him kneel between my quaking thighs and fist himself, rubbing his cock to his desired stiffness before half collapsing over me and introducing himself to my body with one quick, sharp, thrust.

He moaned and bowed his head and I caught *him*, my arms going around him, my fingers finding the softness of his hair as I dragged his mouth to mine.

We kissed, he drew back, and he thrust forward sharply, setting a rhythm that most would call punishing, but I knew it for what it was... *desperate*.

He worked himself in and out of my body at a quick and efficient pace, and no sooner had I begun to come down from my first orgasm, a second was building in its place. I went limp with passion as he lay over the top of me, making as much skin to skin contact as possible, and it was *perfect*. His body moving over mine, both of them working in concert and counterpoint, the pleasure building, expanding, until there was no light, no sound, just sensation engulfing us both and we both climaxed at once, the sensation wholly and uniquely intimate and uniting though we were both trapped in our singular bodies.

It felt as though our consciousness expanded beyond our shells to mingle, both floating entwined and languorously in the warm bath like sensation of our mutual bliss.

I wasn't apt to see the future, of what could be, like Ash… but I saw it then. I saw the laughter and joy, the heartache and pain laid out before us. I saw the long and winding road of all of our years before us. I saw our handfasting, our marriage, our first child, our miscarriage, our second child, and beyond. I saw narrow misses and close calls. I saw gratitude and a little bit of heartache. I saw us, together, celebrating victories and mourning losses. I saw us lose our youthful appearance, the wrinkles set in, the gray at our temples and through it all? A love so deep, a devotion so permanent, there was no decision to be made – we were perfect for each other.

Our house would be strong, built on its foundation of love and respect, the bricks made of the strongest devotion… and I wanted that. I wanted a long, prosperous life with this man. Creating life, saving lives, putting good out there. Shining light into some of the darkest corners of this world… because only light could beat back the dark. Only love could banish heartache and pain.

Jayse blinked his gorgeous hazel eyes down at me as I caressed the side of his face, the light dew of sweat our lovemaking had conjured cooling on our twitching bodies as he asked, "Did you…"

I smiled and whispered, "It wasn't me, but yes."

"*Fuck*," he whispered. "I love you." And those last words were so full of certainty. So full of respect, my heart swelled in my breast and threatened to not be contained.

"I love you, too," I murmured, just as Winter began to relent, the rain starting, pattering against the windowpanes surrounding us on two sides.

He gathered me tightly in his arms and I closed my eyes. Now all that was left was to make our way back *home*…

*J*ayse...

The next morning, I made us breakfast. Though both of us were reluctant to go anywhere, I needed to at least go see Serena. I didn't feel right coming back into Boston and not having my little sister be the first stop. It was breaking a long-held tradition of mine, and it sat uneasy on my shoulders.

Besides that, after talking with Blyn over that breakfast, we had some decisions to make about certain accommodations. As in, I was definitely on board with staying with her, but by the same token, not in this loft apartment. One, it didn't allow dogs and surprisingly, that was a deal breaker for *Blyn*, because she knew it would be for me and how much I loved Shep.

She immediately pulled up real estate on her laptop and was asking about neighborhoods and whether we should start thinking now about schools for our future kids, and all I could honestly do was sit there and grin like a fool.

I didn't know if I just hadn't noticed through the stress of things, or if she was manifesting some of her circle sister's personality traits – Ash specifically, but when you got my woman going, she was, in fact, *very* Type A and I think it was just one more thing I loved about her.

For the first time in forever, I was feeling like I was on the right track. Like *this* was what I was meant to be doing, and I tell you what... I couldn't wait to go ring shopping with my meager savings, because with Blyn's wealth? It was starting to look like for a while, I would be somewhat of a kept man.

Before Blyn, that would have bothered me. *A lot...* but not with her. I couldn't tell you why. I figured, since it was alright with her, while she did her thing with the police and FBI or whoever came knocking looking for her services for the good of mankind, I could and would find what spoke to me. I would figure it out as I went.

I did know that whatever rabbit hole of self-discovery I went down, it would most definitely involve me using my hands.

"I don't know why I feel this way, to be honest," I was telling her. "Like, were it any other woman? I think I'd be freaking out at the prospect of not being able to take care of us in the traditional sense, you know?"

She smiled at me, and a warmth flooded my chest at the sight. It wasn't the smile of a lover, or of a wife even. It was the smile your best friend gave you and the fact that I so easily confessed these feelings to her, felt so secure in doing so, spoke a lot to that, I guess.

"You were raised by a strong, independent woman," Blyn said. "You have been taking care of everyone else around you in that vein, for so long, I think you just got a little lost when you were the only one left to take care of."

She reached out a hand and I took it.

"Now I have you to take care of," I said. "Maybe a darling daughter in our future if we're lucky..." I grinned at the thought and shook her hand back and forth a little.

She laughed slightly and nodded. "You'll have a son to teach, too. I'm sure of it," she said. "To hunt, and to fish. To smith with you and Uncle Ivan." She smiled happily and I grinned too.

"I've never really lived with a *future* in mind. It feels good to plan things," I said.

Blyn nodded. "I know what you mean," she said. She looked me over, her lovely dark eyes roving my face as she sat up a little abruptly.

"What about a fixer-upper?" she asked.

"Yeah?" Now *that* was appealing.

She turned back to her laptop and started clicking through listings and sucked in a breath between her teeth.

"Enough," she said. "This one might be too much."

She turned the computer in my direction and I let my eyes rove the images, reaching forward and scrolling through them. There were holes in sheetrock and in the upstairs, there wasn't even any sheetrock, it was bare studs and electrical.

"Has *a lot* of promise, though," I said eyeing it. "A good backyard for Shep that's already fenced. I could do a nice fence around the front yard for him too. Straight shot through the house front door to back door for a nice summertime breeze and it looks like it's in a part of the city that's slowly getting cleaned up. I'm not real keen on gentrification and what it does to low-income families, but we could flip it for a real tidy sum in the next two to three years. It'll also keep me occupied."

"Yeah?" She searched my face and turned the computer back to her, her gorgeous eyes roving the images while I pointed out some of my thoughts on some of the old house's potential.

Pretty soon, she was into it.

"Could you imagine a kitchen like Miri's?" she asked. "All of the modern amenities, but with that retro kind of vibe?"

"Oh, shit, I mean shoot! Yeah. I loved her kitchen. That tile was *mint*."

She laughed at me and shook her head slightly. "You know, it's okay to swear around me," she said, getting up to round the kitchen's breakfast bar to get herself some more coffee. "I mean, have you *listened* to Ash?"

I laughed and felt myself blush, nodding. I had to concede that point, but still… "My momma didn't raise me that way, to swear in front of a lady."

"Hmm." She sipped her coffee. "I wasn't aware I classified as a lady."

"In the traditional sense?" I asked. "Yeah, probably not so much," I agreed. "But to me? You're all class, Ms. Courtney."

I got up and went over to her, pulling her into my arms and dipping my head. She raised her lips to mine and that was the spark that ignited the inferno of our passion for one another all over again.

I took my woman back to bed.

I FELT a little guilty as we made the drive over to my sister's. It was getting on toward late afternoon. After lovemaking, we'd needed to shower and get dressed, and Blyn wasn't going to be able to concentrate or think about *anything else* until she put in some calls to her real estate people and lawyers and whatnot to get the ball rolling on making offers on that house.

I was excited to get over to Serena's and tell her about it. She was, after all, my original best friend. My biggest cheerleader right alongside Mom for everything that I did. Understanding when I didn't take the path expected of me, but rather when I'd struck out for the woods on my own. Letting me live in her basement to save money, and on more than one occasion, going toe to toe with her husband over that fact.

I owed her a lot, and the first thing I was going to do was what Mike should have done a long time ago and fix her damn broken front steps!

I pulled up to the curb in front of my sister's place and shifted my truck into 'park.' Shep was in the back, pacing and whining. He'd been cooped up with us in the apartment all day and I could tell he wanted to go for a run around the yard or something.

I was going to have to supplement taking him to the dog park for a while until we could get out of the apartment. That is, if we didn't get busted for having him in there before we could make that happen. I hated to ask, but if that happened? I might need to ask Serena if I could kind of board him with her and Mike for a while until Blyn and I got everything squared away with starting our new life together.

She was still dead serious about wintering over back near Loving. Although, she suggested we do it at her family cabin. It was a good idea. I could run trap lines between it and my trapper's cabin and go back and forth.

I was excited at how well our two worlds, for how different they were, were surprisingly compatible in how well they meshed.

"You okay?" I asked Blyn as she stared out the passenger window, up at my sister's house. The silence around her, heavy.

"Yeah," she said, but she sounded distracted and a bit far away.

"You sure?"

She shook whatever it was off and smiled, and it was like the sun peeking out from behind a cloud.

"Yeah, I'm fine," she said and unbuckled her seatbelt.

"Let me get your door," I murmured and I jumped out of my truck, heading around the back and dropping the gate for Shep on my way by.

I helped Blyn down, holding out my hands for her to grasp as the front door to my sister's place opened. Serena stepped out onto the front porch smiling, and I almost missed the tightness around her eyes. I mean, I would have if Blyn hadn't said, "Oh, she looks like she's hurting."

"What?" I whipped my attention back to my sister and sure enough, she was holding herself sort of stiffly.

"What happened?" I called up to her, shutting the truck door behind Blyn.

"Oh, you know. Was carrying a basket of laundry down into the basement, caught the edge of the stair wrong with the sole of my boot and slipped. It's nothing. I'm okay." Serena waved it off.

I reached her and I bent, hugging her very carefully, gingerly and moved out of the way.

"Hi," Blyn said smiling and went in for a similar hug. Serena bent somewhat awkwardly at the waist as though her back hurt her and Blyn pressed her cheek to my sisters.

It was Blyn's sharp intake of breath that rose the hackles on the back of my neck.

"Oh, honey…" Blyn straightened and held my sister at arm's length, looking up into her eyes. "Oh, honey, no. You can't live like this anymore."

I felt the pit of my stomach drop out…

"Serena?" I asked.

*B*lyn...

I couldn't be certain, the first time I had visited Serena's house, that touch to her kitchen table revealing some... intimate images, without sound, without feeling. I couldn't have been certain if the face she'd been making as her husband had her bent over that kitchen table was a good one or a bad one. Sometimes, they were indistinguishable and you just didn't ask your new boyfriend's sister if she happened to enjoy rough sex bent over her kitchen table, or if what I had actually seen was her own husband raping her.

The light touch of my cheek to hers revealed all I needed to know. She hadn't slipped on the stairs. Her husband had kicked her down them. He'd been hitting her a lot lately, and he had been extraordinarily calculated in his abuse. He never, not once, touched her face.

She gripped my arms, her hazel eyes so like Jayse's brimming with tears as she choked on a little sob.

"Serena?" Jayse asked and I ushered them both inside, closing the front door behind us.

She went to her big brother then, and hugged him tight, sobbing brokenly and I felt incandescent with rage, my power coming to the fore, my palms beginning to sweat and itch with the urge to touch things and I do mean *everything* to get the whole measure of the abuse she'd suffered at the hands of that asshole.

"I didn't want to tell you!" she cried. "Mike, he threatened to hurt you if I told."

"That son of a bitch," Jayse uttered in disbelief.

A car door shut outside and I murmured, "Let's take this to the kitchen, shall we?"

Jayse led the way, his sister tucked close against his chest. He lowered her into one of the kitchen table chairs and I laid fingertips against the kitchen table itself, the sights, sounds, and images coming to me in a controlled rush.

"Blyn?" Jayse asked.

"Make your sister a cup of tea, Jayse," I told him, and my voice echoed hollowly in my own ears.

"Okay." He nodded and trusting me to do my thing, let go of Serena, murmuring that it was alright and that we would be getting her out of there.

I went about touching things lightly and was in the living room by the fireplace when the front door opened and the bastard came through.

"Serena!" he called and then he looked up, straight into my eyes, demanding, "Who the fuck are you?"

I gave him a nasty little smile. "The divine feminine," I answered and my voice wasn't simply my own. There was a discordant note, a hint of something older and wiser than I had ever been underlying my voice and she was just as angry as I was.

"The fuck is that supposed to mean?" he demanded and I heard Jayse's bootfalls in the hallway behind the wall of the fireplace passing by the stairs up to the bedroom, heading straight for this malevolent creature just inside the front door.

I made a cutting gesture with my hand in front of my breast and the front door flew open, all the way back, slamming into the wall beside Serena's husband. I heard Jayse's footfalls stop in the hallway as the wind picked up inside the house.

I raised my chin, and ceded control to the divinity within me and with a thrust of my chin, Serena's husband went flying back, arching high above the broken front steps and coming down *hard* on the walkway outside.

"You're leaving," I said and again with the two-toned discordant harmony from my voice box. "Never to return."

"Bitch, I'm going to find you and I'm going to *fucking*—" I stole the air from his lungs and laughed a wicked wild thing and turned my head, stepping out onto the front porch, aware of Jayse holding Serenity behind me.

I delighted in her husband, Mike, flopping around like a landed fish on the ground in front of me and I gave him back his breath.

"You will do nothing except grant this woman her divorce," I said. "Furthermore, I bind you, Michael, from doing harm. Harm against another woman and from entering this house."

I repeated the spell, weaving with my hands the intricate warding needed to prevent him from setting foot upon the front steps, the back steps, or from touching any windows.

"I bind you, Michael, from doing harm. Harm against another woman and from entering this house."

He sputtered. "You can't do that!" he yelled. "This is my house!"

"I bind you, Michael, from doing harm. Harm against another woman and from entering this house."

"What the fuck are you talking about?" He went for denial. "I didn't do anything!"

I turned back to Serena and Jayse and I knew my eyes weren't my own. I felt power drunk with rage and the essence of the divine, and I went to Mike who was struggling to his feet.

The goddess taught me something new that day as I grabbed him by his head and sort of, I don't know... reversed polarity of my power? I poured every ounce of pain, every bit of sorrow and fear that I gathered from the house behind me and I poured it directly into this wretched creature's mind, filling it to overflowing with Serena's tears, her heartache and the cherry on top? Her continued love for him... because she did. Against all odds, she still loved this wretch despite the things he'd done to her.

He stared up at me, wide-eyed, the horror seeping in and I watched as his eyes went blank before rolling up into the back of his head. The divinity in me had a firm grasp on the reins and I stepped back within myself.

The Goddess will it, then so shall it be.

"Now let me show you what you will become if you do not change your darkling ways…"

The voice that poured from my lips was no longer mine. It was both light and dark, held the crash of thunder and the howl of the wolf, the cawing of ravens and the belling of the hounds on the hunt through the woods. It was both order and chaos, immeasurable pain and yet gentle healing as the thoughts, feelings, and imagery poured from every crime I had ever worked through me to him.

He crumbled back down to his knees, screaming as the wind twisted and whipped my hair before my eyes and I let him go.

"Do something with yourself, Michael," I ordered, my voice returning to the discordant double notes of mine and hers. "Do better."

I turned from the weeping man on the walk and put my booted foot on the bottom riser of the slanting steps, slapping my hand against the porch pillar beside me. My magic flowed, the white runes of warding and protection flashing brilliantly and then sinking into the wood.

I looked at Serena and the Goddess voice returned to the fore. "My gift to you, for your aide in restoring balance. I am not through with my need for you, my daughter." I reached out a fingertip and pressed it to Serena's forehead, the divine moving through me to her. Healing, restoring, and something… something I couldn't identify but clearly wasn't for me to know.

I felt the Mother leave me as swiftly as she came as I lowered my hand. The wind died down from a tempest to a soft breeze and the cloud cover above us lightened. I staggered slightly and Jayse reached out to me. I grabbed onto his arm and let him steady me.

The only sounds now, the wild bawling and weeping coming from Mike behind me.

"Let's go inside," I said, shaken and Serena nodded. She, Jayse, and I piled back into the house and Jayse shut the door firmly behind us and Michael out, where he belonged.

"I'm going to call Dax," I said shaking, fumbling my phone out of my pocket. "Get the abuse on official record with the Boston PD

"Then what?" Serena asked, a bit shocky.

"Then I'm calling you a good lawyer. A divorce attorney. This was just a preview of coming attractions. By the time you're done with him, he'll be stripped of *everything*."

I looked to Jayse, and he nodded. He was still seething, I could tell, and he needed some satisfaction.

"I know you want to punch him in the face," I said. "But how about instead you grab his shit and toss it out there with him? One less thing your sister has got to do."

"Right." He nodded and went to do just that.

"Thank you," Serena said, tears coursing down her cheeks, and I shook my head.

"That was all you, baby. You helped us, and the divine Mother took notice. You just keep on being you and I promise, we will all get you through this." I hugged her tightly, and she hugged me back and whispered in awe, "It doesn't hurt anymore."

"Not for right now," I murmured, but there would be pain. Emotional, anyway. This was just the beginning. Hopefully by the end, her pain would be replaced with cathartic anger. She had earned it.

I called Dax, and to his credit, he dropped everything and came to take a report.

EPILOGUE

*J*ayse...

While we waited on the long process of escrow and everything else for the house, we moved most of Blyn's stuff into storage and I started work on Serena's place. She didn't want to be alone and damnit, I didn't want her to *be* alone.

Blyn didn't say a word about it, just had movers put her things in storage and asked if she could turn my old basement room into an office and workroom sort of like Miri's. My sister was all for it and threw herself double time into learning everything she could and then some from Blyn.

I don't know what, if anything, whatever deity that had been riding Blyn had done to my sister, but she began learning magic and it seemed, though she'd had no real magic ability before, there was something there now. Small, a flickering tea light to Blyn's raging inferno, but something nonetheless.

She was taking to the old ways like a fish to water, and it made her happy... so there was that.

We were a little slow to establish a new normal, but by the end of Spring, we were doing okay. We went to the Matchmaker's Festival together. Me, Blyn, Serena and Dax. I mean, they were both going through or freshly divorced – Serena's had been quick, Dax's not so much – and we figured, why not?

Blyn and I made mad love that night, and it seemed like Serena and Dax hit it off. Maybe a little more than they were letting on to the rest of us, but after having watched Dax take care of my Blyn on our first meet, I would be more than happy if he ended up with Serena. We would just have to see.

I was taking to being a 'house husband' without really having the title of 'husband' just yet, just fine. That was coming, though. I'd asked officially, ring and all, just before the clock struck the magic hour at the Beltane Matchmaker's Festival with the rest of Blyn's circle present at the bar.

Ivan had nodded at me, I guess it was his idea of a blessing, before he'd beat a hasty retreat before he could get swept up in the magic.

He just liked being alone, I guess, and wasn't interested in hooking up.

Spring was wearing on into summer, now, and Blyn was still working for the Boston Police, and the FBI on the side. Of course, nothing crossed her desk that was anywhere *near* the level of batshit as we'd gone through with the Savage Torture Killer. Thank whatever gods for that.

"Hey, you." I looked up from where I was patching a hole in the plaster behind a door in Serena's bedroom. A fix that had just kept getting pushed down the list with more immediate needs like plumbing etc. taking precedence.

"Hey," I said softly, killing the *YouTube* video on my phone. That was how I was teaching myself to do most of these things. It was working out pretty well, too.

Blyn went up on her toes and I bent to kiss her.

"You want me to start dinner?" she asked.

"Yeah, yeah. If you wouldn't mind. Where's Serena at?" I asked.

"She's at her interview," Blyn said smiling.

"Oh, shit. Was that today?" I asked, smearing some mud onto the wire-mesh patch.

"Mm-hmm." She leaned her shoulder against the doorway to my

sister's room and crossed her arms over her stomach, her silk blouse open, revealing a really nice view down the crevice between her breasts.

"You, uh, do that for my benefit?" I asked, smiling.

"Mm-hmm," she said, biting her bottom lip and smiling, a more seductive tone to the sound she made.

"You're killing me, babe," I said, laughing lightly.

"Finish up," she said, pushing off the wall. "I'll go make dinner. Just consider it a preview of coming attractions."

I was already hard, my jeans pinching uncomfortably.

"Yeah, fuck that," I said and dropped the trough of mud to the plastic, grabbing for her. She squealed in delight and twisted away, leaving me to grasp only air and I laughed too, going after her, straight into our bedroom.

We were working on kid number one.

The End

ABOUT TIMBER PHILIPS

Timber Philips hails from a land filled with beauty and steeped in magic; the Pacific Northwest. She swears you can see fairies and goblins, magic and promise around every tree and in every drop of water and she shares that magic whenever she can. She loves welcoming everyone to her worlds of romance rooted in fable and fantasy.

Stalker Information:
www.timberphilips.com

Facebook Group
https://www.facebook.com/groups/timberswolves

facebook.com/authortimberphilips
bookbub.com/authors/timber-philips
instagram.com/authortimberphilips
twitter.com/timberphilips